"King is a writer's writer, his voice is utterly convincing."
—Beryl Bainbridge

"No one writes better prose than Francis King."
—Ruth Rendell

"Wryly tender and painful . . . He is writing about love in all its aspects of greed, devotion, happiness and loss."
—Janice Elliott, *The Sunday Telegraph*

"His writing is like fine china . . . This book's strength is its dark stab of feeling."
—Philip Norman, *The Sunday Times*

"[Francis King's] writing is always accomplished and elegant."
—A. S. Byatt

"He deserves the widest possible readership."
—Melvyn Bragg, *Punch*

"Master of a subtle, melancholy style, rich and understated."
—Roxana Robinson, *The New York Times Book Review*

"The author investigates his chosen examples of emotional blight with sympathy, precision, and immense skill."
—*The Evening Standard*

"A most accomplished writer who commands both deftness and feeling."
—Christopher Wordsworth, *The Guardian*

A DOMESTIC ANIMAL

A DOMESTIC ANIMAL

FRANCIS KING

WITH A FOREWORD BY RUMAAN ALAM

McNally Editions
New York

McNally Editions
134 Prince St.
New York, NY 10012

Copyright © 1970 by Francis King
Foreword copyright © 2026 by Rumaan Alam
All rights reserved

Originally published in 1970 by the Longman Group, Ltd., London
First McNally Editions Paperback, 2026

ISBN: 978-1-96134-170-8
E-book: 978-1-96134-171-5

Design by Jonathan Lippincott

1 3 5 7 9 10 8 6 4 2

TO
G.

Nessun maggior dolore
Che ricordarsi del tempo felice
Nella miseria . . .
—Dante Alighieri

To love someone too much is to do him an irreparable wrong.
—Bossuet

FOREWORD

I'll begin with what is either warning or recommendation: *A Domestic Animal* is a love story. So many turn out to be, because the subject—with its attendants of sex, obsession, and other deep feelings—cannot be exhausted. It's maybe one of the tasks of art, to make sense of this most illogical and human thing. At any rate, our novelists seem to keep trying.

Our hero is Dick Thompson, a novelist himself, a confirmed bachelor who is tormented by love, for Antonio. Dick is "fortyish" and has the middle-age worries of the middle class: bills and home renovations. Antonio is an academic, visiting England from his native Italy, who rents a room in Dick's place. A hunky soccer player who's also a philosophy student? Well, this is a work of fiction.

The novel is not that interested in questions of *gay* and *straight*, a book from 1970 that anticipated an understanding of sexuality as spectrum rather than binary. Antonio has a wife and two children back in Italy, and he takes a local girl, the vapid Pam, as a mistress. But there's something between the two men: "All my life I have been embarrassed at touching or being touched by others . . . and even with Antonio I would shrink away. Frequently he would pat my head or run a hand through my hair." Francis King plays this for comedy, fussy British queen meets demonstrative Mediterranean, shades of Felix Ungar and Oscar Madison. At any rate, I laughed.

It's not love at first sight but a gradual awakening to something: "As he shook my hand it was as though some piece of machinery, long left unused and untended, slowly began to grind into movement through hampering encrustations of rust and dust and dirt." But Dick's affection is not returned. "A better choice would be someone who was capable of returning that love," Antonio tells Dick, reasonably enough, when the older man eventually confesses his feeling.

Maybe so. Dick is not apologetic or morose; indeed, he seems to relish his own agony, which he knows is part of the pleasure of being alive. "No, I could not wish not to care for him entirely; I did not wish to step down off that cross. But I wanted to have this intensity of love without this intensity of suffering." Dick sounds rather as I remember feeling in college, perhaps more in love with the "cross" of my unrequited longing than the young man who preoccupied me the entirety of my twentieth year.

I don't want to spoil the plot because King has concocted a surprising one, but I will skip ahead to the book's conclusion:

> I see myself now as the sufferer from an illness which all remedies—surgery, drugs, a change of scene, rest—may palliate but can never cure. Of course, like all such sufferers, I hope for the 'miracle'—the spontaneous regression that, in an infinitesimally small minority of cases, even the scientists agree to be possible. The deeply-rooted growth may all at once being to dissolve

and be absorbed into a system that asserts its long-withheld authority. But somehow I doubt it.

I expected *A Domestic Animal* to be a document of gay life in a benighted past. It isn't, exactly. The American Psychiatric Association notoriously considered homosexuality a pathology until 1973. Dick does them one better; maybe love is a private experience by definition, maybe—gay or straight—it's a disease without a cure.

Francis King began publishing when he was an undergraduate. He was one of those true literary creatures, working as a translator, publishing collections of poetry and short stories, writing a biography (of E. M. Forster), but the novel was his métier. *A Domestic Animal* was his twelfth, and he'd go on to publish more than the same number again before his death, at 88.

There's some natural temptation to understand Dick Thompson, this novel's novelist protagonist, as a stand-in for King. *A Domestic Animal* opens with a stern authorial note: "the 'I' is not I." This is impossible to reconcile with the author's autobiography, *Yesterday Came Suddenly*.

> As I have described in what I consider one of the three best of my novels, *A Domestic Animal*, I became totally obsessed with someone who, although he clearly liked and admired me and although he was no less clearly flattered by my devotion, was totally incapable of the sort of reciprocation for which I yearned. Although married and the father of two children, he had a girlfriend, with whom he spent most of his evenings. Each evening, after he called out to me, 'Ciao, Francesco, I

go now!', I used to suffer a terrible desolation. I would try to settle to some writing, a book, television. But I could not stop thinking of him.

The novel became the subject of a libel case (it was not Antonio's real-life counterpart who objected). "We writers are all too often cannibals," King writes in his memoir, "in devouring family and friends, and cads, in betraying the secrets entrusted to us." *A Domestic Animal* was withdrawn before publication, revised, and published anew. This seems useful context for a reader, and not the uninteresting question of the tension between fact and fiction. King considered this book worth writing twice, and when taking stock of his long career ranked this one of his most significant achievements.

I learned about being gay from books. I was a child in a more innocent era. When the other kids called me a *faggot*, I believed them even if I didn't get it, tried to parse the meaning of the word from that one Dire Straits song. The year I was fourteen, I read John Knowles's *A Separate Peace* and something fell into place. Phineas tells Gene he's his "best pal," and Gene is unable to respond.

> I should have told him then that he was my best friend also and rounded off what he had said. I started to; I nearly did. But something held me back. Perhaps I was stopped by that level of feeling, deeper than thought, which contains the truth.

Before the internet existed, maybe all fledgling queers were confined to that "level of feeling, deeper than thought." Or maybe I was an especially naïve teen. The APA's Diagnostic and Statistical Manual of Mental Disorders told one story—so potent you didn't even need to read it—but at least I had novels. I've no memory of how I came to know about them, but I furtively bought Edmund White's *A Boy's Own Story* and David Leavitt's *Family Dancing*. I could not believe that literature might address the subject of what I was, or that what I was might be worthy of consideration.

It's fashionable, now, to talk about an imperative to cultivate a literature that depicts the panoply of human existence. It's a matter of revising the canon, of publishing writers who would have been overlooked in a different time, of believing that books can and should be about all sorts of people. It's been distilled to the word *representation*, which often feels wrong to me because that's not, I don't think, one of the aims of the novel as a form. Nevertheless, I discovered as a teen that a book has the power to ratify your very existence. It's not fiction's principal endeavor, just a kind of added bonus. I don't know what straight readers make of it, but when I was but a boy, I was determined to catch a glimpse of myself in *A Separate Peace*, like trying to make out my reflection in a mud puddle. That's why David Leavitt and Edmund White were so startling, their books revealing me, clearly as a mirror.

Perhaps it follows that I, a gay novelist at middle age, would be moved by *A Domestic Animal*. If I've reached the point of midlife crisis, how lovely to imagine that what lies ahead might not be the embarrassment of a sports car or a leather jacket or a toupee but something quite beautiful. Dick is in crisis, no question, but he's also in love:

> Naturally morose by temperament, I felt an astonishing exhilaration; naturally critical, I noticed how my judgements of others had suddenly grown generous. Friends would say to me 'How well you are looking!' Or even 'How happy you seem!'

King understands love's power. It alters our perspective. Antonio's voracity at the table repels one of Dick's friends. "But this rapacity, so far from disgusting me, struck me as curiously poignant." Dick can't see an ill-mannered man but a boy going hungry in postwar Italy. Love asks us to submit, and we do, and find pleasure in that. "Like most Italian men Antonio was used to being spoiled by women." Dick runs out to buy his lodger new shoelaces, his feeling elevating the errand to something like sacrament.

It used to be either unthinkable or just bad form to get into the erotic. Maybe that explains a contemporary bias, that this fundamental aspect of human life is a recent invention. King allows Dick his lust: ". . . the day when he called me into his room as he was preparing for a football match and there he was, totally unselfconscious, standing at the window in nothing but his Y-fronted pants, one arm under the other to scratch at his naked, freckled back." (I was struck by the echo of how John Knowles describes Phineas, early in *A Separate Peace*, stripping off his clothes and clambering up a tree, "his back muscles working like a panther's.")

I am, as I write this, about the age Francis King was when he wrote *A Domestic Animal*. If I'm reading Dick as some proxy for myself, that is presumably how all the other boys in ninth grade read *A Separate Peace*. How nice that this doesn't require acrobatics of my imagination; how nice to simply tell it as it is. Of course, identity—gay, Black, trans, what have you—cannot supplant the demands of a novel: plot, character, ideas. And that this is a gay novel does not mean it will not yield to a straight reader.

But that this is a gay novel is worth saying, worth celebrating. I can't be the only gay reader who thrilled at the scene of Dick stealing into Antonio's bedroom, "excited, as I was always to be, by the smell rising up from the garments that littered the floor and from the bedclothes that were so much twisted and rumpled that they suggested hours of frantic lovemaking." I read this and thought, yes, that's right. It's sexy and naughty and funny. It's not pitiable but powerful. That Dick's love goes unrequited is neither here nor there. He is at midlife, but he is more than *not dead yet*. He is alive.

Rumaan Alam
New York City, 2026

AUTHOR'S NOTE

Since this is a story supposedly told by a novelist in the first-person singular, readers may be tempted to identify the narrator with the author. I should therefore like to put on record that the 'I' is not I and that the 'they' derive their existence only from myself.

A DOMESTIC ANIMAL

1

'I write *a lume spento*—the hours all seem dark.' That was how, fourteen months ago, I began my first letter to Antonio when he had returned to Florence, his wife and his two children for the Easter vacation; and that is how I now begin this account after he has left England for good. The light is still extinguished; and like a blind man in a room strange to him, I blunder about among these memories, bruising and cutting myself on their vicious edges.

It all began when Penny Ashleigh asked me, 'I suppose you don't want a lodger?'

If Penny had listened to anything I had told her during our daily telephone calls for the past three weeks, she would have known that a lodger was, at that moment, the last thing I wanted. But Penny rarely listens, so acute is her craving to talk. 'How are you this morning, my dear?' she asks, and as one begins to tell her that one has a headache or a temperature or a bad tooth, she rushes on: 'I'm really not feeling *at all* well.' So it did not surprise me that she had failed to take in that I had left my old house and was camping out in the basement of my new one, while the builders were still in possession of most of the rooms above.

'I wouldn't know where to put a lodger,' I said. 'There's that slip of a room in the basement flat, but it would only do for a child. Why?'

'Well, that nice Miss McComber from the University has just been on to me to ask if I can take an Italian philosopher. Apparently he's in some dreadful digs in Newen and he's feeling far from happy.' She looked at her watch: 'He should be here any moment now. Except that Italians are always so unpunctual.'

Penny is full of such generalisations about her foreign lodgers: Greeks are always so unreliable, Arabs are always so dishonest, Koreans are always so dirty.

'Why don't you have him yourself?'

'With Jim due back next month, I don't really *want* more than one lodger. I only have Masa for the fun of the thing. For company. It's not as though one made a penny out of them.' Since Penny usually charges her lodgers eleven guineas a week, this repeated plaint that her lodgers bring her in no money always baffles me. 'And I'm not sure that I want another Italian. You remember all that trouble I had with Gino—a dear though he was.' It was unlikely that I could have forgotten the telephone calls, sometimes two or three in a day and lasting for several minutes, in which Penny detailed all Gino's enormities and shortcomings: the bath that was never cleaned out, the underclothes that were never changed, the coffee that was brewed in the early hours of the morning, the sluts (a favourite word of Penny's) who thronged the house, apparently scattering cigarette-ash, powder and hair-slides wherever they went. 'Italians—let's face it—are not really domestic animals.'

'No. They are predators,' I agreed.

At that moment the doorbell tinkled out 'Boys and Girls Come out to Play' and Penny lumbered upwards from her chair. 'That must be him.'

It would be easy to say now that as soon as I saw Antonio I fell in love with him—indeed, I have often told him this—but it would not be strictly true. As he shook my hand it was as though some piece of machinery, long left unused and untended, slowly began to grind into movement through hampering encrustations of rust and dust and dirt. It was to be several days before the machine was functioning properly; and now, as it whirrs remorselessly, crazily on and on and on, I wonder how many years it will be before it can be stilled.

My first impression was of the contrast, later to grow so familiar to me, between the extraordinary vivacity of his manner and an appearance that suggested extreme fatigue or actual illness. Wearing green corduroy trousers, suede bootees the colour of ash and one of the many pullovers that were so prominent a feature of his otherwise exiguous wardrobe, he swaggered across the room, extending an arm to me.

'Antonio Valli.' The voice was high and slightly nasal.

'*Motto piacere.*'

'*Ah, parla Italiano!*'

'*No, no, pochissimo.*'

'*Ma, è stato in Italia?*'

'My first post was in the British Consulate in Florence—in Firenze,' I explained, relapsing into English.

'But my home is in Firenze! You liked Firenze, I am sure! Beautiful city!'

'Very much.'

Then, as on so many subsequent occasions, I regretted my inability to match this euphoric expansiveness of tone—how was he to know that that mumbled 'Very much' implied that my year and a half in Florence had been the happiest period of my whole life?

'Yes, Firenze is very, *very* beautiful,' he went on.

Penny was glancing anxiously back and forth, now at me and now at him, with that look of rising panic that one sees on the face of a little girl whose ball is being tossed between two older children cruelly determined to ignore her presence. Penny is always terrified of exclusion: so that her endless chatter is really her way of saying 'Here I am, this is me, you must interest yourselves in me, you must not get taken up with each other.'

Eventually she touched Antonio's arm. 'Come—do please sit down.'

Antonio sat, in a position that I was soon to know so well, on the edge of the chair as though preparatory to getting up again in a hurry, with his arms on his knees and his hands dangling between them. His battered briefcase rested against one of his legs.

'Would you like some tea?'

'Thank you. Only a glass of water.'

'The tea is made. Mr Thompson and I have just been having a cup. Do have some too.'

'Thank you.' Antonio shook his head. 'Just a glass of water.' I was soon to learn, as Penny never did, that he hated tea.

'And a crumpet?'

'Please?'

Penny held out the dish in which a single charred crumpet was embedded in congealed butter like a burned candle-wick in wax. 'An English speciality.'

'Thank you, Mrs Thomp-son. I am not hungry.'

Obviously Penny failed to realise that he was under the impression that we were husband and wife, mother and son or perhaps brother and sister. Instead she asked archly, 'Do you know the word crumpet? It has two meanings in English—its real meaning and its slang meaning. My Japanese lodger—Masa—and I have many a laugh about it.'

'I do not understand.'

'Mr Thompson will explain. I think it's better if a man explains to you.' She gave her braying laugh. 'I'll get you your water.'

As she went out, Antonio looked at me for the promised explanation: but 'Miss Ashleigh is my friend. We're not related,' I had started to tell him.

'Ah! I thought . . . Then you are Mr Thomp-son and the lady is . . . ?'

'Miss Ashleigh. Miss Penny Ashleigh.' I wondered whether I should explain that Penny was short for Penelope.

'And it is with you or with Miss Ashleigh that I am to stay?'

'Not with me, I'm afraid. And it's not at all certain that you'll be able to stay with Miss Ashleigh.'

'But Miss McComber told me . . .'

At that point Penny returned, carrying the glass on a saucer. 'I've made a *delicious* supper,' she announced—irrelevantly, since neither Antonio nor I was to eat it. 'Sautéed kidneys, peas with mint from the garden and a slice of Brie. Masa should soon be home. I gave him kippers for breakfast. It made a change—he usually has a fried egg.'

Antonio took the glass of water, threw back his head and drained it at a single gulp.

'You must have been thirsty,' Penny said. 'More?'

'No. Thank you. That is fine.'

'I'd better explain the position.' Penny sat down, folding her long legs at the same moment that she began to lower her cylindrical body into the sofa, in the manner of a camel. 'I told Miss McComber that of course I'd see you but that I was by no means sure that I could help you out. You see, my brother and I share this house—it's half his and half mine—and I'm expecting him back from Poland either at the end of this month or in the middle of the next. He's in the Foreign Service—if you know what that means? The Diplomatic Service. He's a diplomat. Now in this house I have four bedrooms—well, five bedrooms if you count an attic room that I use just as an ironing room and a storage place for junk. Though it has got a bed, a camp-bed, in it. As things are at present there's Masa, this brilliant young Japanese biochemist, staying here, and my *au pair* girl—she's from Switzerland and really a dead loss—and then of course from time to time I have the odd relative or friend . . .'

Penny ran on and on, while Antonio gazed at her and I gazed at him. People have often complained to me of the boredom they have suffered in Penny's company: but I can truthfully say that when I am with her I am no more bored than I am bored when I am alone. With her I *am* alone. She holds forth, stopping only to take a deep gulp of air, and I busy myself with my own thoughts. I do not have to listen since she will never concern herself with whether I am listening or not; and if, subsequently, I am caught out in having entirely failed to assimilate something she has told me, she will be delighted to repeat the whole speech for a second and even a third time.

As he looked at her, his strange sherry-coloured eyes fixed on her plain, beaky face, Antonio's right knee jerked spasmodically as though all that electric energy that crackled through him must always demand some outlet. He was, I learned later, thirty-three years old, but at that moment I assumed him to be in his early twenties. The face struck me then as curiously Slav, with the high flat planes of the cheekbones under the sunken eyes, the square jaw and the long, heavy eyelids that swept upwards at either end. He was—is—beautiful; and beautiful not only to me but to almost everyone, man or woman, with whom he has ever come into contact. Repeatedly I have tried to analyse that beauty, as I tried to analyse it then, Penny's voice clacking on and on between us, and as I try to analyse it now; and always I have decided that of all his attributes the most extraordinary is his colouring. The hair, which that day was untidy and over-long, is dark brown but with a curious reddish sheen; and the pallor of his face, scattered with small freckles on the forehead and across the bridge of the nose, also flashes from time to time with the same reddish glints. The other two things that I noticed then, moved by them as though by some deep physical pang, were the teeth and the hands. The teeth were apparently perfect. (Antonio has always been proud of them, even maintaining that he has never had to visit a dentist in his life; but once when I went into his bedroom to find him lying, unsleeping but totally abandoned to the exhaustion that from time to time would strike him down like a physical illness, I saw at the back of his open mouth—the lips drawn away alarmingly as though in the last agony of death—the glitter of one of those costly gold inlays so rarely seen nowadays in England but so common in Italy.) The huge and immensely powerful hands might have belonged to one of the Tuscan *contadini* from which he was descended, were it not for the care he lavished on them: the cuticles carefully coaxed back, the nails filed each to a perfect semi-circle. Reddish hair sprouted in tufts at the base of each finger and was thick at the wrists.

Suddenly he became aware that I was staring at him and his eyes left Penny's face and slowly, almost dreamily, sought out mine. He began to smile; but in contrast to the nervous mobility of the mouth, opening to reveal those teeth that were so large, white and square, and in contrast to the nervous mobility of the body that even in sleep never seemed to be truly in repose, the eyes that now held my gaze had an unfathomable weariness and an unfathomable sadness in them. Plunging his hands deep into his pockets and kicking out his legs, he gave a small shrug of his shoulders as though to say 'I suppose we'll have to stick this out for a long time yet.'

It was then that I decided to cut in on Penny. 'I don't think that Signor Valli would be awfully comfortable in my basement flat. But if you could have him for the next two or three weeks—at least until Jim gets back—then once I've made the move upstairs, I can take him over.'

'Well, as I said, my dear, I don't know that I really *want* another lodger. Quite frankly'—she turned to Antonio—'with prices being what they are these days, having a lodger is more trouble than it's worth. I have this brilliant Japanese biochemist—Masa—as I told you, and I find that by the end of a week I am actually out of pocket.' But while she said this, she was looking at Antonio for the first time, her pale blue eyes travelling over the tight corduroy trousers, the suede bootees, the pullover and the reddish glint on the prominent cheek-bones beneath the huge, deep-set eyes. I knew now that she would eventually say yes; Antonio, I had recognised even then, was one of those people to whom everyone says yes.

'It's only a matter of two or three weeks,' I said again. 'Once I've got the builders out . . .' But I had been trying to get the builders out for almost three months.

Penny sighed. 'I don't like my lodgers to come home too late,' she warned. 'Masa—my Japanese—is very good about that. There are so many burglaries in Lymstead—I had one less than six months ago—and I like to make sure that everything is locked up before I turn in. And there's the question of shoes. The Swiss girl will make beds but she doesn't clean shoes. You'd have to clean your own shoes. The Swiss girl won't do them.' There was a great deal more of this; but to each fresh condition Antonio merely nodded his head—that leg still jerking ceaselessly, as he leant forward in his chair to gaze into Penny's face—and murmured either 'Yes, I understand' or 'Perfect.'

Finally Penny came to the question of payment. 'I can give you breakfast and dinner every day and also lunch on Saturday and Sunday. For that I suggest eleven guineas a week. I really can't do it for less—there's the central heating and the terrible rise in the price of food, and the way in which the rates go up and up and up. That's really the absolute minimum—and by charging it I make nothing at all.'

At that time Antonio knew too little about the cost of living in England to recognise a barefaced lie. 'Perfect,' he said again. 'Agreed.'

'What have you been paying in Newen?' I enquired, maliciously hoping to embarrass Penny.

'In Newen? Oh, five guineas per week.'

'Well, of course, in Newen rents are much cheaper. But I bet the house isn't properly heated.' Penny was vehement. 'And I bet you don't get fed as you'll get fed here. I don't like to boast but Mr Thompson will confirm that I'm one of the best cooks in Lymstead.'

'My room in Newen is very uncomfortable,' Antonio agreed. 'That is why I have decided to leave. No heating except from an oil-stove that smells horribly. And I must pay two shillings for every bath. And no hot water for washing.'

'Well, there you are!' Penny exclaimed. 'Isn't it scandalous'— she turned to me—'the way in which these landladies exploit their foreign students! I must have a word about it with Miss McComber. You'd think the University would take better care. After all, the first impression a foreigner gets on arriving in England is so very, very important.' She turned back to Antonio: 'Now when would you like to move in?'

'Tonight?'

'Tonight!'

'I have paid until tomorrow—one week of rent in advance. So I can leave when I wish. It does not matter if I lose one night.'

'But don't you think that perhaps you should give them a little notice?'

'Why?' He laughed. 'They have not been very kind to me. One night I came home very late and very cold and I made myself some cocoa and the next morning Mrs Berridge—she is the landlady—says to me "Mr Valli—next time you want some milk, would you please ask my permission first?" Did she expect me to wake her up at one o'clock?'

'Well, in that case . . .' said Penny.

At the time Antonio's attitude seemed to me wholly reasonable. Only now do I see in it a symptom of the ruthlessness that lurked, a dangerously submerged rock, beneath that smooth summer surface of kindliness, gaiety and charm.

Antonio got to his feet, the green corduroy trousers so tight on his muscular legs that he had to stoop to tug them down. 'Then I go to fetch my luggage.'

'I could take you in the car. But not now,' Penny said. 'We always eat at six-thirty.'

'No, no! No car is necessary. I am strong. I can carry two suitcases. And at Lymstead station I will take a taxi.'

'Shall I keep some kidneys for you?'

'Please?'

'Would you like me to have something for you to eat when you arrive?'

'If that is not too much of trouble. Of course that would be very convenient—very nice for me.'

'Well, it is rather an extra-special meal,' Penny said. 'You'll see that English cooking is not as bad as foreigners imagine.'

'I am sure it will be—delicious.' He lingered for a moment on the last word, at the same time giving me a surreptitious glance that made it plain that he was gently mocking at her earlier boast that she had prepared a 'delicious' meal for Masa.

Out in the street Antonio turned to me: 'Mr Thompson—I will say thank you and goodbye.'

I thought for a second of the review I had not written and of the television programme I was supposed to watch; then I said: 'I've nothing to do. I'll walk with you to the station.'

'Good.'

In Penny's room Antonio's physique had seemed to me slender; but though his waist and his hips were both astonishingly narrow I saw now, as from time to time I glanced sideways at him, that his chest, arms and legs were as powerfully muscled as those of a prize-fighter. He had a curious walk, slightly bowlegged and with the right foot turned a fraction inward. When he was not himself talking he kept up a faint, tuneless whistle between his clenched teeth. Later, this habit was to get on my nerves.

Inevitably it was of Penny we conversed. Antonio asked if she had ever worked and I then began to explain that she had had a distinguished public career, its climax coming—as for so many women of her age and type—during the war; that she now served on a number of committees concerned with juvenile delinquency and hospital management; and that her family was one famous for two centuries for producing colonial administrators, diplomats and clerics. Unconsciously, as I spoke about this friend who had done me so many kindnesses, I presented her to him in terms of faint derision; here were we two and over there stood Penny, a distinguished and even admirable figure at whom, nonetheless, we could enjoy the superiority of laughing a little. Later, and again unconsciously,

I would adopt the same tone of subtle denigration when talking of other of my friends; and more dangerously, since this Antonio resented, when talking of friends of his. I see now what motive prompted me and my recognition of it makes me feel ashamed.

'. . . I doubt if you will have many really *delicious* meals, but they'll always be wholesome and edible. Miss Ashleigh is what is called in England "a good plain cook". In Italy you might call her a damned bad one. But as English cooks go, she ranks fairly high.'

'You are a university teacher?' Antonio eventually asked me.

'No. I'm a writer.'

'A writer!' He stopped in the middle of the road we had been crossing, his hand on my arm. 'But that is exciting! What kind of book do you write? Tell me, please.'

I told him, flattered by his interest, and even offered to lend him one of my novels, recently translated into Italian. But 'No, no, I wish to read you in English. Please let me read one of your books in English,' he insisted.

At the station I overcame the impulse to buy a ticket and accompany him to Newen. But I went with him on to the platform.

'Do you smoke?'

'No.'

'Then here's an empty carriage.'

'Oh, this one will do.'

He climbed, not into the carriage I had indicated but into a smoker, in one corner of which an etiolated girl sat running the nail-bitten fingers of a bony hand through her lank blonde hair.

Antonio pulled down the window and leant out. 'You are very kind. I shall be happy when I come to live at your house. I know that already.'

'But don't you want to *see* the house before you decide?'
'Of course not. I know that I shall be happy. *Basta.*'
'Well, I'll leave you to it,' I said.
'Again—*grazie mille.*'
He put out a hand and gripped mine firmly.

I looked back once but his head had already vanished from sight. At that I felt the same disappointment that one experiences when on a journey one has promised oneself a view of a mountain, only to find it swathed in mist.

2

There are a few periods in my life—my eighteen months in the Consulate in Florence soon after the war, two weeks on Mount Athos, a leave spent in a one-room flat off Kensington Church Street—of which I can say 'Then I was truly happy.' Friends tell me that they themselves usually associate such periods of happiness with successful love-affairs but with me that has never been the case, perhaps because for me success in a love-affair has always dragged along with it on its high tide a detritus of remorse and guilt. In Florence I was happy merely to have escaped from the prison of England; on Mount Athos I was happy merely to wander from monastery to monastery unaccompanied and in perfect weather; in my little flat off Church Street I was happy merely because I was working on a book in which, I knew with a growing exhilaration, I had at last found a voice of my own. Only those first weeks with Antonio constitute a period of happiness that was also a period of infatuation.

But of that infatuation I was, at first, totally unaware. Deep within me, as I have said, that rusty machine was beginning to grind and clank into movement; but I preferred to ignore its signals, telling myself and even others that Antonio was 'charming', 'quite exceptionally intelligent', 'such fun to be with' (all of which was true), but never admitting that for the first time in almost fourteen years I was in love.

After that first encounter I remember how I woke up in the shabby little basement flat beneath the elegant and spacious Regency house that I hoped one day to inhabit, and instead of feeling my usual despair at the continuing presence of the builders banging and bawling above me and my usual anxiety at the continuing arrival of bill after bill, I was dizzy with a euphoria I had not known for months. Only as I wallowed in my morning bath did I connect that euphoria with Antonio; and even then I ascribed it merely to having at last found a lodger of whom I felt I could also make a friend.

After breakfast I telephoned Penny instead of waiting for her to telephone me—poor dear, I told myself, it shouldn't always be she who makes the call—and I was rewarded by the obvious pleasure in her voice as she cried out: 'Dick! How nice of you to ring, my dear! I was just about to pick up the phone to you. What a coincidence!' Since Penny rang me daily at just that hour it was not really the coincidence she felt it to be; but for Penny all life is a web of miraculously fortuitous happenings, and were it not for her belief in the existence of that web she would flounder and drown, like a child deprived of its water-wings.

'How are you, Penny dear?'

'Well, I can't say I had an awfully good night. Heartburn . . . I suppose it was a mistake having a cup of hot milk before turning in.' I let her go on while I flicked over the pages of a book I had for review. Then when at last there was a momentary pause, I got in: 'And how is your little family?' 'Little family' was the phrase Penny herself almost invariably used to describe her household.

'Well, would you believe it, I said to that silly gel, now the China tea is in *this* caddy and the Indian tea is in *this* and for breakfast we always—*always*—have Indian tea . . .'

I turned over several more pages of the book.

'And Masa?' I asked at last.

'Well, the poor dear's piles seem to be better. Why do all these Japanese suffer from piles? I suppose it must be the rice. Yes, he's much more his usual cheerful self—not that one could really describe him as *cheerful* at the best of times . . . He's giggling at that . . . Yes, he's right here beside me, having his breakfast. I gave him a kipper yesterday to make a change but this morning we're back to fried eggs. I think he really prefers fried eggs. You really prefer fried eggs, don't you, Masa?'

I had turned over another three pages before I could come to Antonio:

'And the Italian?'

'My dear, would you believe it, he was up at six-thirty and downstairs waiting for breakfast at seven. Well, he can't expect that poor gel to get up at that hour for him. I told him so. I showed him how to make the tea and how to use the toaster and said that he'd just have to get on with it on his own. I mean, don't you agree, if he wants breakfast at that sort of hour, I really can't ask Giselle to get it for him.'

'He seems very charming. And intelligent.'

'Oh, yes.' I could hear Penny give one of her deep sighs, and imagined her narrow, pointed chin drawn down on to her wattled breast as though to transfix it. 'Of course I don't really know how he's going to fit in. Masa is such a treasure, one can't expect every lodger to be like Masa. Italians are just *not* domestic animals. And they do tend to be awfully inconsiderate. I mean, there he was running a bath at six-thirty in the morning and actually singing in it. And God knows what time he went to bed. I heard the chain clanking in the loo long after midnight.'

'Seems to have lots of energy.'

'Yes. I only wish he'd use some of it on keeping his room tidier. Giselle called me into it after he had left for the University. "Just look at this, Miss Ashleigh!" she said, in that challenging way of hers, always looking for a grievance. Well, I took a look and I did see her point. You've never encountered such a mess. Dirty laundry—weeks and weeks of it, one would think—littering the floor. Pyjamas flung over that dear little Sèvres shepherdess of Jim's on the table by the window—it was a miracle it wasn't broken. Photographs of his wife and children scattered everywhere . . .'

Trivialities of a kind which, when enumerated about Masa and Giselle, filled me with boredom, already fascinated me if Antonio was their subject; so that instead of now occupying myself with something else, I was listening intently.

I learned how Antonio had left traces of marmalade on the butter; how he had borrowed ninepence worth of stamps—'I doubt if he'll ever return them'; how his luggage seemed 'surprisingly ramshackle'; how he had not offered to pay her in advance; and how finally he had raced off down the road to catch the University train 'like a schoolboy late for school'.

Eventually, minutes later, she concluded with another sigh: 'Yes, I really don't know *how* it's going to work out—if it works out at all. One must just hope for the best, I suppose.'

'Well, it's not for long, is it? I expect to take him over in two weeks at the outside.'

'I don't know if you're going to find him the ideal lodger, my dear. You're even more pernickety than I am, and pernickety people like ourselves ought to avoid Italians like the plague. I hope you're not going to regret agreeing to have him.'

At odd moments throughout that day I would think of Antonio; and at half-past five that evening, when I took my ancient boxer, Kitty, out for a walk, it was in the direction of Penny's house that I began to wander. Although Penny is the sort of woman—unmarried, lonely—whom one would assume to be a lover of animals, she in fact distrusts and, in the case of dogs, even hates them. But with Kitty, as with some of my friends whom she finds equally unlikeable, she nonetheless always makes an effort to be amiable. 'Well, how is my dear old gel?' she asks, thumping Kitty on the head or the flank. 'Eh, how is my old gel today? Would she like a choccy biscuit?' But Kitty, too shrewd to be taken in, usually responds with a bad-tempered growl, and in alarm Penny then draws back.

'Dick! Lovely!' she greeted me on this occasion. '*Darling* Kitty! Come into the kitchen. I'm just making the supper.' Penny never has supper later than at seven. 'I'm doing them proud. An onion soup with onions from the garden, a delicious casserole of chicken and a baked custard. They couldn't ask for better than that, now could they?'

I sat in the kitchen, sipping at a glass of Cyprus sherry, and listened to Penny's ceaseless chatter, rather as one involuntarily listens to the transistor in the next door garden. I was waiting.

Masa, not Antonio, was the first to arrive home.

When he had first come to Penny, some three months before, both she and I had labelled Masa 'a bore'; but what had then seemed to us a clod-like unresponsiveness arose, we soon realised, from a deficiency in English and not from any deficiency of either intellect or character. Masa was then in his early thirties, with the physique of someone much younger than that age and the personality of someone much more mature. He was wearing on this occasion, as usually when he visited the University, a shiny blue serge suit, too short in the trouser legs and the sleeves, with a black tie tugged into a hard little knot, shoes that were at least one size too big for him and glasses that had the habit of gliding down the greasy bridge of his small, beaky nose.

'Good evening, Masa.'

'Good evening, Mr Thompson.'

I had often asked Masa to call me 'Dick', not 'Mr Thompson'; but to a Japanese, so conscious of age and status, such a request was unthinkable.

'Do I disturb you?'

'Not at all,' said Penny. 'Come and sit down and talk to Mr Thompson, while I go on with the preparation of supper. Onion soup, Masa. I know you like that.' But Masa was given no opportunity to talk to me; as she cooked, Penny continued to hold forth ceaselessly.

Then suddenly a door slammed; footsteps thumped across the hall.

'Hello!'

In the weeks that followed I was so often to await to hear that dissyllable, the accent invariably misplaced: when Antonio, grey with fatigue after a day at the University, would rush into the house, banging the door behind him; when, bleary-eyed after a late night out, he would shuffle down to breakfast in his pyjamas; when, again in his pyjamas, he would appear, no matter how late the hour, at the top of the stairs to greet me on my return from an evening in London. Penny frowned, I noticed, as she peered down into her saucepan. What she resented in Antonio, I was soon to learn, was the effortlessness with which he always captured the audience that she regarded as her own unique role to hog. 'How are you, Mr Thompson? You have had a good day?' His hand rested briefly on my shoulder.

'I could hardly call it a good day. It's difficult to work with builders playing pop-tunes over one's head. But I've managed to write the review I had to write. So that's something at least. And you?'

'For me also there are distractions. No one warned me that this is the university of two thousand miniskirts.'

Masa giggled, raising a tiny, limp hand to his mouth. 'For a Japanese this probably presents no problems. He can absorb himself in his studies and ignore what goes on outside this window. Am I right, Mr Masa? But for an Italian . . .'

'Now you'll have to move a little from there, you know. How do you imagine I can get at the refrigerator?' There was plenty of room for Penny to get at the refrigerator; her mouth with the usually drooping lower lip was now pulled taut into a line.

'Excuse me, Miss Ashleigh.' Antonio leapt to his feet and dragged his chair towards mine. When he sat down his knee touched my knee; curiously he made no attempt to move it away.

'Would you like to stay and have a bite with us?' Penny asked.

Usually when Penny invites me to supper I make some excuse: the idea of eating at half-past six fills me with horror. But now I said: 'Thank you, yes. If you have enough to spare. Cooking and eating a lonely meal is something I always hate.'

'Do you live alone?' Antonio asked.

'Yes, I live alone.'

'You are not married?'

'No, I'm not married.'

'It is not good to live alone!'

'No, it's not good. That's why I'm looking forward to the time when you come to live with me.'

Antonio turned his head sideways, his knee jerking against mine; then I noticed a faint flush spreading upwards along the flat planes of his cheekbones to his forehead.

'Mr Thompson is what is called a confirmed bachelor,' Masa put in.

'That means that he is far too selfish to think of sharing his life with anyone forever,' Penny took up on an uncharacteristically sour note.

'I didn't decide not to get married because I'm selfish. I became selfish because I've never got married.'

'A subtle distinction! . . . Now if someone would give that gel a shout, we could start to dish up.'

As usual, Giselle munched her way through the meal in silence and with lids lowered over her protuberant pale blue eyes. She had a habit of pausing from time to time in the methodical demolition of the food piled before her to gaze down at it as a surgeon might gaze down at his patient before deciding where to make the next incision. Penny paid far more attention to the girl's needs than to those of the rest of us, urging her: 'Oh, you must take more of that!' or 'Have a piece of breast' or 'I know you'd like another spoonful of this delicious gravy.' Penny's protectiveness towards her *au pairs* has always made me feel sad that her one chance of marriage should have been destroyed by the war: motherhood would have suited her. Patiently she will identify herself with all aspects of these girls' lives—bar one: garrulous on all other subjects, however meagre her knowledge of them, she becomes stiff and silent if ever sex is mentioned. Once, when I knew her less well, I referred to an acquaintance, a probation-officer, who faced the ruin of his career after being arrested in a public lavatory; but she refused to listen to me, disappearing in panic into the kitchen, from which she called out a moment later: 'Do come and see this junket I've made for lunch.' How much she was to guess about my relationship with

Antonio I was never to know; neither of us, even at my time of acutest unhappiness, was ever to speak of it.

After supper I suggested that Antonio and Masa might like to be shown an English pub. I also felt obliged to invite Penny to join us, but to my relief she announced that she had to write a letter to *The Times*—it was a period when she was writing letters almost daily to the newspapers in support of better conditions for the nursing profession.

In the street Antonio at once began to discuss Giselle: Swiss girls had no chic, it was a pity she had such dandruff, her legs were far too fat. There was something brutal in the way he had appraised the poor girl and found her wholly wanting, and I think that Masa's giggles at each fresh criticism demonstrated that he was as shocked as myself.

I took them to a 'thirties pub, as vast as an aeroplane hangar, all oak beams and stone fireplaces and barrels of port and sherry that gleamed as though burnished with shoe-polish. When Antonio said 'Ah, this is the traditional English public house! This must be very old,' I did not contradict him.

I knew that Masa only liked the sweetest of drinks and so ordered for him a glass of port; but Antonio wanted a gin, neat, with ice, which he tossed down at a single gulp, to say immediately 'Now I get you a drink.'

'But I haven't started yet.'

'Never mind! . . . Lady! Please, young lady!'

I noticed how the barmaid, neither young nor a lady, at once hurried over. I could seldom command such service.

Antonio, unlike Masa, was generous, I was to learn, even if the generosity sprang in part from a hatred of ever being under an obligation. With the frankness with which Italians habitually speak about money, he told me on that first evening about his salary, £120 per month, as a research fellow at the

University, and explained that half of it he had to remit to his wife. The thought of the eleven guineas he had to pay each week to Penny made me angry for him.

'You'll find it difficult to manage.'

He laughed, shrugging his shoulders. 'I always manage.'

'I'm sure you do.'

Masa said, genuinely worried: 'But you receive only half the money I receive.'

'In this crazy world a philosopher is worth only half a biochemist.'

'What exactly is your subject of research?'

Antonio was usually extraordinary sensitive to the reactions of anyone to whom he was talking—in this being unlike Penny; but when he spoke about philosophy, his conversation became a kind of thinking aloud and he never then considered whether his interlocutor was able to follow or not. I could not follow him either then or on many subsequent occasions; but he never noticed this. Masa could follow him. There were few subjects which Masa was incapable of following: I have met no one equipped with an intellect so formidable and so various in the multitude of its responses.

As Antonio talked, he kept gulping one drink after another, leaving Masa, who had the lightest of heads, and myself far, far behind him. But the countless gins affected him not at all.

When we quit the pub at closing time he announced: 'Tomorrow I have to play football.'

'Football!' Masa exclaimed.

'Yes. Unfortunately, because I am a graduate not an undergraduate, I am not allowed to play with the first team. Do you like football?'

'Very much,' Masa answered.

'Where do you play?'

Masa was convulsed with giggles. 'Oh, I cannot play! I have never played!' he got out eventually. 'No, no, no! I am not a sportsman. But I like to watch.'

'I was once a professional footballer,' Antonio said.

I was astonished. 'Were you really?'

Antonio began to tell us how his father had died when he was still a boy of ten; of how his mother had had to go out to work during the war years in order to support him and his brother; of how, at fifteen, he had had to leave school, first to do a variety of jobs—in a brewery, in a garage, in a restaurant—and then, after some successes with a local team of amateurs, to play professionally for Florence. As a professional footballer he had made a lot of money—'far more than I shall probably ever make as a philosopher'—and having saved it, he had then taken himself first back to *liceo* while already in his twenties and then to the university. As he told the story, with justifiable pride, I could not help comparing the circumstances of his life with my own easy progression from private school to public school and from public school to Oxford. In the weeks that followed Antonio would often speak in this fashion about his early life. He knew that I was interested; he would sometimes even say to me 'One day you must write a novel about all this.'

As we strode out along the front, the wind plucking at my coat and making my eyes smart and water, I noticed that Masa was falling behind us.

'Masa! What is the matter with you?' Antonio called back over his shoulder. 'Are you tired?'

'I think that I must go home,' Masa said. 'I have much to do tomorrow, I am a little tired.' In him the instinct of self-preservation, so feeble in Antonio and myself, was always strong.

'Tomorrow is tomorrow, today is today!'

'But today is almost tomorrow—it is past eleven o'clock.'

'Come, Masa. Come with us!'

'No, no! I will leave you here. I must write a letter to my wife before I go to bed.'

'How often do you write to your wife?'

'Two times each week.'

'Well then! I write to my wife each day—each day, every day. But I am not going home.'

'I do not have your energy,' Masa sighed with simple regret.

He said goodnight, shaking us both by the hands, apologised repeatedly for having to leave us, bowed his thanks for our company and made off sedately into the night.

'Poor Masa!' said Antonio. But there was no reason, as I learned later, why Antonio should pity him. Masa, unlike us, was someone who had reached a perfect accommodation with life, knowing exactly both what he could demand, and what he could never expect, from it.

Antonio linked his arm with mine, drawing me in my heavy overcoat against his own body in the thin trousers that were blown tight against his legs and the thin olive-green pullover of a shade that so beautifully matched his colouring. He began to laugh for no reason that I could see. Then he turned solicitously: 'You are also tired.'

'No. I'm never tired.'

It was a silly boast; but in those early days of our relationship it was something that was true—I was never tired.

'You know, I think I shall be happy in England.'

'Aren't you happy wherever you are?'

'Yes,' he agreed. 'I am usually happy. *Now*.' He unlinked his arm from mine and then thrust his hands deep in his trouser pockets, hunching his shoulders. 'But not when I was a child. And not even when I was older. I owe much to football.'

Suddenly, as though to shake off the melancholy that had begun to settle on him, he leapt up on to the rail that separated the promenade along which we were struggling from the shingle several yards below and began, arms extended, to run perilously along it.

'Antonio! Get down!'

Passersby, blown along by the wind, turned their heads to stare. Antonio was laughing. Then he swayed, began to topple.

'Antonio!'

For a second I thought that he was about to disappear. I jumped up to grip his arm and simultaneously he fell heavily across me, jolting my left shoulder so fiercely that for a moment I wondered if a bone might not be broken.

'Idiot!' I shouted, half-amused and half-exasperated by his recklessness and the pain he had caused me. 'You might have killed yourself.'

He hugged me. 'No, no! I must always *vivere pericolosamente*! But I do not kill myself. I have far too much for which to live. No, no! I never kill myself.'

3

At that time and for several days more I was unaware of any sexuality in the attraction he exerted on me. He seemed to me beautiful as my Siamese cat, Selima, is beautiful, or as Kitty was beautiful before motherhood and overeating between them wrecked her figure. When he talked in that quick, high-pitched, nasal voice of his, his body jerking about and his hands making ample gestures, I used to watch him absorbed as much in his animal vigour and grace as in the substance of what he was saying. Naturally morose by temperament, I felt an astonishing exhilaration; naturally critical, I noticed how my judgements of others had suddenly grown generous. Friends would say to me 'How well you are looking!' Or even 'How happy you seem!' The house, which for months had fretted me like a thorn beneath a fingernail, had now come to seem totally unimportant. I only wanted it to be ready quickly so that Antonio could move in.

Much of my time was spent either thinking about him, planning how next to see him or performing for him this or that minor service. I hardly knew where I was wandering with Kitty, absorbed as I was in remembering trivial mannerisms of his or trivial details of his behaviour: the way in which, for example, the winter sunlight brought out the reddish gleam on his cheekbones; the hands clasped around one knee, as he rocked himself ceaselessly back and forth while talking to me; or the day when he called me into his room as he was preparing for a football match and there he was, totally unselfconscious, standing at the window in nothing but his Y-fronted pants, one arm under the other to scratch at his naked, freckled back.

I was always making some excuse to myself in order to call on Penny; and suspecting nothing, poor dear, she was delighted by my attentions. 'Oh,' she would cry out, 'how you spoil me! You knew I wanted these cuttings for the front bed!' Or: '*Dear* Dick! You really are the kindest of friends. How did you guess that a pineapple was the one thing for which I had developed a morbid craving?' Ashamed, I would mumble something inarticulate. Often Penny would have to go away, to attend some committee meeting in London, to visit one or other of the feckless relations whose lives she was always attempting to straighten out, or to take over the household of an invalid friend. 'I really don't know how that silly gel can possibly manage,' she would complain and at once I would say 'You must send them to me for their supper.'

'But that's far too much bother for you. You have quite enough on your plate already.'

'No, no. I'd *like* to have them.'

Invariably Penny would then warn me: 'You know, of course, that Antonio has *the* most enormous appetite.'

'Yes, I do know.'

It was curious how profound a pleasure I used to get out of satisfying that enormous appetite to the full.

Like most Italian men Antonio was used to being spoiled by women. Just as he expected the Swiss girl or even Penny to pick up his dirty clothes, to fold his pyjamas and to scour out the bath when he had used it, so he expected someone to buy him his shoelaces, take his parcels to the post office and give his films to be developed. Since there was no woman on hand to perform these chores, he was willing for me to be the substitute. I remember how, when he had broken one of the laces of those ash-coloured bootees, he asked me where he could find a similar pair and I at once volunteered: 'Oh, I'll get some for you when I'm shopping this afternoon.' I never told him how I had gone from shop to shop, determined to find laces that were exactly the same length, exactly the same shade and exactly the same texture. Eventually I ended up in a remote wholesale shop and the laces were found. 'You are very kind,' he said casually when I handed them to him. How kind, he never guessed.

Often the bell would ring and I would know at once 'Yes, that's Antonio!' 'You must help me, Dick,' he would begin and I would answer 'Of course, Antonio. Anything you want.' Sometimes it was a letter that I had to correct, written in English to a fellow scholar in Cambridge or Oxford or the United States; sometimes he would ask me to explain—a difficult task—a sentence in *Mind* or *Philosophy*. Sometimes he merely wanted me to recommend a cleaner's or to tell him where to buy a typewriter ribbon, and I knew that that meant that he wished me to go to the cleaner's or the stationer's myself. Having lived almost exclusively for myself for so many years, it was odd to begin living almost exclusively for another.

Antonio soon asked me if, when he and Masa came to eat a meal, he might be allowed to cook it.

'Have you cooked before?'

He laughed. 'No. At home my mother cooks, my wife cooks. But here I wish to try.'

'What do you want to cook?'

'Well . . .' He thought. 'You know, Dick, since I went to stay with Miss Ashleigh, I have not once eaten *pasta*. So for our first *piatto* that is what I should like to make for you. Do you like *pasta*?'

'Very much.'

'Good. Let us then begin with a *spaghetti alla bolognese*. All right?'

'Fine.'

'And then—perhaps—*entrecote pizzaiola*. How about that?'

I was dubious. 'Won't that be difficult to do?'

'No, no. Not difficult at all. I can make it easily.'

'But have you ever made it before?'

'No. But I know what to do. Really.'

Eventually we made out a shopping list together and I then scoured the town, as I had once scoured it for the shoelaces, to get him exactly what he wanted.

That evening he and Masa arrived from the University together: Masa in his dark blue double-breasted overcoat, an absurd black trilby hat that, like his shoes, seemed one size too large for him, and the shiny blue suit; Antonio in those tight corduroy trousers that always made me think that any material less durable would long since have split on those squat, muscular legs of his, one of the many pullovers above it, and of course the suede bootees.

'Hello!' he shouted out from the hall. 'Here we are!'

Antonio's face again had the greyness of exhaustion in it; the eyelids were heavy. But at once he dashed into the kitchen, talking all the time. 'Wonderful! You are the most wonderful man in the world! You have found'—he began to examine my purchases—'*maggiorana*—and the best parmesan—and even Italian spaghetti. Wonderful, wonderful man!' He whirled round, whipped an apron off a peg, pulled off his pullover to reveal a singlet torn under one arm, and then placed the apron round his waist. 'Masa and I have bought the wine,' he announced. 'Chianti!'

'But I have plenty of wine,' I protested.

'No, no. You have bought enough. You have bought all these things. Now you must leave me alone and when I am ready I will call you.'

'Don't you want some help?'

'No help. None at all. Talk to Masa. Except'—as I reached the door he called me back—'bring me some gin if you have some. Just gin—no vermouth, no pink, no tonic.'

When I handed him the glass he threw it back at a single gulp and then, with a bow, returned it to me. *'Grazie, signore.'*

Masa was standing in the centre of the living-room of the gloomy basement flat, his eyes fixed ruminatively on the table which I had already laid.

'Do sit down,' I urged.

Awkwardly he placed himself on the edge of the settee, his hands clasped before him. However long I knew him, there was always to be this shyness for at least the first half-hour of any of our encounters.

'What news of your wife?'

Masa was waiting from day to day to hear of the birth of his first child.

'She is well. But we are still waiting.'

'You must miss her.'

He was too stoical to say that he did, though to Penny, who knew him so much better than I, he had often enough confided how difficult he found it to live by himself. Now he shrugged his shoulders. 'Like this it is easier for me to concentrate on my work.' He stared for a while down at his shoes, wriggling first one bony ankle and then the other, before he looked up to ask: 'I think you like to do things for other people?'

'It depends on who the other people are.'

'But you like to look after others?' he persisted.

'Yes, I suppose I do. I'm really rather a bossy sort of person. I always think I know what's best for my friends.'

'I am not a man who wishes to look after others. I like others to look after me . . . You see'—in a sudden rush now he choked out his confidence—'I was an only child, Mr Thompson, and my parents—perhaps like your parents—were rich people. My father was a merchant, a rich merchant. When I was a baby I had everything I wanted. And it has been the same ever since. Now my father is dead and my mother lives with us, and she and my wife are always there to do exactly what I tell them. Perhaps I should be more independent,' he ended on a sigh.

'You must find life difficult in England then.'

He nodded, blinking the luxuriant eyelashes that made a fringed shadow on the cheek he was now averting from me. 'But I have much to occupy me,' he said, with a calm fortitude that then, as so often later, I was to find both so moving and so admirable. 'This is a great opportunity for me, you know. And after my six months here, I am to go on to M.I.T. That is an even greater opportunity.'

From the kitchen we could hear Antonio singing '*La donna è mobile*' in his light, not unpleasing tenor. Masa smiled. 'He is lucky,' he said after a pause.

'Lucky? Why?'

'Everyone likes him.'

Later I was often to wonder whether for Antonio that was luck or a curse.

Eventually the meal was ready. Antonio ripped off the apron, plunged his head through the neck of the pullover, ran a hand through his tousled hair and then dashed back into the kitchen to emerge with a plate piled high with spaghetti.

'But Antonio,' I protested. 'There's enough there for at least a dozen people.'

'Wait and see!'

The food was delicious, as were all the meals that he ever prepared for me. He was, quite simply, what Penny had never been—a born cook, who needed no lessons and no receipts in order to prepare any dish he had ever tasted.

Penny had often enough complained to me about his table-manners and now, as he shoved the spaghetti into his mouth with loud sucking noises, gulped his wine and snatched across the table for bread, I saw what she had meant. But this rapacity, so far from disgusting me, struck me as curiously poignant. I remembered the stories he had told me of how, as a child, he had been dispatched by his mother to a soup-kitchen run by American missionaries; and as he now sprawled across the table, one elbow on it and the other flung across the back of his chair, I seemed to see behind the burly, almost gross, figure stuffing his mouth with food, the timid, sickly child that once he had been. Suddenly he caught my eye, watching him as he ate, and for a moment he paused, his fork, overloaded with spaghetti, stopping in midair and the colour mounting under the profusely sweating skin of his neck and forehead. His gaze was shameful, almost pleading. Then he hit Masa on the shoulder: 'All right, Masa?' he demanded, himself to provide the answer, 'All right!'

'You have given me too much,' Masa pleaded. 'I have not your appetite.'

No one I have ever known has had Antonio's appetite, whether for food or for experience.

At that time I failed to realise that much of this feverish voracity was sexual in origin. I had known many Italian men for whom an interest in women was a mere convention, no different in kind from the convention of the ambitious American woman's interest in the arts or good works. A female colleague of mine in Florence had once summed up such men contemptuously: 'Oh, with them it's all talk and no do,' and I had assumed that with Antonio the case was the same. Habit, I used to say, when at the moment he was telling me something serious, his eyes would suddenly begin to follow some woman, often middle-aged and plain, across the floor of a bar or down the street. Habit, I used to say again, when he started to tell me about this or that secretary or this or that girl student encountered at the University. Often Masa and I would tease him about the 'two thousand miniskirts', about his possible unfaithfulness to his wife back in Florence and even about the Swiss *au pair*; and on these occasions he would laugh with a trace of self-consciousness that should have put me on my guard.

I think that he was trying in those first weeks to remain faithful to his wife; but for someone of his temperament the deprivation was hard. More than once he told me how, as an unmarried footballer of some renown, he had been able to take his pick of the women in any town in which he happened to be playing. 'Not just light women,' he would hasten to explain—I was always amused by that translation of *donne leggere*—'but respectable, married women, rich or of good family. You would be surprised.'

'Not surprised. Horrified.'

'I have made love to every kind of woman. In Ancona I had a love affair with a prostitute. She was a young girl, only seventeen, but already she had been working for three years at the profession . . .'

Dreamily he would reminisce and I would listen, thinking it was worse than hearing Penny talk about meals she had prepared or eaten.

In his frustration he was always leaping up after we had finished dinner to exclaim: 'Come, Dick! Let us go for a walk!' or 'Let us go to have a drink!' He walked fast, as though hastening to some appointment, his eyes darting from side to side of the road or up and down the promenade. In those days he was always touching me—later he was to come to avoid any contact—his arm moving round my shoulder or his hand gripping my forearm with a fierceness that often made me want to shout out 'Hey! Be careful!' All my life I have been embarrassed at touching or being touched by others—when I have lived abroad the constant necessity of shaking hands with all and sundry has filled me with unease—and even with Antonio I would shrink away. Frequently he would pat my head or run a hand through my hair.

Looking back, I see that it was then that, had I had the courage, I might have achieved what now I shall never achieve. He was desperate for the meeting of his body with another body and even my body—male, fortyish, fattening—might have done for him. But I have always suffered from a sexual diffidence in my relationships with men that contrasts with the almost contemptuous self-assurance that I have brought to my relationships with women; and since all love is a kind of confidence trick and a confidence-trick must be based on confidence in oneself, this may perhaps explain the irony of why I have always found it so easy to have the women I have wanted so little and so difficult to have the men I have wanted so much.

My first awareness that I desired from Antonio something more than his daily company came to me on an evening when he brought his friend, Pam Mason, to the basement flat for dinner. He had spoken to me about this girl, as he had spoken about other girls whom he had met either at the University or at parties at the houses of his colleagues.

'Is this the one who came across to you at that party and kissed you on the mouth?' I asked, not remembering which she was.

'No, no. That was another girl. Of that girl I do not even know the name.'

The incident had obviously both astonished and excited him: an unknown girl first pushing her way through a milling crowd of guests and then, drunkenly impudent, throwing her arms round him and pressing her lips to his own, finally to insert her tongue.

'This is a good girl. Not a light woman. She is from Australia,' he added as though that proved it.

'Does she work at the University?'

'For an architect. But she comes to our canteen to see her friends.'

I remembered now that he had once told me of meeting this girl—'carina' was the adjective he had used to describe her.

'Wouldn't it be better to wait until we're in the house?'

'No, no. Pam is a very simple girl. Very home-loving. She will not expect a grand house or a grand meal. Truly.'

'Yes, but everything here is in such an awful *mess*.'

'I want you to meet her. And she is eager to meet you. I have spoken a lot about you to her of course. And she has read some of your books. You will like her.'

I could not say to him—though perhaps it would have been better if I had done so—'Look, dear Antonio, you are a normal man and you are an Italian. You will want to have women friends and I cannot prevent that. But I don't want to meet your women—firstly because I prefer to see you alone and secondly because I doubt if your women are the kind of women I like.' Instead I merely nodded weakly: 'All right. What evening will you bring her?'

At once he began to plan the meal: he was going to make *lasagne al forno*—I should like that, wouldn't I?—and then, since she was so fond of chicken, he would prepare *petti di pollo ai funghi* in the way his wife prepared it. 'You will see. This time it will be a *cordon bleu* meal! And of course we must invite Masa too.'

We fixed a date; and then, after we had fixed it and the girl had been invited, I remembered that it was the day the curtains for the basement flat were going to be delivered. 'Marvellous!' Antonio exclaimed. 'Then I will come and hang the curtains for you as soon as I get back from the University—before I start the cooking. All right?'

'All right.'

We agreed that he would be with me at six, that the girl would arrive at eight and that he would get the wine if I bought the food.

At six he had not arrived and when I telephoned to Penny at six-fifteen she said that though Masa was at home waiting for him, Antonio had not appeared. At quarter to seven, exasperated, I began to prepare the table and at seven I decided I had better take over the cooking.

At ten past seven Masa arrived, obviously perturbed, such was his own invariable punctuality, that Antonio had not turned up. 'It is very strange,' he said, drawing in his breath in his embarrassment and I replied acidly 'It's not strange at all.' I felt on edge; and my efforts to prepare the *lasagne* with the aid of a cookbook—something I had never done before—seemed unlikely to be successful.

It was twenty past seven when Antonio finally rang the bell. 'Shall I go?' Masa called; but I hurried, red-faced, out of the kitchen—by then it seemed to have become unbearably hot—and made for the door.

'*Well!*'

'Dick—please forgive me!' He was breathless, his face greenish in its pallor and pearled with silvery beads of sweat. 'But the supermarket was closed and I have been going all over the town to find the wine.'

'That was not very clever of you then. There's an off-licence just at the corner.'

Pulling off his jacket—as usual he was wearing no overcoat, indeed later I discovered that he did not possess one—he went on; 'I had to go all the way to Market Square—to the Wine Lodge. You remember the Wine Lodge? You introduced me there last week.'

'And it took you—' I glanced at my watch—'one hour and twenty minutes to get to the Wine Lodge and back. You must have been walking extremely slowly.'

'Don't you believe me?' Suddenly he realised that I was angry. He stared at me, the lips drawn back from the gleaming teeth as though in a snarl, the eyes with a beaten, sulky expression in them.

'Frankly, no . . . Look, my dear Antonio, no one spends one hour and twenty minutes in Lymstead looking for a bottle of Chianti. Do they?' Masa had suddenly appeared beside me from the sitting-room, looking from one to the other of us with a smile that could have been expressive either of amusement at our argument or of embarrassment.

'But that is what I did,' he persisted obstinately.

'Don't tell me a lie. I don't know what you were doing but you were certainly not looking for a bottle of wine for all that time.'

'You can ask Kostas Stangos.'

It was not the first time I had heard the name of this young Greek colleague; and in future I was to hear it yet more frequently.

'Kostas Stangos? What has he to do with it?'

'He was with me. He was looking with me.'

'I should have thought him more intelligent. If you don't know where to find a bottle of wine, why not ask a passerby?' I knew that I should not go on, but as so often in our relationship in the weeks that followed rage and a desire for destruction both overmastered me. 'Antonio, you may not realise this but I'm an extremely busy person. I've a lot of work to do and in addition I'm in the middle of a move. You asked me if you could bring this girlfriend of yours to dinner and because I knew it would please you to do so, I said yes. I didn't really want to have as a guest someone I had never met before but I said yes because that was what you wanted. In return I asked you to do something very small for me—to be here early to help me to hang some curtains and to cook the meal.'

'But the meal will take me only a short while to prepare.' He was speaking in a congested voice, like a child on the verge of tears.

'Never mind.' Suddenly I relented. 'It doesn't matter. I'm making the *lasagne* after a fashion.' I forced a smile, propelling him into the sitting-room. 'I get angry easily, but it doesn't mean a thing. Here, sit down. Let me give you a drink.' Already I felt ashamed of my outburst and particularly ashamed because Masa had witnessed it. I pushed him into a chair. 'Gin?' My hand was shaking as I filled the tumbler almost to the top.

'Too much, too much!' Antonio cried out. 'And in any case I must hang your curtains for you. That was my promise.'

'Never mind your promise. People like you have no need to keep promises—or to be punctual or useful.' I gulped my own gin and this time my smile came naturally in answer to his.

Masa, who had had a Christian upbringing, now put in: 'Antonio is one of the lilies of the field. Is that what you mean, Mr Thompson?'

'Yes. A very decorative lily . . . Now you sit here, Antonio, with your drink, and Masa and I will go on with the preparations.'

But in a moment, his drink consumed, Antonio appeared in the kitchen, jerking the pullover off his head to reveal bare arms and shoulders on which the orange hair was thick and furry. 'Now I work!' he shouted.

'No, no. Leave it to me. You're tired after all that rushing about in search of the wine.'

'Truly, Dick, I am sorry. I know that you are angry with me, but it was not my fault.'

'I *was* angry with you. But I'm never angry with anyone for long and certainly not with you, Antonio. Forget it.'

He put an arm round my shoulder, his body, with its smell of healthy sweat—how well I came to know that smell, how evocative it still is for me when I catch it faintly from the drawers into which he used, higgledy-piggledy, to stuff his dirty clothes—pressed against mine. All at once I felt limp and enervated in contact with all that remorseless vitality.

When I saw the girl I thought that I recognised her and I began to search in my memory, even as I helped her off with her coat, for some clue. Then it came to me: the girl in the corner of the compartment on the train to Newen when, on that first day, I had seen Antonio off. This was not that same girl—Pam was better-looking—but both had the same etiolated appearance, as of a plant deprived of the sun under overhanging leaves in some mouldering recess of a garden. As I held the coat against myself, her back to me, I noticed the fragility of the bare arms and the curious blueness, as of watered milk, of her skin. The long, blonde hair might have been a wig in its deadness; and she had a way of running her fingers through it, head on one side, as though it did not really belong to her. She carried herself badly, with a hint of being over-conscious that she was tall above the average, and in this self-effacing stance, hands often crossed over her stomach as though in an attack of abdominal cramp, she always filled me with an unwilling pity for her, even at the times when I hated her most. Certainly she was not the type of woman I had expected Antonio to choose. He had often told me that he had no use for the kind of intellectual women that, alone, attract me—'If I want to talk about philosophy or politics or literature, I do not do so with a woman,' he was fond of saying—and to that extent Pam fulfilled my expectations. But I had supposed that Antonio would opt for someone of a vitality that matched his own, of a strident glamour, of an obvious, even tarty expensiveness and chic. Everything about Pam was muted: her vestigially cockney voice, which was often so faint that, being slightly deaf, I used to be obliged to lean forward to hear her; her clothes which were invariably pastel in shades and soft to the touch; her vague, dreamy movements and her vague, dreamy way of using phrases like 'sort of', 'you see', 'when you come to think about it'. But as I was quickly to learn, she was basically tough, sensible and ruthless.

Antonio fussed over her, dashing between the kitchen-stove and the sitting-room where she sipped, with an odd wrinkling of the lips, at the glass of sherry I had given her. I remember deciding that it was probably too dry for her and finding a certain base satisfaction in that. I had not yet started to think of her as a rival, but I had already decided that Antonio ought not to be wasting his time on anyone so vapid.

As I attempted to talk to her—it was not easy since she showed vitality only when Antonio appeared—I examined her carefully. The large green eyes, with the slightly inflamed lids smeared with a silvery makeup, were her most remarkable feature; there was a defencelessness about them as about the eyes of people who have temporarily removed the glasses they are accustomed to wear. Often when it was cold or when she was reading, these eyes would begin to water slightly and that would add to their pathos. Her teeth were bad—uneven, even crooked, with a dark stain on one in the corner of her nervous smile—and though the slightly beaked nose was now attractive, it was easy to see that with the years it and the pointed chin would inexorably come nearer and nearer to each other, giving her a witch-like appearance.

The *lasagne* were a failure—no doubt because I had botched them in the beginning—but even so the way in which Pam ate a mouthful or two, then put down her fork and took a cigarette from her bag, struck me as ill-mannered. One elbow on the table, with the hand perpetually stroking that seaweed-like blonde hair, she blew smoke across the table at me as she gazed dreamily at Antonio.

'You do not like this?' he asked.

She shrugged and gave a little smile.

'Never mind! The next course will be *marvellous*—or, as Miss Ashleigh would say, *delicious*.'

Having learned how important praise was to Antonio and how deeply he felt any failure to give pleasure, I hoped for his sake that this common bitch (I was already thinking of her in these wholly unjust and ungallant terms) would show a little more enthusiasm.

'Do you like it?' Antonio asked, watching her take her first dainty mouthful.

She masticated, head on one side as she gazed at him. 'H'm,' she said. 'Yes. Not bad. Not bad at all, Antonio.'

'Could *you* do as well?' I wanted to ask. But I contented myself with saying 'It's marvellous, Antonio.'

'Yes, excellent,' Masa confirmed. Unobtrusively sensitive to the feelings of everyone around him, he had recognised, as clearly as myself, Antonio's constant, if unspoken and even unacknowledged, need for applause.

'And you've turned up trumps with this wine,' I added.

Pam raised her glass reflectively to lips that, like her eyelids, had been given an artificially silvery sheen. 'H'm. It's rather good. I always say that you get the best value at the Wine Lodge.'

It was possible that she had merely noticed the name on the label; but at that moment I was convinced that here was the true reason for Antonio's lateness—he had been sitting in the Wine Lodge with Pam. This suspicion seemed immediately to be confirmed by the false heartiness with which he now brandished his glass in the air, shouting:

'Let us drink a toast! Or a number of toasts! To Italy—and to Japan—and to the town of two thousand miniskirts—and above all, to the success of Dick's book.'

'Cheers!' Masa took up in a feeble attempt to imitate this conviviality.

Pam and I merely raised our glasses in silence, our eyes fixed warily on each other.

After dinner I do not now remember how it was that we got on to the subject of sacrifice. I did not intentionally introduce it—though both Antonio and Pam were always to believe that I did. Masa had asked me something about my years in the Foreign Service and I had then begun to tell the story of how, on an impulse, at the moment when I had been offered the post of Head of Chancery in Athens, I had decided to resign in order to devote myself to writing.

'Do you regret your resignation?' Antonio had asked.

'Not really. Though sometimes I regret no longer having that monthly sum of money paid into my bank account, no matter how little work I may have done.' I then spoke about the difficulties of earning a livelihood as a literary freelance, of the freelance's constant fear that either he or the commissions will dry up, of his no less constant fear of an illness that will prevent him writing, of the drudgery of reviewing and reading for publishers and giving broadcast talks.

'You made a sacrifice,' Masa said.

'I suppose so, yes. I believe in sacrifice. Sacrifice gives value to the thing for which it is made. I never really felt wholehearted about my career as a writer until I had cut myself adrift.'

'And do you think the same thing is true about personal relationships?' Masa prompted, as though he and I were in some unspoken conspiracy against Pam. How innocent was he being? I shall never know. If I were to ask him, he would, I know, feign a total incomprehension even of the drift of my question. 'Yes, in personal relationships too. That is why I believe in fidelity between people—tiresome and difficult and even painful though it is.'

'My fidelity to my wife is certainly tiresome and difficult and painful,' Masa giggled.

'But don't the sacrifices you make for your wife give your relationship with her an additional value?'

Masa thought for a while, drawing in his breath on a muted whistle. Then he nodded. 'Yes.' He turned to Antonio who was sitting uncharacteristically mute and uncharacteristically motionless. 'What do you think, Antonio?'

'Antonio,' I took up, 'is like most Italian men—he would like to have his cake and eat it.'

'Cake and eat it?' Masa echoed, puzzled.

I explained the idiom, Masa nodding his head gravely and Antonio meanwhile continuing to remain stiff and still. Pam appeared not to be listening to us, as she patted Kitty, lying on her distended side before the fireplace.

'You see,' I went on, 'this isn't a matter of morality. I don't mean that men shouldn't be unfaithful to their wives or wives to their husbands. I only mean that one should decide what one wants in life and be prepared to make sacrifices for that one thing. A priest can't have sanctity and also a full sexual life, a writer can't have his vocation as a writer and also a career of ambition in the Foreign Service.'

'And a man like myself cannot have a successful marriage and also a successful love affair,' Masa took up.

'Well, it all depends what you mean by success. But no— not in the fullest sense—no.'

Masa sank back in his chair as though satisfied.

At that same moment Antonio leapt to his feet, obviously determined to cut off our discussion: 'Come on! Let's all go bowling! Pam—let's go bowling!'

'Oh, Antonio,' I pleaded, 'aren't we all quite happy as we are?'

'But it is fun to go bowling. Come on!' He caught Pam by both of her wrists and dragged her to her feet.

'No, no, I don't want to go. I hate that place,' she protested. Antonio began to struggle with her playfully. 'Come *on*! Come!'

He was dragging her, still gripping her two fragile bony wrists in his peasant hands, and she was squirming from side to side and pulling away from him with little cries of 'Let me go! You're hurting!'

It was then that I suddenly saw the erection that was thrusting up in the tight corduroy trousers; and it was from that precise moment that my infatuation, until then never consciously sexual, revealed its true nature. I stared, fascinated.

Pam had pulled free, massaging her wrist with a hand, and Antonio's sherry-coloured eyes, clouded with a kind of stricken languor, came up to encounter mine. We gazed at each other, until as though from far away I heard Pam's slightly cockney, slightly adenoidal voice say first 'Beast!' and then ask 'Where did you put my coat, Antonio?'

'I put it in the hall,' I said.

Pam had an ancient Volkswagen, painted not sprayed a black that seemed to cover it like a giant scab. I came to hate that cockroach-like car and everything for which it eventually stood in our lives. There were two imitation leopard-skin cushions on the front seats; the front pockets always seemed about to spew out an undigested diet of used Kleenex tissues, empty cigarette cartons, gloves, chocolate wrapping, maps and guidebooks. The atmosphere was laden with the fumes of petrol. Masa and I got in behind and Antonio got in in front.

'Let me drive,' Antonio urged as she began to start the engine.

'Not on your life!'

'Come, let me drive.'

'The cheek of it!'

Suddenly she had ceased to be remote and vague; there was the same sexual combativeness in this verbal contest as in the physical one that had preceded it.

'Come!'

'I wouldn't dream of it! You'll have us all dead in no time at all!'

After some more of this banter, eventually we were off.

I felt a growing desperation in the brightly lit, voice-filled bowling alley and Antonio must, I think, have realised this, since from time to time he would break off from his attentions to Pam to cross over to me. 'Come on—your turn!' he would shout—and he would thump me between the shoulderblades, grip my arm or give me a push. The artificial conviviality of it all, so much in contrast to other occasions when the conviviality between us had been genuine, filled me with gloom.

Not content with flirting with Pam, Antonio would from time to time turn away from all of us to carry on a conversation with this or that stranger, regardless of sex.

Suddenly I asked 'Do you have to try to charm *everyone* here?'

'What do you mean?' I think that it was my vicious tone, rather than my words, that had taken him aback.

'This Mary Pickford complex is so absurd.'

'Mary Pickford?'

'She was once the World's Sweetheart.' Still he looked baffled. 'Oh, forget it.'

Suddenly I realised that Pam was gazing at me, a bowl clutched awkwardly in one hand, as though she were beginning to revise some opinion already formed of the kind of person I was: not disapproving, not shocked, but certainly surprised and wary, as she had been wary when I had talked of sacrifice.

Soon after that Antonio shouted: 'O.K. Let's go. Dick is our champion.'

'I thought that *you* would be our champion,' Pam said in a challengingly pert tone.

He shrugged. 'I have seldom played this game.'

Later, when I learned that Antonio hated to be a loser, I foolishly used to allow him to defeat me at bowls and any other game at which I could, in fact, excel him.

Outside my house, Antonio, Masa and I got out of the car; then, having thanked me, Antonio got back into it. 'You are not coming?' Masa asked.

'I wish to talk a little to Pam.'

'Let me get Kitty,' I told Masa, 'and I'll walk as far as Penny's with you.'

As we climbed the hill in silence, Kitty waddling breathlessly between us, Masa suddenly said: 'She is not a beautiful girl.'

'No, she's not beautiful.'

'Italians like blondes.'

'Perhaps they do.'

'I thought his girl would be different.'

'So did I.'

'He is the kind of man who can take his pick.'

There was a long silence and then he announced, 'I think my baby will be born this week.'

'Wonderful.'

'I hope my wife will be all right.'

He was anxious, I knew that; and I should have done something to comfort him. But I could only think with a rising desolation of Antonio and the girl seated in that vile little car.

Outside Penny's I said goodnight to Masa, telling him that no, thank you, it was too late, I would not come in. Then I walked back down the hill.

The car was still there and out of the corner of my eye I could see Pam sitting upright at the wheel and Antonio leaning over her, an arm round her shoulder. I do not know if they saw me or if they were so much absorbed in each other's company that they did not notice my passing or hear the click of the gate as I let myself in.

I went down into the basement flat and began slowly and methodically to clear the table while Kitty, always hungry, pattered after me back and forth between sitting-room and kitchen. Then suddenly I could no more bear to look at the remains of our meal and I sank into a chair, dragging her up on to my lap. I put my head down to hers and pressed my cheek against her ear. There was something reassuring about the stubbly feel of her fur and the doggy odour that began to fill my nostrils.

I thought of the erection that had bulged in the tight corduroy trousers—somehow the size of it had surprised me—and of the febrile quality of that silly argument about which of them was to drive. Then all at once, in a moment, I was terrified as, firewatching in the war, I would suddenly be terrified when on an impulse I looked down and down from the roof of my Oxford college into the dizzying quadrangle below.

'What is to become of us?' I asked the dog. I felt what at first I thought was a spasm of abdominal cramp; until I realised that there was a growing pressure in my trousers, mounting to an agonising throbbing, as of some deep-hidden abscess.

4

'What did you think of Pam?'

It was the next day, a Sunday, and Antonio and I were travelling up to London to attend a party given by my brother.

'I thought her a nice girl.'

But Antonio could always see through my pretences, with the same devastating clarity that I could see through his.

'Really?'

'Yes, really. Why?'

He shook his head. 'I do not think you liked her.'

'She's not the kind of girl that greatly interests me. You've met some of my women friends and you know what they're like. Intellectual, worldly, elegant. I think Pam is exactly what I said before—a *nice* girl.'

'What is this "nice"?' He was smiling.

'*Simpatica.*'

'She liked you.'

'Did she?'

'But she said she found you frightening. She is not the first person to tell me that.'

'And who else finds me frightening?'

He shrugged. 'When I first met you *I* was frightened.'

'Then you put up a very good pretence of not being so. But why on earth should I frighten you—or Pam for that matter?'

'You see too clearly.'

He said, simply, what I was so often to say in turn about him.

'Did you sit for a long time in that little car of hers?'

The colour mounted along the flat planes of the cheekbones. With one hand he played with the plastic spoon that lay stuck in weeks-old encrustations of mustard in the pot on the table before us. 'What is this?' he asked.

'What is what?'

He held the caked spoon aloft.

'Oh, that. Mustard.'

'*Mustard!*' He laughed.

'You haven't answered my question.'

'We talked for about two hours. Miss Ashleigh was angry because I came home so late and she had locked the door and I had to ring the bell and wake her up.' He gave me a mischievous look from under his sandy-coloured lashes.

'Only talk,' he said.

'Only?'

'Only. I am telling you the truth.'

'Be careful, Antonio.'

'You have no need to worry. Pam is *carina*, I like the company of a woman from time to time, I like to talk to a woman or to go dancing with a woman.'

'Or to sit with her in her car for two hours after midnight.'

'Yes, also that. But I am not in love with her. I am in love with my wife. And I wish to be faithful to my wife.' He fumbled in the breast pocket of the badly cut grey suit that he so seldom wore—he had none of the usual elegance of Italian men—and pulled out his wallet. 'I have never shown you my wife. Or my two children.'

She was a pretty woman, already on the verge of middle age even though Antonio told me that she was two years younger than himself: her thick black hair parted in the middle and falling to her shoulders on either side of a square, symmetrical face; the bust high and ample; the eyes, as large as Pam's but dark, expressing ill-health and a kind of querulous exasperation even though the mouth, with its full lower lip and the faint traces of a moustache above it, was drawn back in an artificial smile. I felt no twinge of jealousy then, as Antonio leaned forward over the table to stare at her image upside down in my hands; I was never to feel any jealousy of her.

'She is a handsome woman,' I said.

'Yes,' he agreed, curiously dispassionate, as about every woman whom he ever discussed with me, with the exception of Pam. 'She is handsome. From Napoli. Her father was once the Mayor. He did not wish her to marry a footballer, but now that I am a philosopher we are reconciled. You will like her, I think. When you come to visit us in Firenze'—it was the first time that he had suggested that I might visit them— 'you will see what a good cook she is.'

'Does she speak any English?'

He shook his head vigorously. 'No, no. She is not an intellectual.' I did not remind him of the chambermaids and the secretaries and the shopgirls in Florence who spoke English and yet were also not intellectuals. 'Not at all, she is a simple housewife. I prefer it like that.'

From the wallet he drew out another two photographs. 'This is my son—he is now five. My wife writes continually that since I have gone he refuses to do anything she tells him. He is very devoted to me. Sometimes that makes my wife jealous.'

The child in his dark pinstripe suit, his carefully knotted tie, secured with a golden pin with the name 'Carlo' across it, and his slicked-down hair the same colour as Antonio's, seemed perfectly to merit the description 'little man'; and the little man was a replica, but one finer, more delicate, even sickly, of the big man sitting opposite to me.

'He's a handsome boy. He takes after you.'

'That is what everyone says—that he looks like his father. And for some reason my wife is always angry to hear it!' He said it as a joke, but the sentence seemed expressive of some deep-seated grudge. 'When I spoke to my wife yesterday on the telephone she said she wanted me to come back—she could not control our Carlo, she was desperate.'

'But how could you go back?'

'How could I? Of course I could not. I told her it was impossible, impossible. But it was difficult for her to understand. For a woman it is always difficult to understand such things.'

'Not for all women.'

'She believes that one day my work will make me famous. She is proud to be the wife of a philosopher, just as she was once proud to be the wife of a footballer. But the football was something she could understand, the philosophy no. She has no conception of what philosophy demands of a man—the concentration, the self-discipline, the hours of solitude. And she does not understand how important this research fellowship is for me. She only thinks that we are spending more money like this—me here, she in Firenze—than we spent when we were together and that I am learning less. You know, it was difficult to make her agree that I should accept the offer to come here.'

She seemed to me even then a thoroughly tiresome woman, at once obtuse, querulous and selfish.

'The boy—Carlo—gives her headaches. My wife suffers very much from headaches,' Antonio went on. 'He is a good boy, really—very intelligent—but he is—how do you say?'— he paused as he sought for the word.

'*Cattivo?*'

Antonio considered, head on one side. 'More *capriccioso*,' he said. 'A boy needs a man in the house.'

'Is your wife alone?'

'My mother lives with her. But my mother now has angina, she cannot move much or do much.'

Again he searched his wallet and this time drew out a photograph of a grossly fat baby with an upstanding quiff of black hair. It lay on its stomach on a shawl. 'My daughter—Valentina. We call her "Tina". She is only four months old. If it had not been for her my wife would have come here with me and we should not have had all these problems.'

I never know what to say when I am shown babies or the photographs of babies. A bachelor friend of mine usually exclaims 'Now that's what I *really* call a baby,' and the parents are invariably satisfied. 'She's sweet,' I said.

'It is strange, I cannot feel for her what I felt for my son when he was the same age—what I feel for him now. It may be because she was—how do you say?—an error, but I do not think so.'

'Didn't you want the second one?'

He shook his head. 'Not at this moment. That is to say, *I* didn't want her. Perhaps my wife did.' He gave a dry laugh. 'Maybe she thought that a new baby would keep me from going away.'

'But it didn't.'

'No. It didn't. If I want to do something—if I want something—then nothing can stop me.'

'We are like each other in that,' I said quietly.

'Yes, we are like each other.' He smiled at me, still stirring the mustard. 'We are both egotists.'

•

My brother and his wife had invited some fifty people to come in for drinks before lunch and I had promised Antonio that he would meet a number of personalities famous in the world of the cinema (my brother is a film-director), in the arts and in public life.

Antonio, unlike myself, is the perfect partygoer, giving each person to whom he talks the impression that of all those crowded into the room there is no one with whom he would more like to be isolated. His knowledge of English literature is slight, his knowledge of English politics even slighter; yet with a writer here and a Treasury chief or a Member of Parliament there he gave an impression of being not merely totally at his ease but totally in command. When I was in a bitter or vindictive frame of mind, I used to accuse him of having a 'professional' (i.e. insincere) charm; but that was unjust. Antonio genuinely likes the majority of people just as I genuinely dislike them.

Most of the guests were known to me; and as I went among them I never ceased to glance over to see what Antonio was doing, like some prewar mother anxiously supervising her debutante daughter from afar at a ball. How long he was talking to that pimply girl who worked for the British Council—she always liked to give the impression that she was something more important than a secretary—and how much they both were smiling! Ah, now he was with Sir Andrew Masters; that should be interesting for him! But that overdressed bitch who was a film agent of some kind was going to prise him away . . .

Swollen with the heart and kidney complaints that were to kill him off in a few weeks, my old friend, Michael Hart, probably the world's greatest authority on Leibniz, lay back in a chair, his puffy eyelids almost wholly covering his watery, pale blue eyes and his hands crossed over his paunch. Antonio must meet him at all costs, I decided.

'Antonio—may I drag you away?' As I took his elbow, he said to the girl to whom he was talking: 'Well, *ciao* for the moment. But we shall meet again.'

'*Ciao!*' She wrinkled her little nose and raised her hand to wiggle the fingers in a farewell salute.

To the dying old man Antonio was enchanting: at once reverential and affectionate, as he perched on the arm of the chair in which he was sprawling and began to speak of what a first reading of his *Leibniz* as a teenage boy had meant to him. Michael Hart had never married; certainly he had never slept with a woman and possibly he had never slept with a man. I had always thought of him as a homosexual eunuch; but the homosexuality, like the death he knew to be imminent, he always kept even from a friend as old, as intimate and as understanding as myself. But it was impossible not to see and to be touched by his delight—pleasure would be too muted a word—not only in the homage of this brilliant young man but also in his physical presence. Michael had always been an ugly man—morbidly conscious of his ugliness he had once confessed to me that if the gods had offered him one single gift he would have opted for the gift of beauty—and his illness had now made him not merely ugly but grotesque. Yet some of the splendour of Antonio seemed now to be reflected from him, as the sunshine in the street outside glimmers fugitively from the tarnished recesses of a mirror in a shuttered room.

Eventually my sister-in-law came over: 'Oh, Dr Valli, I do so much want you to meet Annie Powell. Do you know who I mean?'

Antonio, who had acquired a taste for pop-music during his years as a footballer, nodded eagerly, jumping to his feet.

'Of course!' He began to whistle Annie Powell's latest song as he followed my sister-in-law across the room.

'What a remarkable young man,' Michael huffed, scratching with the long, yellowing nail of a forefinger at the wen on his chin. 'Quite remarkable! I am sure he'll go far.'

'Do you think him a good philosopher?'

'Possibly. Oh, yes, possibly. But it's the personality—the presence—of which I was really thinking. Quite extraordinary.' When people praised Antonio I always suffered, as now, the same conflicting emotions: pride, as of a parent for an outstandingly brilliant son, and jealousy that, if everyone shared my view of him, he would have no need of me.

The phlegm rattled in the back of Michael's throat, as he coughed, the tears forcing themselves into the small, red-rimmed eyes. Then he jerked a handkerchief out of the breast pocket of his tweed coat and spat into it. 'He's'—he cleared his throat again—'that young man of yours—he's rare, you know. That physical beauty of his. It's not just an external thing, you know. Oh no. It's merely the—the outward manifestation of something within him. A—a beauty of nature. Yes, a quite exceptional beauty of nature.' He gasped for breath; then he fixed his eyes on me, squinting in a startlingly malevolent way, as he said, 'When I first met you—remember?—in Martin Tiverton's rooms in Balliol, you were also an extremely *pretty* young man. Quite the toast of Oxford—even if the toast was beginning to get a little charred. But no one ever suggested that your prettiness—or beauty, if we were to believe dear, sentimental Martin—had any *internal* origin.' He wheezed, as though in joke; but the words seemed to carry all the bitterness of the rejection, so long ago, that nonetheless did not prevent us from remaining the closest of friends or my name from appearing in his will.

'Bring him to dinner this evening, if you've nothing better to do,' Michael suggested at the end of our conversation, levering his huge bulk out of the chair with so much difficulty that I put out a hand to aid him. 'No need to decide now. I'll be at the Club. All afternoon. Ring if you can come. If you don't ring then I'll know that you have other, more succulent fish to fry.'

My first reaction to this suggestion was not even to pass it on to Antonio; then I saw how foolish I was being and at once I felt ashamed. It might help Antonio's career to get to know Michael better; and in what way could the dying man, incapable of admitting his inclinations even to himself, let alone to another, be a rival to me?

After we had lunched with my brother and sister-in-law, I told Antonio about the invitation and at once he looked at his watch, a mannerism with which I was later to become familiar, before asking. 'Which train do we take home?'

'It doesn't matter which. There are two every hour.'

He hesitated. 'I think Miss Ashleigh expects me home for supper.'

'Oh, you needn't worry about that. I can ring her up.'

'She likes to have warning the day before.'

I had guessed already that he had an appointment with Pam and that he was embarrassed to tell me this; but as so often, instead of allowing him the protection of pretence, I felt impelled to force the truth from him.

'Nonsense. On Sunday she never has anything but a cold meal. So she can put the gammon or the sardines in the fridge until tomorrow.'

'Also I must do some work. I have a lot of preparation for my seminar.'

The argument continued, with Antonio getting increasingly embarrassed and increasingly entangled in a web of contradictory lies. But he refused either to give way or to admit that it was for Pam he was hurrying back.

In the train I said to him: 'It was a pity you missed that opportunity.'

'What opportunity?'

'To have dinner with Michael Hart. He was a friend of Wittgenstein, you know.'

'Yes, I know. He told me that.'

Wittgenstein was the philosopher to whom Antonio had often told me that he felt the closest affinity.

'He has a lot of letters from Wittgenstein. He might have let you see them.'

'I can meet him another time.' I was silent. 'Can't I?'

'Yes, I suppose so. If he hasn't died first.'

'Died?'

I explained about Michael's rapidly deteriorating health, concluding:

'You were not really thinking about Penny or about your work when you wanted to hurry back to Lymstead. Were you?' Antonio turned his head aside, to look at the wintry countryside scurrying past the window. 'Were you?'

'Yes.' He spoke the monosyllable with the angry force of a child insisting on something he knows to be untrue.

'You wanted to get back because you have a date with Pam.' Silence. 'Weren't you?'

At that his gaze met mine, suddenly beaten. 'Yes. I am going to meet Pam. But only for a moment. The other things were also true. Miss Ashleigh does not like me to miss meals unless I warn her in advance. And I do have a lot to read tonight.'

'It's odd. If I went to Italy and Moravia or—or Mario Praz or—or Silone invited me to dinner, I don't think I'd let a date with any girl—however beautiful, however brilliant—stand in my way. But I really believe that if Wittgenstein came back from the dead and you were bidden to meet him, you would stand him up for Pam—or someone like her.' I laughed; many of the cruellest things I said to him were said in the guise of jokes. 'Wouldn't you, Antonio?'

He smiled; but the smile had no humour in it, only bafflement and shame. 'Possibly. That is the difference between an Italian and an Englishman. For an Italian women are *important*.'

'More important than a life-work?'

He shrugged and again looked out at the dimming countryside.

'How will you ever become the great philosopher you could become if you have no self-discipline, no singleness of purpose? You spoke just now of your wife not understanding the demands that philosophy makes. But how can she, if you yourself so often ignore those demands?'

Wearily he replied, 'I will never be a great philosopher. You are right. I am a good philosopher, but I will never be a great philosopher. Too many other things interest me.'

At that he closed his eyes and either actually went to sleep or pretended to do so. Fixedly I watched him. His arms were crossed over that deep chest of his, his head lolling sideways almost to touch a shoulder. His legs were thrust out ahead of him, one ankle against mine, and the trousers, drawn up tight to the crotch, revealed the outline of his genitals. The long carriage was deserted and I suddenly had a crazy impulse to put out my hand, either to stroke that smooth cheek or to touch that swelling between the out-thrust legs. I never felt more tender towards him than when I had savaged him.

All at once his eyes clicked open, to stare at me for a second as though I had, in fact, yielded to that impulse. Then the hostility vanished from them and he gave that private smile of his that was so totally different from the public smile with which he had charmed my brother's guests. 'Why don't you also sleep?'

I shook my head; perhaps because of the drink, it had started to throb.

'Tell me, Dick.' Suddenly he straightened himself, ran a hand through his tousled hair and then leant forward. 'Last night—all that talk of yours about—about sacrifice—was that planned for Pam and me?'

'Good heavens no! Why should you think that? I was talking in the most general of terms.'

Again that private smile, welling up out of some deep resource of good nature within him, irradiated his face as it turned towards the window. 'Pam thought you intended it for her.'

'Did she?'

'Yes. In the car she told me that perhaps—that perhaps our relationship was an error.'

'Perhaps it is, Antonio.'

'It is only a friendship. Nothing more.'

I remained silent.

'Don't you believe that?' he pursued.

'I believe it for the moment. And yes, I believe that *you* are not in love with *her*. But I think that she's in love with you.'

'Nonsense!' But he said it without conviction. 'She is a sensible girl.'

'Even the most sensible people lose their heads.'

'She said she wondered if we should continue to see each other.'

'If she wonders that, then she must see some danger. If it were just a friendship between you both she wouldn't wonder that, would she?'

'What you said made her wonder that.' He spoke without any recrimination, quietly reflective.

'I should hate to be the voice of her super-ego—or of yours.'

He sighed. 'Perhaps you're right. Perhaps we should not see each other.'

'Oh, Antonio, I don't know, I just don't know.' Suddenly I felt frightened of the responsibility of separating them. 'You're probably a different type of person from myself. For me there comes a moment when I can't turn back, when I'm—lost.' The last monosyllable seemed to fall between us dully, like a stone. 'Perhaps you can turn back.'

Again he smiled, but this time sadly. 'I have often turned back in my life. I like to—how do you say?—*vivere pericolosamente.*'

'Live dangerously.'

'Live dangerously. But I can always stop.'

'I wish I had the same faculty,' I said, conscious that the train was now swaying along the immense viaduct above the outskirts of the town and that with each jolt of it the throbbing over my eyes was becoming more intense.

'I will go so far and no further. Pam for me is just a *passatempo.*'

'Poor Pam.'

'*Siamo arrivati!*' He rose to his feet, looking at his watch as he did so.

'I hope you're not late for her.'

'No, I'm not late. And even if I were—what would it matter?'

5

'I don't really like him sitting out in that car with her until all hours. There's bound to be gossip. And I certainly don't like him coming in at three or four and blundering about the house and even taking a bath. But he's not a child after all.'

Penny was talking so loudly in the supermarket that heads were turning in our direction and one old woman, a tin of soup in a grubby paw, had even stopped to listen.

'I wonder where it will end.'

'Oh, I don't think he's serious about her. Do you? You know what Italian men are like. Look at Gino and that little slut with whom I had all that trouble.' Penny's previous Italian lodger had made a shopgirl pregnant and the family, assuming from Gino's own bragging that his family was far richer than it was, had made a determined effort to force a marriage. It was Penny who had first extricated the boy and had then arranged both for the girl's confinement and the adoption of the child. 'Antonio is far too hard-headed. And hard-hearted,' she added. 'You're going to take him over on Sunday, aren't you?'

'That's right. The builders will still be in the house but he says he doesn't mind that.'

'He seems awfully eager to get away from me,' Penny said with one of her all too rare flashes of perception. 'And I can't say that I shall really be sorry to lose him . . . Do try this breast of lamb. It's a bargain. I know it looks awfully fatty but I make a really delicious stew from it . . . No, in many ways he's a dear—great fun to have around—but he's not like dear Masa. Not considerate at all.'

'But he's kind, Penny. Kindness and consideration are not the same things and Antonio *is* kind.'

Sensitive to any apparent rebuke, Penny said: 'Oh, I'm not *criticising* him, dear. We're the best of friends . . . Oh, and that reminds me'—she stood on tiptoe to reach for a tin of the baked beans that Antonio told me he so much hated—'I wanted to have a word with you about poor Masa.'

When Masa's baby had been born, four days before, he had invited me to join him, Penny and Antonio in celebrating the occasion with a bottle of sickly Spanish champagne.

'Yes?'

'You know that—now that the baby is born—he wants the wife and infant to join him here in Lymstead before they go on to the States?'

'He did say something about it to me.'

'Well—he's been trying to find a flat—furnished of course—and has drawn an absolute blank. I looked through the *Post* for him and we made appointments for him to see a number of possibles but as soon as he presented himself on the doorstep and mentioned that baby, the flat was mysteriously *gone*. The trouble is obviously that the people who are prepared to have orientals are not prepared to have squalling at all hours of the night, and the people who are prepared to put up with the squalling are not prepared to put up with yellow skins. He's desperate about it. Whether he has an inkling that his colour may have played some part—even a major part—I just don't know. But I do feel awfully sorry for the poor dear.'

I knew already where this conversation was tending and was saying to myself: Now don't be an idiot, you must harden your heart, you can only afford that far too large house because the flat will help to pay off the mortgage. 'It's bad luck,' I said.

'Now there's nothing *I* can do for them,' Penny said. 'But I did think that perhaps that basement flat of yours . . .'

'They could never afford the rent.'

'What *is* the rent?'

'The agents say that with good furniture in it and redecorated it should bring in about twelve guineas a week.'

'Masa could never pay that,' she said in a shocked voice, at the same time glaring with half-closed eyes and bunched lips at a woman who had banged into her with a trolley.

'No, I'm sure he couldn't.'

'He said he could manage eight.'

'That's a big drop. And when would he want the flat?'

'He said at the beginning of May.'

'So I'd have to leave it empty for two months.'

'Miss McComber could probably find you some students for the interregnum. I could have a word with her.'

'Thank you!'

'Some of those University kids are perfectly all right.'

'I'm sure they are. But knowing my luck, I'd get some who were far from all right.'

'I feel we ought to do all we can to help poor Masa. After all he is a quite exceptional person.'

I wanted to say: 'If you're so eager to help poor Masa, why don't you offer to subsidise his rent?—a thing you could easily afford to do with your savings on your purchases of baked beans and stewed breast of lamb.' But instead I merely replied: 'Well, I must think about it.'

'Yes, do please do that, my dear.'

In the hours ahead I did think about it: setting the accumulated bills, the mortgage and overdraft against my affection and admiration for Masa and my memories of innumerable kindnesses in Japan. Then, reluctantly, I decided that he would have to become my tenant.

When I next saw Antonio, a day later, he said to me, apparently apropos of nothing: 'You are a good man, Dick.'

'Thank you. But what has made you decide that now?'

'Miss Ashleigh told me the story of the flat. You will lose money.'

'Well'—I shrugged my shoulders, embarrassed—'I felt sorry for Masa.'

'You are a good man. A kind man.' We were walking down the hill towards the sea and now he linked his arm in mine.

'My kindness is not like your kindness. It is easy enough to be kind to people of whom one is fond—to be kind to Masa or to Penny or—or to you. But I can't be kind to people to whom I am indifferent—I haven't got that kind of generalised benevolence. You can, you have.'

'We shall have a nice time with Masa and his family as our neighbours.'

Antonio had already come to speak of the house as though he were to share it with me and not merely be my lodger; and I myself spoke and thought the same. It touched me that he should take so much interest in it, wandering round even when the builders were at work and then making suggestions, usually so tasteless that I immediately rejected them, of how this or that room should be done up. Many of my pictures and some of my furniture were stacked in what was eventually to be the sitting-room, and I would often look for him only to find *him* in there on his knees in the dust examining some table or chair or peering at a Japanese woodblock print or a Chinese screen. He never ceased to be surprised by the number of my possessions—'So many cups!' he would exclaim, gazing stupefied into a cupboard. 'Why so many? Do you ever have teaparties for fifty guests?' Or: 'What is the use of all these pictures you never hang?'

'I suppose I collect possessions as you collect women,' I answered on one of these occasions. 'If I were happier,' I went on, 'perhaps my cupboards and attic would be less full.'

Antonio's fascination was like that of a hungry child, let loose in an expensive confectioner's; and when from time to time I would say, in one of those excesses of generosity that for me had come to have some of the excitement of the caresses I could never bestow on him, 'Oh, take that, if you like it—it's no use to me,' he would stare down at the ikon, the Imari bowl or the Victorian sand-picture exactly like that same hungry child, incredulous at his luck when a meringue is thrust into his hands.

'You should have seen the house in which I grew up,' he said to me more than once. 'Nothing in it was there except for use. Useful objects can of course also be beautiful—like your stainless steel knives and forks from Finland—but all was ugly, ugly, ugly. Now in my home I try to have a few beautiful things. But for a married man, with a wife who wants clothes and with children who want food . . .'

'Oh, I expect you're really better off than me. Who wants to be a lonely bachelor with only roomfuls of junk, a dog and a cat for company?'

It was then that he first asked me the question: 'Dick—why have you never got married?'

'Because I have never met anyone that I cared for enough.'

'Is that a reason?'

'I think it is.'

'There are many decent, intelligent women who want a home—a husband—even children—but who do not want a profound love.'

'Yes, I know there are. The trouble is that I'm such an absolutist. I always demand far too much from life. As a child, you see, I was the exact antithesis of you—I was brought up in India with innumerable servants and everyone spoiled me outrageously. "Nothing but the best"—that was the phrase my parents liked to use. And so for all my life I've demanded nothing but the best. Sometimes I've achieved it. If I don't, then I fret myself and feel frustrated. The second best doesn't interest me, I'd rather make do with nothing... Yes, of course, I could have a marriage of a kind. But I don't want anything but a perfect relationship.'

'No relationship can be perfect.'

'Once or twice I've achieved one that almost was.'

'It is so sad. You would make such a wonderful father. You like looking after others, you like making sacrifices for others. You need to be needed.'

'You know me well.'

He shrugged. Then, turning away, embarrassed, he said 'Yes, I think I know you well.'

All at once I felt an overmastering urge to unburden myself to him. 'Some women attract me sexually, others become my close friends. But once I have slept with a woman I become bored and exasperated with her—sometimes even profoundly depressed for days on end.'

'Your psychology is strange,' he said, facing me in the dusty attic out of which the afternoon sunlight was beginning to seep away in the same way that I felt all my energy withdrawing from me, leaving me weak and chill.

'Yes, my psychology is strange.' I put out a hand and lifted up a heavy chunk of agate; Antonio looked down at it as though he were afraid that I was about to dash it against his head. 'I'm a mess,' I said.

'Life must be a compromise—always.'

'But the kind of compromise I should offer wouldn't be fair to any woman.' I put down the piece of agate, my hand cold and trembling from its weight, and made for the door. 'So there it is.'

That was the nearest that I came to speaking about my secret feelings until he came to live with me; and the attempt made me feel faint and queasy as, Antonio behind me, I groped my way down the narrow stairs from the attic to the basement flat. Most homosexuals, however great their reticence in youth, begin by middle age to undergo a process of loosening-up. Many, as I know from my acquaintances, even suffer from a suicidal impulse to betray themselves at every turn. But as I had grown older the carapace of secrecy had become not softer but more and more impenetrable around me. To a few of my closest friends I would speak freely of my secret life; but when at some chance encounter a homosexual, divining my true nature with that extraordinary instinct most inverts possess, embarked on the humiliating process of 'letting down hair', I would feel both panic and horror and would at once pretend to have no inkling of the trend of his remarks. Entering a room full of men at a dinner given by a well-known publisher, I remember overhearing a sinuous moustachioed theatrical producer hissing to his companion 'Here's that closet queen! The airs she gives herself!' Only a week before, this same man had frozen me with a series of outrageous confessions about his activities in an East End Turkish bath. Yes, I suppose that description was right: a closet queen.

I thought that this discretion, which all my life had made me seem stuck-up, frigid or prissy to my fellow homosexuals, had remained intact in my relationship with Antonio; but now I see that was wrong. I did not, after the fashion of many of my friends, rush round our circle to vomit out every detail of my infatuation; I did not even speak of it. On one occasion a woman friend of mine, a retired actress who likes to collect about her a small circle of what she calls 'the boys', seemed blatantly to be inviting my confidence by asking me who was 'that absolutely gorgeous foreigner' I was going around with; but I would not commit myself. Yet to this woman and to many other people far less perceptive and far less knowledgeable about the subject, my feelings must have been plain; and the belated realisation of that fact, so humiliating in all its implications, now fills me with shame and self-disgust. Not only at that party of my brother's did I follow Antonio with my gaze as I talked to one group of people and he to another. Like some fatuously doting parent, I would encourage him to show off his parlour-tricks: drawing him out on the subject of philosophy if the occasion was an academic one; teasing him about his conquests at the University when we were among a group of his friends; urging him to sing *'Arrivederci Roma'* or *'Ciao, ciao, bambino'* if we visited the public house where the pianist, a ceaselessly giggling figure with improbable red hair, would greet Antonio as 'Signor Jelly Belly' and would then bawl out for him in a throaty tenor a series of Italian love songs, punctuated by comments, the trend of which Antonio either did not understand or pretended not to understand, that were in the nature of declarations of love.

No less obvious than the pianist's fluttering of his eyelashes, his coy drawing of his flaccid lips together as though the strings of a purse were being tightly pulled, and the occasional maniacal fits of laughter, must have been my more restrained, though no less idiotic attentions. When we were at a party, it was always to him that, without thinking, I took the first drink; it was next to him or near to him that I always seated myself; it was at his jokes that I laughed the loudest, to his stories that I listened the most intently.

Just as I imagined that I was successfully concealing my infatuation from others, so I also imagined that I was successfully concealing it from Antonio himself. Normally a man who shrinks from any enthusiasm or demonstration of affection, I flattered and wooed him outrageously; and he, so far from being embarrassed or annoyed, took an obvious pleasure in my homage. Normal men, it has always been my experience, may on occasion be infuriated or disgusted by the physical intimation of the love of other men; but the love itself, like all love, only brings them pleasure. Antonio is vain, and he has the desire for attention of someone who as a child never received his due share of it. When I am paid a compliment, even one which I know to be true, I feel embarrassed; for Antonio a compliment is like a sudden warming ray of sunshine on an English winter's day. I never wearied of either implying or saying directly that he was exceptionally handsome, exceptionally clever, exceptionally perceptive (all of which was true); and he in turn never wearied of listening to me.

I can see now my blindness in imagining firstly that others did not perceive that I was in love with him, and secondly that he himself did not perceive it. Women friends would come to the house as frequently as men friends; but Antonio must have noticed that my attitude to the opposite sex—comradely, egalitarian, matter-of-fact—was totally different from his. Then there would be the occasional indiscreet friend who in front of Antonio would—no doubt in many cases deliberately—let fall some remark—'You never told me that there were those two divine students living opposite you', 'I thought I'd never be able to park my broomstick in your street', 'Do you like my Jean Harlow rinse?'—that must have made their proclivities entirely clear to him.

Finally there was the incident of our visit to Maurice Rhodes.

This painter, now in his middle eighties, had become a friend of mine after I had written to suggest I might drive out to see his pictures and had then, on an extravagant impulse, bought one of the superb male nudes that at that time he had never put on public exhibition. Later, two friends of mine, an unobtrusive 'couple' who shared a huge Victorian house crammed with works of art, had asked me if I could take them to see the old man and I had asked Antonio if he would like to accompany us. Apart from Wittgenstein, the other modern philosopher whom Antonio most admired was Roberto Siqueiros, the young Spaniard who had been a friend and colleague of both Russell and G. E. Moore at Cambridge and who had died, while still in his thirties, of typhoid during the First World War. Somewhere Antonio had read of the friendship between Maurice and Siqueiros and had even seen a reproduction of the famous Rhodes portrait of the Spaniard, probably the only one in existence, which now hangs in the Tate.

In the car Antonio said, 'It will be interesting to speak to the man who was the closest of all Siqueiros's friends.'

Ralph, the younger of the 'couple', turned around in his seat in front of us. 'Not only friend. Lover.'

Ralph's is a quiet voice and it may indeed be that Antonio did not hear him. Certainly at that point the Italian showed neither interest nor surprise.

Mervyn, who was driving the car, then took up: 'It's odd that the old boy didn't object to all those revelations about his amours in that piece in *Encounter*.'

'Perhaps no one realised he was still alive,' I answered.

'He must have been a great dish in his time,' Ralph said. 'What emotionally packed lives they all led! All those confessions of undying love—all those scenes of fiery jealousy—all those sublime renunciations! And we imagine that ours is a permissive society.'

Still Antonio gave no indication of understanding the trend of the conversation.

Yes, Maurice must have been a great dish in his time, I agreed in thought, as the old man sat talking to us before the huge Russian-type tiled stove that filled a corner of his studio in a recess over which he himself had painted gods and nymphs in voluptuous battle. He was tiny now and his voice was tiny, a mouse-like squeak which made us all lean forward in our chairs. But even in advanced old age, his face lined as though some rough hand had screwed up a piece of tissuepaper and then smoothed it out again, he could bear comparison with Antonio. He was all delicate bones and elegance and grace; so that the antithesis between his body and that of the muscularly solid body opposite struck me as being both funny and sad. If Antonio were to give him one blow of that peasant fist that he was now kneading between his knees, the beautiful old man would, one felt, disintegrate into dust.

'. . . So young men like you still read Siqueiros,' he was saying in a tone of wonder, as though the Spaniard's growing fame all the years since his death had never been known to him till now. 'But you know, I could never understand a word that he wrote—or indeed a word he said on the subject of philosophy.'

'That is exactly my situation with Antonio now,' I put in; and then, realising that my words might imply a relationship that paralleled that between the painter and the Spaniard, I at once felt embarrassed.

'And does he understand your books?'

'He never reads more than the first chapter, so how can I say?'

'Tell me about Siqueiros,' Antonio demanded, with that childlike directness of his when something interests him or he wants something.

'Tell you about him? What do you wish to know?'

'Firstly, how did he come to Cambridge?'

'Well, I suppose indirectly I can be said to have brought him there.'

Like the amatory warfare composed into a formally perfect if muted work of art above the stove, all that jarring turbulence of love, betrayal and jealousy, of which one had heard so often, now seemed to be harmonised by Maurice's slow, silvery voice. 'Yes. Oh dear yes,' he would sigh from time to time, the startlingly green eyes, the colour of the wings of some exotic insect, fixing on one of our faces or another. How much did Antonio understand? And of what he understood, how much shocked him? There was no way of telling, as he sat leaning forward, hands dangling between his knees and gaze fixed on the face opposite.

Somewhere in the recesses of the house a bell tinkled faintly and the old man broke off. 'Let's have some tea. And then if it would amuse you, I'll show you some of my pictures.'

The studio, built on to the eighteenth-century farmhouse in the 'twenties, had been over-warm, making me sweat in my rough tweed suit and causing Antonio to drag off his pullover; but the dining room, in which we sat at a huge round table decorated, like the walls, by Maurice and his long-dead sister, was icy and clammy. There was a homemade date-loaf, a homemade chocolate cake and China tea which we drank out of Japanese-style cups without handles. These last, Maurice told us, had been a gift from Bernard Leach.

It was on such occasions, liberated both from the distraction of feminine company and from that insistent need to woo and charm, that Antonio was at his best. All his questions to the old man were marked by perception and intelligence; and it was touching to see how, tending to be rough in his manners with Penny and myself, he showed to Maurice a marvellous consideration; I could see that the old painter, like the old and dying philosopher at my brother's party, had taken to Antonio at once; so that as we went back to the studio he even murmured to me, the others preceding us:

'How nice your Italian is! You're very lucky.'

Like other of my friends he had obviously assumed that Antonio and I were lovers; and I could not bring myself to explain that he was not 'my' Italian at all.

Ralph and Mervyn were particularly interested in a folio of drawings about which I had told them. Executed in the 'twenties and 'thirties and shown only to a small circle of friends, these were male nudes, sprawled out on unmade beds, putting on their clothes—often the clothes of labourers or sailors—or making love. Many people maintained that all the huge still-lives and portraits in galleries around the world were not worth this one folio of some two hundred exquisite drawings.

'Now I know what your friends want to see,' Maurice said, disappearing into a closet, from which he emerged carrying a huge folder. 'Just one moment.' Twice more he entered the closet, each time emerging with a similar folder. On the second occasion Antonio rushed forward to help him.

'Now, Dick, you can amuse yourself with this one.' He placed a folder on the floor and then set a cushion beside it. 'Your two friends over there had better take this one. And for your Italian friend I'll put *this* on the worktable.'

I opened my folder and began to turn over sketches—as technically faultless and dull as Brangwyn drawings—for those allegorical frescoes which, in the 'thirties and 'forties, Maurice had so often executed for liners and public buildings.

Ralph and Mervyn were muttering to each other, as they lifted up drawing after drawing.

Maurice was standing over Antonio, one hand on the worktable so that his weight was supported on it. There was a small smile on his soft, red lips. Antonio was now holding one of the drawings at a tilt to catch the light and I suddenly realised that it was one I had once admired, of a middle-aged negro and a brutalised-looking white youth, the former's mouth open as though in a scream of horror while the two of them froze, rigid, in hideous erotic contest. I tried to make out the drawing that followed it, but since Antonio did not lift this one to the light, as he had lifted the other, this was harder. But I was sure that it was one, in chalk, of a pathetically emaciated boy, almost a child, lying with closed eyes, a vast erection reaching up almost to his protuberant navel.

Evidently the folios had been muddled. Or had they? Perhaps the switch had been intentional. From all that I had read about Maurice—had not his nickname in the Bloomsbury Group been 'The Angel of Destruction'?—and from all that I had heard about him, it was not impossible.

At first I felt angry at the error, but then as I saw Antonio looking gravely at drawing after drawing, with no sign of astonishment or shock, I was content.

'Could we see that other folio?' Mervyn asked, when they had run through theirs.

'Which one?' Maurice queried. 'Dick's?'

'No. The one Antonio has.'

'Oh that one. Yes, of course.'

There could be no doubt that he was teasing them gently.

When we left, Ralph and Mervyn had bought one of the nudes: beautiful in its draughtsmanship since their taste is unfailing, unexceptionable in its subject since their discretion is absolute. Antonio nursed it across his knees.

I peered at it in the failing light of evening. 'It might be yourself,' I said. Indeed it might.

'Except that I am much more hairy,' he replied literally.

'Yes, except for that.' There was a silence; then I said on an impulse, 'You know, when I have some money to spare, I'd like to commission him to do a picture of you.'

Mervyn turned round in the front seat. 'In the nude?'

'Why not?' I said boldly. 'Those male nudes are the best things he's ever done.'

'Yes, you're right about that. Your picture was a shrewd buy.'

'And your drawing.'

Antonio seemed as totally unembarrassed by this conversation as he had been by the folio of drawings. 'I liked Mr Rhodes,' he said slowly. 'I liked him very much. He is one of the nicest—and most interesting—people I have met in England.' He turned to me: 'Can we visit him again?'

'Of course.' I smiled: 'We shall have to visit him if I commission a portrait.'

That Antonio should so obviously have taken to Maurice and that in the days ahead he should so often refer to him, both when we were talking together and when we were with others, inevitably exacerbated my jealous nature; but it also gave me hope. The drawings in that folio, shown to him either by accident or design, had not shocked him; indeed, so far from being shocked, he wished to see the artist again.

At that time I was always looking for some indication, however oblique or fugitive, that Antonio 'understood'. His behaviour over the drawings seemed to be one; his occasional references to an American missionary who had befriended him as a boy and to what he called his 'trauma' seemed to be others. This missionary, who came from Texas and to whom Antonio always referred as 'Joe', apparently had arrived in Florence soon after the war to work, not as director but as assistant, in a boys' club opened by an American religious sect of which until then I had not even heard the name. It was Joe who first discovered in the boy a talent for football and who had appointed himself his coach; it was he who had found for him, when he had been obliged to leave school at fifteen, a job in a laundry; it was he who used to give him cast-off shoes, shirts and underclothes, which the boy would then sell in bulk to buy some single article of clothing that would fit him. The previous summer the missionary, who in his forties had just married a girl some twenty years younger than himself, had come to Italy for his honeymoon and there had been a reunion first in Florence and then in Viareggio, where the two couples had stayed in the same hotel for four days. Antonio did not approve of Joe's wife—she drank too much, she painted her face too heavily, she had even made to him a number of remarks that suggested that she would not be indifferent to his attentions—and in this disapproval, the symptom perhaps of an unconscious jealousy, I also found cause for hope. I had already convinced myself that the missionary must have seduced the beautiful, destitute and fatherless young boy.

This supposition seemed to be confirmed by Antonio's curious references to his 'trauma'. He would allude to this often, but for a long time it was difficult to get him to be specific about the details. Apparently when he was fifteen one of his schoolfellows had asked him whether he would like to make love to a girl whom he knew. Antonio, then still a virgin, had agreed. The girl, who was sixteen and whose widowed mother went out to work each day in the Palazzo d'Oro Hotel as a sempstress, was suffering from some illness that Antonio could not define but which on the evidence I assumed to be muscular dystrophy. Most of the day she sat in the two-roomed apartment, reading what Antonio called 'yellow novels', thrillers. The boys would have her in turn, one looking on while the other, his trousers lowered but otherwise fully clothed, would grapple with her on the floor, the sewing which she would be doing for her mother scattered around them. 'She was sick,' Antonio would repeatedly say when he talked about her, and I knew that he was referring not to the mysterious paralysis which was destroying her piecemeal but to a sickness of the soul. Insatiably she would demand the attentions of the two adolescent boys; and when, wearied and disgusted, they would attempt to leave her, she would at once badger them to return the next day. There were times when, having returned, Antonio was unable either to achieve an orgasm, or, on some occasions, to achieve any kind of erection at all, and then she would taunt him by making comparisons between him and his friend. It was to Antonio that she was particularly attached. For a while, loathing her but fascinated, he gave in to her voracious will; then he told his friend that he did not want to go back again and his friend, who had by now met another girl, agreed with him. Coming home, Antonio started to avoid the narrow *calle*, at a high-up window of which the sallow, emaciated girl would perch, looking downwards, like some famished bird of prey.

Then the obscene letters started arriving. By good fortune his mother, who invariably got up the first of the family, happened to be ill, with the first intimation of the angina that was eventually to make her a cripple, and so it was Antonio who picked up the letter in a house to which letters rarely came. With growing nausea he read the desperate phrases. His upbringing by his widowed mother, a deeply religious woman, had always been severe. Some of the words he had never dared to speak in his life, though he had heard them of course at school or in the street. He began to tear the letter, written in a large, sloping hand in green ink on violet paper, into innumerable tiny pieces which he then stuffed into the pocket of his shorts to throw away somewhere far from his home. He was trembling all over; his mouth had filled with a bitter saliva.

Day after day the letters would come, now obscenely amatory and now viciously accusing; and inevitably his mother, having made a temporary recovery from her illness, at last came to read one, as she read all letters that reached her children. He would never forget how she rushed at him, white-faced and arms flailing wildly, to demand 'What is this? What is this?' and then to rain blows on his unresisting head and shoulders with her bony fists. Exhausted, she finally collapsed in noisy weeping across the kitchen table, calling on his dead father, on Christ and on the Virgin to witness their shame.

For months it went on, day after day; and his mother never once proposed that she should go to see the mother of the girl or even the girl herself. This, she seemed to imply, was the punishment for his terrible sin, each letter like the sting of a lash across his bare back to drive out the devil that had housed within him. Then at long last, with a mixture of horror and relief, he had heard from that same friend who had shared the whole experience but who, mysteriously, had never been a recipient of a single similar letter, that the girl's body had one afternoon tumbled out of the high window into the street, crashing on to a cart loaded with vegetables that was standing below, and so frightening the horse that it had bolted. Everyone had tacitly agreed, as so often in a Catholic country, that the tragedy had been an accident—*la poverina* was ill, no doubt she had lost her balance, no doubt she had been taken giddy or had a sudden fainting fit. But for Antonio there was no doubt that it had been suicide—'In a way I can say that I killed her.'

From then until he was nineteen he avoided all women. 'Yes, they still fascinated me, of course. Sometimes I had erotic dreams about them, I would masturbate thinking about them. But even when I had to talk to a woman I would feel myself begin to tremble, my face to redden, my eyes to blink or look away.' At nineteen he had gone to a brothel, drunk, with a party of his fellow-footballers—he had been terrified that he would be unable to do anything but he had been even more terrified of their mockery and contempt if he refused to accompany them—and there, on the worn-out body of a Jewess with greasy black ringlets and huge earlobes transfixed with gold studs each the size of a lira piece (he described all this with fastidious exactness), he had at long last recovered his manhood.

It was in those years from fifteen to nineteen that now I sought for hope. A fatherless boy, unable to draw near to his mother because of a religious fanaticism in which he could not share, must have had some emotional outlet outside his family; and if not with a woman, then surely with a man. My novelist's imagination then got to work: the outlet must have been Joe, who else? It was, after all, significant that it was during Antonio's nineteenth year that Joe had finally left Florence for good. I often used to try to coax or exact from Antonio an admission that Joe had been his lover; but since at that time we had never once openly discussed or even mentioned the subject of inversion, it was as difficult for me to force the issue as it was easy for Antonio to evade it.

'This Joe—you were very attached to him I suppose?'

'Yes, I liked him. He was a good man.'

'He must have been a kind of father-figure to you at that time.'

'He did me many kindnesses.'

'It's strange that he married so late in life.'

'He is a man who lives almost entirely for others. Perhaps he did not marry sooner because he never had time to think about himself.'

Round and round we went; and I never knew if Antonio was aware or not of the question that I never dared to put point-blank to him.

'I should like to meet this Joe,' I said on one occasion.

'I don't think you would like him.'

'And would he like me?'

'I don't think so.'

'Why?'

He thought a moment. 'You are—different. Completely different.'

'In what way?'

Again he thought. 'Joe is a very simple man. Basically very simple.'

'And I am not?'

He smiled. 'Of course you are not. How can you ask that!'

Whether this comparison was in my favour or not there was no way of telling.

'He's handsome?' I pursued.

Antonio shrugged his shoulders. 'I do not know. Perhaps. Now he is getting fat.'

'Like me.'

'Worse than you.' Again he smiled. 'But he is stronger than you,' he added.

It was curious to feel jealous of someone I had never met, married and living hundreds of miles from us; but mine is an abnormally jealous nature. I remember how, many years ago, I had a love affair with a Polish boy who had survived the concentration camps. In the camps he had been befriended by an older man, who had later become his lover; the older man had died in the gas-ovens, the boy had precariously survived. In the boy's room there had been a faded snapshot of the dead man, in a cheap passe-partout frame beside the bed, and often, after we had made our savage, sterile kind of love, I would find myself staring at that smudged face in a sudden access of loathing.

Making Antonio talk about Joe was the present equivalent to that obsessive staring at the snapshot; and the feelings both situations evoked were exactly the same.

6

In the months that followed I was to say or to think many bitter and even vicious things about Antonio: that he was selfish and ruthless and egotistical, and that he had exploited me and betrayed me. But then I would think of his kindness to me over my move and at once I would feel remorse.

Some of my friends said to me 'If there's anything I can do, you will let me know, won't you?' secure in the knowledge that I certainly would not bother them. Some, like Penny, said after the move was over: 'Oh, I'd completely forgotten that you were going to move. I do wish you'd let me know.' Only Antonio actually did anything.

The builders were still in possession of the house, having long since become a joke to all my neighbours. The central heating had been installed, and, complaining of the cold, they had persuaded me to keep it functioning all day. As I emerged from the basement or as my neighbours passed, there the builders usually were, squatting in the sunshine that flooded through the amply swelling bow-window of the drawing-room, with their thermoses and packets of sandwiches and their newspapers and their transistor-sets around them. When

I had said firmly to the contractor that on March 1st I was going to move, he had answered 'Oh, but that's quite out of the question.' But I had found some students to take the flat from that date until Masa required it, and I had insisted that move I must.

There was, not unnaturally, chaos as the remover's men started trying to carry pieces of furniture into rooms that were only half-decorated or from which floorboards were missing. 'You'll have to shift that trestle, mate, if we're going to get past.' 'If you want it moved, you'll fucking well have to move it yourselves.' 'Mind that bleeding stair-rail! Can't you see the fucking paint is wet?' 'I can see it's fucking wet on me trousers.'

The marble top of a Victorian break-front wardrobe, its milky texture veined as though with orange wisps of smoke, was dropped in the drive and shattered in two. The largest of the remover's men flung himself down in feigned exhaustion on to a Regency settee and, to the uncontrolled hilarity of everyone but myself, managed to break a leg. A pot of paint was kicked down the stairs, splashing the carpet that was in process of being laid.

Eventually my daily and I retreated to the kitchen where we sat drinking tea, a rampart of kitchen equipment, furniture and still unlaid linoleum growing higher and higher around us. Neither of us spoke. The transistors blared; the voices grew louder and louder in the directions, or, more often, the insults that they shouted at each other.

Then suddenly I heard from the hall: '*Ecco mi!* Dick, I have come! I am at your service!'

It was Antonio, rushing into the kitchen to fling his battered and bulging briefcase on top of the pile of linoleum, to pull off first his jacket and then his tie and to roll up his sleeves to reveal those muscular arms with the orange hair thick on them. 'What do I do? Instruct me.'

'But you shouldn't have come. I know how much you have to do at the University this week. You have that seminar of yours—'

'Nonsense! Come—what do we do?'

He did many things—carried the heaviest furniture, snatching it from the astonished remover's men; hung pictures; even helped to lay the carpets—but his chief service was somehow, God knows how, to persuade remover's men and builders to cooperate. Perhaps it was his charm; perhaps the example of all that irresistible energy which he squandered with a recklessness that contrasted cruelly with the parsimony with which they hoarded theirs. He never for one moment let them think, as I must have done, that he was in the 'boss' class. 'Come along!' he would rally them as one of themselves, helping to hoist a wardrobe to the top of the house or humping a bed on his back. Me they would never call anything but 'Mr Thompson', but already they were all referring to him as 'Tonio'.

It was on such occasions that he was always at his best. The trivial expressions of gratitude, the trivial acts of good manners or kindness with which most of us maintain the convention of caring about our fellows were usually beyond him; but in what was important he would seldom fail. Weeks later, when I had a wisdom tooth out, no one could have been gentler or more helpful; yet he was the kind of person who habitually forgot to say thank you for a present, who would change the television channel without a by-your-leave and who would race up the stairs, making the whole house vibrate, at five o'clock in the morning.

The day following my move Antonio moved in too. 'Wouldn't you rather wait until the house is really in order and the builders have left?' I suggested; but he was gratifyingly eager to join me at once.

Penny drove him over with his luggage, booming out at me as soon as he left the sitting-room: 'Well, now I make him over to you—and good luck to you. I've nothing really against him but I can't say I'm sorry to have him off my hands.' Antonio, going up the stairs with his two suitcases, must have overheard her.

I gave him the choice of two rooms: the one huge, with a ceiling that I had mistakenly made to seem even more cavernous by the device of painting it a dark blue above the white walls in an attempt to bring it down; the other much smaller, with a bow-window overlooking the garden. It was the latter that he chose. At the time I thought that this showed a natural taste; but in the light of subsequent events I came to wonder if the reason for his choice may not merely have been that to go to the big room he had to pass my bedroom door and that if he came home late or if he came home accompanied the other would therefore be more convenient.

This small room had white-painted shutters, against which hung some red damask curtains. On that first day Antonio stood by the window, running the damask through his fingers much in the way that, in an intense heat, one refreshes one's fingers in the waters of a stream. 'So soft,' he said. 'Beautiful.' 'I got that silk in Japan.' 'Beautiful.' But when I went into the bedroom the next morning after he had gone to the University, excited, as I was always to be, by the smell rising up from the garments that littered the floor and from the bedclothes that were so much twisted and rumpled that they suggested hours of frantic lovemaking, I was appalled to see that in an attempt to exclude all light he had pinned the edges of the curtains to the shutters with drawing pins. Later I remonstrated with him.

'But it's nothing. I can repair the holes for you in the wood. I need a little—what do you call it?—*gesso*, that is all. You must not worry about such trivial things.'

I knew that it was typical of a homosexual to be worried by a dozen small holes in some freshly painted wood. But his casualness rankled then, as it still rankles when I see the holes, never—needless to say—repaired despite all his promises.

Those first ten days were, I now think, the happiest I have ever known. Even at breakfast, a time when normally I wish to be silent, he would dazzle me with his talk. Then shouting '*Ciao*' he would race out of the house, leaving me to make his bed, fold his pyjamas and clean his shoes—tasks I should be reluctant to perform for anyone else. All day I would work, with no desire to see anyone else of my friends or even to leave the house. At six he would return, often carrying a bottle of wine or a bag of fruit. 'Now I cook,' he would announce and, if I protested, he would at once silence me: 'No, no! You are tired! I cook!'

After eating we would go to a cinema or for a walk on the front or for a drink at the local. Once he went out alone to meet Pam, coming home God knows how late—that was a period when I was still able to sleep before he had come home; once she joined us at the pub for a drink. I thought that he was losing interest in her and of course that pleased me.

That next weekend she was apparently going to visit some distant relatives, cousins of her mother, who ran a boarding-house in Bournemouth. 'Why don't you come over for the day?' she suggested to him in front of me. But Antonio shrugged his shoulders—he had a book he must read and a number of letters to write.

When he came home from the University on Monday afternoon he said to me, more amused and puzzled than distressed: 'It is very strange—Pam seems not to wish to meet me.'

'How do you mean?'

'Usually I have lunch with her in the canteen at one. But today she was not there. And when I asked for her on the telephone, they said she was too busy.'

'Perhaps you've done something to annoy her.'

He shook his head. 'How could I have annoyed her? It is very strange.'

Twice more that evening he reverted to Pam's behaviour: he had been growing bored with her but now his interest had revived.

The next evening he described to me how he had waited for her outside her office, how she had remained inside, apparently knowing that he was there, long after the hour she usually left, and how she had then tried to hurry past him in the company of a frumpish girl who lived in the same lodging-house. But he had caught her arm, saying 'Pam, what is all this? What is the matter? Let me talk to you for a moment.'

They had sat out on a bench in the square, Pam shivering from the cold but wrenching away from him when he had attempted to draw her close into the shelter of his body. She had explained that she had decided that what they were doing was 'wrong' and 'pointless'. He was a married man, he loved his wife and his children, she knew very well that she would never get anywhere and that she would only make herself unhappy. They had better part before there was anything really serious between them.

Antonio had tried to argue with her—why could not they just be friends?—but she had jumped up off the seat, drawing her coat tight about her, her hands deep in its pockets. 'Oh, don't go *on*!' she had cried out; and when he had also risen to his feet: 'And I don't want you accompanying me to the station.'

As he recounted all this Antonio was seated at the kitchen table, while I peeled the potatoes for our supper. 'She is a good girl,' he concluded. 'A very good girl. You know, she is deeply religious. Perhaps when she was in Bournemouth, she consulted a clergyman. Certainly she must have talked with her relations.'

'Oh, you'll see her again, don't you worry.' But I said it not to console him but out of the certainty that such good fortune could not possibly come my way.

He shook his head gravely. 'No, no. She has a very strong will. You do not realise that, because she seems such a quiet and timid girl. But I know—if she wants to do something she does it.'

'Antonio, Antonio!' I cried out in desperate mockery. 'Stop thinking in terms of Italian opera! In *Traviata* Violetta's renunciation is something beautiful, I know, but in real life *la grande rinuncia* seldom takes place. You'll see!'

Impervious, he again shook his head. 'She is that kind of girl. I admire her for it. She will suffer.'

I could see then that, whether intentionally or not, she had played her cards with the skill of a professional. Antonio was vain, as only Italian men can be vain; he could not let himself believe that she had given him up except as a gesture of supreme renunciation made with a maximum of agony to herself; and he could not accept that gesture without a struggle to regain her. To test my analysis, I now said:

'Well, you may be right . . . Poor girl! . . . You know, it's probably best that it should all end like this before you become too deeply involved with each other. You must now make the break as easy as possible for her.'

'As easy as possible? How?' Obviously he had already decided to make the break as difficult as possible, if not unthinkable.

'Write her a little letter,' I suggested. 'That would be the kindest way to do it. And send her some flowers—a present of some kind. Say that you want to thank her for her friendship, that you are sorry that it has to end like this, but that perhaps she is right and it is better for you to separate.'

I watched him closely: obviously my suggestion had little appeal for him. In his world women might occasionally indulge in gestures of renunciation, but men never.

'It is better to do nothing,' he said at last. 'That will make it easier.'

'How do you mean?'

'If I write to her then she will feel that she must write to me and so it goes on. But this way a break is possible.' He knew that all this sounded lame; shamefaced he glanced up at me: 'Don't you agree?'

'Not really. But never mind.' I left the potatoes and came and sat down opposite him, willing him to raise his eyes to mine. 'Antonio—I'll take a bet with you. Antonio!' Now he glanced up: but at once he looked down again. 'In two days—or three days—or even perhaps a week—Pam will be round again.' He shook his head in simulated woe, but I could see that my words had cheered him. 'Yes. Wait and see. I bet you anything, of course she will.'

'She is not that kind of girl.'

Suddenly I spoke with passion. 'Of course she's that kind of girl—every girl is. Do you think she's going to give up a man like you unless she has to? What kind of men do you think she has attracted in the past? You're way beyond her league—she's like the captain of a village football team who suddenly sees an opportunity of getting hold of a first division player. A miracle! Do you think she's ever had a boyfriend as brilliant as you—or as handsome as you—or as generous as you? Of course not. And she never will. Never, never, never!'

He seemed to be elated by my vehemence; he broke into a smile. 'You are too cynical,' he said, still smiling.

'No, Antonio. Realistic.'

In the event it was two days later that she telephoned to the house, to ask in that flat, slightly nasal voice of hers: 'Is Mr Valli there?'

She must have known that she was talking to me and I felt angry that she should neither greet me nor refer to Antonio by his Christian name. 'It's Pam, isn't it?' I said sharply.

'That's right. Is Antonio in?'

'He should be here any moment now.'

'I'll ring him later.'

When I told Antonio of the call he attempted to conceal his elation but with little success.

'What did I tell you?' I asked.

'No, no. This is not a reunion.'

'What else can it be?'

At that the telephone rang again and Antonio dived for it.

'Yes... Pam... How are you? How are you, Pam?... You are well?' When Antonio talked on the telephone, it always amused me to watch him. All the cajoling smiles, all the gestures, all the little moues that he used in ordinary conversation would be deployed as though visible to his auditor at the other end of the line. He would move about, place his head on one side, suddenly perch on a chair and no less suddenly jump to his feet.

'Well?' I asked when he had replaced the receiver.

'She wishes to give me back a torch.'

'A *torch*?'

He was obviously aware of the flimsiness of the pretext. He smiled in mingled embarrassment and pleasure. 'I lent her my torch one night. She had dropped something—an earring—on the floor of the car. Now she wishes to give it back. She wants to meet me to give it back.'

'Antonio, Antonio! You see, I was right!'

I cried it out as though in joke but I felt an intense vexation. Antonio began to laugh. 'No, no. You will see. It is only for the torch. Only to return the torch.'

Until then I had not disliked Pam, because she had seemed to me to be a victim no less than myself. But her ruse (for that is what it then seemed to me, though now I cannot be sure) had shown that she knew both how to look after her interests and how to 'play' Antonio with a coolness that I, so much older than her and so much more experienced, could not emulate. When his interest had begun to flag, she had known exactly how to stimulate it; whereas I, incapable of dissimulating my devotion and unwearying in my discovery of ways to express it, did exactly what was needed to make Antonio bored and exasperated with me. The sad truth is that though I am adept at the small insincerities that go to contribute to the smooth functioning of social intercourse, about the big emotions of love any concealment is repellent to me. To attempt to make another person jealous by feigning an interest elsewhere, to retreat only with the motive of being pursued, to pretend provocative indifference—all such things strike me as blasphemies, I cannot do them. I loved Antonio and I had always to behave as though I loved him, whatever the annoyance to him or the damage to myself.

It was from that telephone call that I date the slow clouding-over of a relationship that, until it, had seemed to be irradiated with a perpetual sunshine. The process was, of course, a slow one; it might have been slower if my jealousy had not precipitated a series of confrontations between Antonio and myself.

He ran out of the house as soon as supper was over, shouting 'I will be back in time to watch that television programme.' A Cabinet Minister was due to appear to explain the economic situation and Antonio was eager to see what he would make of a task so difficult. In the event I watched the programme alone, hardly listening to the glib, sibilant voice as I waited for Antonio's return. At eleven I took Kitty for her usual late-night walk, glancing in turn at the cars parked up the road to see if I could pick out that obscene cockroach of Pam's. Eventually I lay in bed, half-awake and half-asleep, as I was to be so often in the weeks that followed, *The Times* crossword propped on my chest and my transistor set tuned to 'Night Ride'. 'This is absurd, turn off the light, go to sleep,' I told myself; but still I waited. Once I heard the voices of a man and woman, carried up to my window on the still night air; once the gate creaked open and shut but it must only have been one of the students, I never knew their number, who had become my tenants.

It was long after one when I heard from far away the sound of Antonio whistling '*Ciao, ciao, bambino*' as he made his way up the street. The gate creaked open and then banged shut—later I always knew from that bang that it was he and not one of the students—and then the front door opened and also banged. He was in the kitchen below me now. I imagined him draining a bottle of milk or cutting himself two huge slices of bread and then placing a slab of cheese between them. But when he appeared at my bedroom door—purposely I had left it half-open so that he should see the light—it was an apple he was munching.

'Why are you awake?' he asked. 'It is late for you.'

'It's late for you too.' I patted the eiderdown. 'Tell me what happened. I was right, wasn't I?'

He came slowly over to the bed, without speaking, the apple held to his mouth but his teeth no longer tearing at it.

Still without speaking he sat down, raising one knee off the ground so that his body was sprawled over towards me. 'We talked,' he said at last.

'You *talked*? And what did you decide?'

'We decided that we can still be friends.'

'Friends!'

His face darkened at my derisory tone. 'Yes, friends. Only friends. We enjoy the company of each other. But we are adults, we are sensible people. She knows that I am a married man and that we can never be lovers. And I know that I must not become her lover.'

'But you will,' I said softly. Suddenly I was transfixed by despair, as though some rusty stake, driven through my breastbone, was holding me rigid against the pillows. 'Oh, you will.'

'Why do you say that?' he demanded, with the anger of someone who does not wish to face what he himself knows to be true. 'I love my wife. I do not want another woman.'

'Yes, you may love your wife. But of course you want another woman. That's your nature.'

'If Pam were another kind of girl—a light woman or a married woman—then perhaps it might be different. But it would be very wrong for me to seduce her when I have no intention of marrying her.'

'Perhaps she will seduce you because she has every intention of marrying you,' I said in bitter joke.

'What kind of girl do you think she is?'

'I think she has an immensely strong will. She knows that if she's skilful she may hit the jackpot. She's certainly not going to give up the chance of doing so.'

'The jackpot?'

I did not bother to explain; I could see that he had got the gist of what I was trying to tell him.

He leant closer to me across the length of the vast Victorian brass bedstead. 'Dick—I have always been pure with her,' he said. 'I have always been pure for the sake of my wife.'

I wanted to ask brutally 'What do you mean by "pure"? That you've kissed her but not been tossed off? That you've been tossed off but not sucked off? That you've been sucked off but haven't fucked her?' Instead I merely gazed at him, my eyes suddenly pricking as though there were grains of sand beneath the lids.

'You think I have no self-control,' he went on. 'I like to joke with women, to flirt with them, to boast of what I have done with them. But I am a serious man, truly I am a serious man. I like to *vivere pericolosamente*—yes, I know that. But I am always in control of my emotions. I can go to this point and I can turn back.' He gripped my leg under the bedclothes. 'You must not worry about me. You worry too much about me, Dick. I am not a child. I have had to look after myself since I was fifteen. I know how to do it.'

Yes, he knew how to look after himself; it was my mistake to imagine that he needed me to look after him. 'Why did you not go to sleep?' he asked, with that tenderness so common between normal men in Mediterranean countries and so uncommon in Anglo-Saxon ones. 'Were you waiting for my return?'

I nodded.

'But why?'

'Because—oh—I suppose because I was anxious.'

'About myself and Pam?'

'Yes, that too.' Once again I was consumed by a suicidal impulse to unburden all my secret feelings. 'And about yourself and me.'

I watched him closely, with thumping heart, to see the effect of these last words.

'About us?'

I nodded.

'But why should you be anxious about *us*?'

'I think I have become too fond of you.'

He stared at me in silence, the bedside lamp fretting a jagged shadow across his left cheek and the eye above it.

'These last weeks—with you here'—the words seemed to come out of me as though in spasm on spasm of effortful retching—'I have never been more happy.'

'I have also been happy.'

'Yes, perhaps. But not in the same way.'

'But why should all this make you anxious?'

'Because I have been happy, very happy, but I know I must be unhappy, very unhappy.'

He laughed. 'What do you mean? I do not understand you. Why should you be unhappy?'

'Because nothing lasts. Because, oh, because the whole situation is—is absurd.'

'I do not know what you are trying to say.'

I still could not shout: 'Idiot! I love you!' Instead, still prevaricating, I went on: 'You're married, you have your family. Our friendship can't possibly mean to you what it means to me. Soon you'll go back to Italy and that'll be the end of it.'

'But your friendship does not end when I return to Italy! Why do you think such a thing? You will come and stay with us in Firenze, we will come and visit you in England. You do not understand what friendship means to me, Dick. I have many acquaintances but only a few friends. You are one of those friends. I never forget my friends.' Again his hand pressed my knee through the bedclothes.

'Yes—but we'll never again be as we are now. I know that. And it saddens me.'

'I do not understand you!' he exclaimed in good-humoured exasperation; but I wondered if he really did not understand me or if he found it less embarrassing to pretend that he did not.

'Perhaps I am more complex than you imagine... Anyway forget what I've said.'

'Why must you always think so far ahead?' he asked, getting off the bed and looking down at me with eyes that were blurred with tiredness. 'We are together now. Forget that one day we must separate and enjoy our being together.'

'You're lucky. You can live in the present—without regret for the past, without anxiety for the future. I can't, I wish I could.'

Some of the clarity of my despair seemed at last to have got through to him. His lower lip trembled slightly as he gave a small smile: 'That is life,' he said in a husky voice. '*Tout casse, tout lasse, tout passe*. You know that French saying?'

'Yes, I know it. And how dreadful it is.'

'Sleep, Dick. You must sleep.'

'Yes, I must sleep.'

He put out a hand and first took the crossword from me, then switched off the bedside lamp. 'Goodnight, Dick.'

'Goodnight, Antonio.' I forced myself to add: ' I'm glad it all worked out all right. With Pam, I mean.'

He left the room without answering.

I listened to him moving about in his room, going to the lavatory, then brushing his teeth. I thought I even heard the creaking of his bed as he climbed into it. Then there was a long silence in which I listened only to a thud, thud, thud in the eardrum that was pressed against the pillow. On and on it went, like an amplified extension of the heartbeat that I longed only to be stilled.

7

I remember one of my women friends once confiding in me that she thought that her husband was being unfaithful. 'What on earth makes you think that?' I asked, though I knew that she was right, and she answered, 'He's started to be so generous with me.' Antonio had always been generous with me—with everyone he gave as freely of his possessions as of himself—but now he surpassed himself. Rarely a day passed when he did not bring in a bottle of wine, a box of chocolates or some cigarettes. But of his time he gave me less and less.

'Would you like to come with me to see that Italian film?' I would ask, for example; and he would then say in a hurried, oddly breathless voice: 'I must go over to Kostas—we must do some work together in preparation for our seminar.' 'Penny is giving a little party for someone who is staying with her and has asked me to bring you,' I would tell him: and again in that same voice, as if he had just been running, he would excuse himself; 'Kostas has invited me to join some friends at the Top Rank.'

Antonio and Kostas shared a room at the University; but the Greek was a silent, morose youth, single-minded in his research, and I could not believe that Antonio would wish to spend almost every evening in his company.

My suspicions were confirmed when one Sunday evening I ran into the Greek outside the post office, where we had both gone to buy stamps from the machine. At first, although we had met on two or three occasions and although he had even visited my house, Kostas pretended not to see me, busying himself clumsily with the machine while I stood at his shoulder.

'Hello, Kostas.'

'*Ah*, Mr Thompson!' He swung round, the thick lenses of his glasses making his eyes bulge enormously as they reluctantly sought out my face. He licked one of the stamps on a greyish tongue and affixed it to his letter, then he licked two more. 'It is many days since I wrote to my mother,' he explained. 'She is a widow and I am the only son, so I must write to her often. But I have been so busy with my work.' He crossed to the box, examined the envelope for the last time and then popped it in. 'How is Antonio?' he asked.

'I thought that he was with you.'

'With *me*?' He was astonished. 'Oh, no, Mr Thompson. I have not seen him since Friday.'

'I must have been mistaken.'

Awkwardly, in silence, we began to walk away.

'You are going to Greece for your holiday this year?' Kostas was one of those shy people who repeat the same conversations over and over again with others. We had had this one before.

'I'm not sure. Antonio would like me to go to Florence. But really I prefer Greece to Italy.'

Kostas gave a little smirk. 'If you visit Patras I hope that you will visit me and my mother.'

'Thank you. That would be very nice.'

Each of us knew that both the invitation and its acceptance were merely politeness.

'Here I must leave you.' He pointed in the direction of where he lived. 'Please give my greetings to Antonio.'

'Yes, I'll certainly do that.'

That evening I had a review to complete, and since the novel was one which had interested me intensely I was able to absorb myself in my writing to the exclusion of any thought of Antonio's lie.

He came home early, soon after eleven, to burst in on me in my study while I was hammering at the typewriter.

I looked up: 'Did you have a nice time?' My tone was distant.

'Very nice, thank you. But the room in which we danced was far too hot and so I decided to come home.' He gazed over my shoulder, one hip pressing against my arm. 'And what have you been doing?'

'Writing this review.'

'All evening? Dick, you work too hard.'

'Except that I walked to the post office to buy some stamps.'

'I could have bought them for you. I passed that way to catch the last post with my letter for my wife.'

'Do you still write to her daily?'

'Yes, of course. Why?'

I knew that he had already begun to suspect from my tone that something was amiss.

'I met Kostas.'

'Kostas?'

'Yes, he was also buying stamps. He sent his greetings to you.'

'Thank you.'

There was a long silence. I typed another word, then lowered my hands from the keyboard and turned to ask:

'Why did you tell me you were going to a party at Kostas's?'

'Did I say that?'

'Of course you did.'

'But how could I have said that? You are mistaken, Dick. I went to Professor Valenti. He is the Professor of Italian. I told you that.'

'You told me you had been invited by Kostas.'

'No, no. You are mistaken. I never told you such a thing. Why should I tell you that I am going to Kostas if I am going to Professor Valenti?'

'I suppose because you were going to neither.'

Angrily he retorted: 'If you do not believe me—if you think that I am lying—then why not ask Professor Valenti?'

'I can hardly ring up and ask him such a question. Even a jealous wife might shrink from doing so. But you know very well you were out with Pam. Weren't you?'

'If I am out with Pam why should I not tell you? Why should I conceal it from you?'

'Perhaps she asked you to. Or perhaps you feel ashamed of going out with her almost every evening?'

'Why should I feel ashamed? Our relationship is entirely pure.'

I shrugged; then I smiled, without any humour. 'Perhaps I have become for you the voice of your conscience. And you would rather that your conscience did not know what you are doing.'

'I am doing nothing bad.'

'Then why conceal it from me?'

He stared at me with what was almost hatred in his eyes. 'Because you are jealous,' he eventually said in a tone of contemptuous brutality he had never used to me before.

'Jealous?'

'Yes. Jealous.'

'And why should I be jealous?'

I pressed both hands against the cold metal of the typewriter in an attempt to stop their trembling.

'I do not know. But you are jealous of Pam.'

'Don't be silly! I have no reason to be jealous of her. But I admit,' I went on, 'that I hate to see you getting deeper and deeper into this relationship with her. It'll only mess up your work and mess up your marriage . . . Anyway, it doesn't matter.' I typed a word and then another.

Looking round, I found that he had gone.

8

Several days later I was working alone in the house, after midnight.

It seems to me astonishing now that through all that time of obsessive love and of the sleeplessness, loss of appetite and misery it caused me, I was able to go on writing. People must have read my articles and reviews then as in the past, and not one of them can have guessed with what weariness and self-hatred I thumped them out on my typewriter and out of how cold and echoing a void I seemed to dredge up all the bright, trite things that went to their composition. 'How hard you work!' Antonio was always telling me, sometimes with admiration and sometimes with pity; and it was true. All my life I have worked hard but at that period I immersed myself in work as the only drug effective against the ravages of jealousy, frustration and despair. Hour after hour I would stoop over the typewriter, my eyes sore and my back aching from the posture. 'How hard you work, Dick!' Once in answer to that exclamation I replied 'Yes, I work hard because I must.' 'You mean you need the money?' 'Yes, I need the money. But that is not what I mean.' 'What do you mean then?' 'I mean that if I did not work so hard perhaps I should kill myself.'

'Dick! Dick!'

Suddenly that evening I was roused by the sound of Kitty barking, people laughing and chattering and Antonio shouting my name. Frozen, I made no move.

'Dick! Come on! *Come!*' Now he was at the door of the study, his face flushed with happiness. 'We have come to make spaghetti for you and to drink some wine with you. Come, Dick! You have worked enough.'

I see now that he had brought Pam and her dismal circle of friends back to the house in an effort to placate me and even give me pleasure; but tired and tense I could not then recognise the kindly if clumsy gesture for what it was worth.

'Oh, for God's sake!'

'I have brought two bottles of Chianti—Chianti Antinori, the kind you like best. You have nothing to do. I will cook the spaghetti. Come!' He caught my arm to drag me up from the typewriter.

'But I don't *want* to come. Oh, Antonio, can't you understand? I'm tired, I want to go to bed. Don't you understand what it means to do any intellectual kind of work? I must have tranquillity, I must have my peace of mind.'

The excitement left his face. I knew that I had hurt him deeply; and I was glad that I had hurt him.

'I will tell them to go,' he said in that veiled, husky voice, so unlike his usual clear, nasal tones, that always signified that he was upset or disturbed.

'How *can* you tell them to go?' I cried out. 'What would they think of my hospitality?' All my life I have had almost morbid punctiliousness about my duties to a guest, however little liked and however much wished away. 'If only you had had the sense to telephone first!'

'But in Italy'—he began, to be cut off by me:

'This is *not* Italy! Why won't you understand that?'

Silently he left the study.

When I came down Pam, Antonio and five strangers—two girls and three boys—were standing in the kitchen. 'Good evening,' I said. I forced a smile, now at one of them and now another. 'Hello, Pam.'

'Hello, Dick. I'm afraid you may think this is a bit much. But Antonio insisted on our coming back.'

'I'm delighted to see you.' I motioned them to the table in the bay. 'Do sit down.' Awkwardly, whispering to each other, they one by one took their seats. 'Antonio, aren't you going to introduce me?'

Unnaturally stiff and speaking through barely parted lips, Antonio muttered the names; but I did not take them in. The prettiest of the girls was a hospital nurse; the only man who, of the whole party, had not a cowed, embarrassed look was a postgraduate of economics. It was he who chose the seat next to the one before which I was standing.

As soon as we were all settled, Antonio shook himself like a nerve-racked actor when he hears his cue, to assume his public role of stage Italian. Clowning, he wrapped an apron around himself. '*Ecco!*' he shouted. Then, singing '*Funiculi, funicula*' in a *basso profondo*, he began to set about preparation of the food, to the delighted squeals of the girls. 'You will see. Never in your lives have you tasted such spaghetti. A dream!' At that last word he even kissed his fingertips. Pam, her elbows propped on the table and her chin cupped in both hands, watched him, her usually vague green eyes glittering with a brilliance I had never seen in them before.

The young man next to me began to talk. He had read my books, he had particularly admired one, he himself had made an abortive attempt at a novel. I barely listened to him and never looked at him, answering him with a few perfunctory words or by a mere shrug of the shoulders. All my attention was for Antonio and Pam.

Then all at once it came through to me, with amazement, that I was the only person in the room who interested this boy; and that, whether with an unconscious or a conscious coquetry, he was making every effort to woo me. He was not handsome—the nose was too long and thin, the eyelashes almost albino in the square, ruddy face—but in other circumstances I should certainly have been flattered and possibly I should also have been attracted. Yet now his unremitting attempts to please only filled me with exasperation.

The other boys—gauche students who seemed inappropriate companions for a brilliant don already reaching his mid-thirties—never spoke except in whispers to their girlfriends, until a few glasses of Chianti had loosened their shyness. Then their voices grew strident, their joking crude.

Antonio was everywhere, now dashing to the stove, now topping up our glasses and now standing in the middle of the kitchen, hands on hips, and holding forth. At one point his eyes caught mine and he came over and thumped me on the shoulder: 'Aren't you glad you came down to join us?' he demanded.

'Of course.' My voice was cruel in its irony. He felt the cruelty, and I knew that and was glad.

After the spaghetti, one of the girls said 'Why don't we dance?' and Antonio, dubious but eager as always to please, turned to me to ask if they might borrow my transistor set. I nodded.

'We turn off this light,' Antonio said, having brought the set down from my bedroom. He switched off the light over the kitchen table. 'We put on this light.' He switched on the light over the sink. 'O.K.? Much more romantic . . . Pam—come.'

She got up with an awkwardness that contrasted sadly with his grace. He was holding out both arms to her. 'Come!' he called again, as though summoning her not to the dance but to his bed. 'Come!' He held her very close to him, his eyes almost closed. Her own eyes were open, her lips were parted as though she were out of breath. Her nostrils looked pinched.

The young man and I were now left alone at the kitchen table.

'I'm afraid you're tired.'

'Oh, I'm never tired.' But the old boast was no longer true; I felt a deadly weariness, not merely of the flesh and of the bones but of the whole spirit.

'We shouldn't have come here so late. It was inconsiderate. I told Antonio it was inconsiderate.' He was, I realised, an exceptionally nice young man. 'May I come one day and see you alone—so that we can really talk? I mean, not against all this din—and when you're not tired.'

'Yes, do.'

I knew that my voice must sound unfriendly, even forbidding; but I was watching Pam in Antonio's arms, I could see that he had an erection as on that previous occasion when they had wrestled together.

'Did you catch my name? Roger—Roger Parker.'

'Roger Parker.'

'May I write it for you, with my telephone number?'

'Please do.'

He tore a sheet out of his diary and began to write in a large, clear, immature hand. 'It's been wonderful meeting you. I never knew you lived in Lymstead. I always imagined you spent most of your time abroad.'

'I did until recently. But now I've come back to England to roost.'

'Shall I try to break up the party for you?'

'No. Let it burn itself out.'

He looked at me curiously. 'But you'd like it to end, wouldn't you?'

'Oh, yes, I'd like it to end.'

'Well, then . . .' One of the boys had just subsided into a chair opposite to us, tugging from his trouser pocket a grubby handkerchief with which he began to mop his heavily sweating face. Roger whatever-he-was (I had already forgotten his surname) leant across and whispered. The boy nodded and gave me a nervous glance.

Soon all of them were at the door, except for Pam and Antonio who still circled on and on in each other's arms, oblivious to what was happening.

Roger touched Antonio's shoulder; his hand was large and slightly pudgy, there was a snake ring on the little finger. Antonio roused himself like someone emerging from a deep sleep. Pam still kept one arm round his neck long after they had stopped dancing and Roger had turned off the music.

The others began to mumble goodbye; one of the boys shook my hand, gripping it so fiercely that I suspected, not excessive friendliness, but repressed aggression.

'I will just take Pam home,' Antonio said. 'I will not be long.'

'Goodbye, Dick.' Was there a note of triumph in Pam's voice, a flash of triumph in those eyes with their silvery lids? Her hand was hot and moist in mine; one might have guessed she had a fever.

'What will you do about the washing-up?' Roger asked.

The whole kitchen was littered with pots and pans, plates and glasses. Antonio is a brilliant natural cook but the kind of cook who invariably needs a kitchen-maid.

'Oh, let's leave it till tomorrow.'

'But tomorrow is Sunday.'

'So it is.' My daily would not be coming.

'No one wants to wake up on a Sunday morning to find a mess like this. I'll do it for you now.'

'Are you coming, Roger?' one of the girls fluted from the hall.

'You all go on. Mr Thompson and I are going to do the washing-up.'

'Want any help?' another female voice, not Pam's, shouted.

'No, no. I'm an expert.'

There was a chorus of goodbyes, and then the door slammed.

'It was kind of you to have us at such an hour,' the boy said. 'Now you sit down, let me give you what's left in this bottle and then I'll do it all myself.'

'Certainly not. I'll help you.'

He was astonishingly neat, quick and methodical, in spite of his heavy build and the apparent clumsiness of his large hands. While he worked he hardly talked at all except to ask 'Where does this live?' holding up a knife or spoon or plate, or to say 'Sorry' when he leant across me to take something more to wash from the table.

'Antonio might have helped,' I said bitterly at one point.

'Oh, he wanted to see Pam home.'

'Come to that, so might she.'

'When people are in love they tend to be selfish.'

I thought with a new access of despair, like the sudden return of a toothache: So even to this twenty-two-year-old boy it is obvious that they love each other!

'Have you known Antonio for long?' he asked.

'No, not for long.' How long? It was difficult to think of a time when each hour had not been gorged with his presence or the memory of his presence or the expectation of his presence.

'He's fun.'

'Yes, he's—fun.'

Again he gave me that look, at once enquiring and pitying. We did not say anything more until the washing-up was finished.

'So that's it,' Roger then announced. 'It wasn't as bad as it looked, was it?'

'You were very kind.'

'I'm an expert washer-up as I said. You must call on me whenever you need my services.'

'I'll remember that.'

I followed him into the hall and opened the inner door for him. 'Thank you,' he said; and suddenly I realised that, so phlegmatic and calm before, he was now manifestly nervous. 'Thank you very much.' He raised his chin a little, the albino lashes fluttered, and then he momentarily closed his eyes. He swallowed hard, the adam's apple bobbing up and down in the throat that was disproportionately massive for his features. Suddenly I thought with complete certainty 'He wants me to kiss him! That's why he let the others go on ahead.'

But I could not do it.

'Well, goodnight,' I said, my voice almost frosty. 'And again—thanks a lot.'

'It's I who must thank you.' He was beginning to blush. 'And I may really come again?'

'Of course.'

'I'd like that. I'd like that a lot.'

He gave a little wriggle, as though his clothes were uncomfortable, and then held out a hand, oddly limp at the wrist.

'I'll be seeing you.' Our fingers barely met.

I climbed upstairs, Selima leaping up ahead of me, her claws, from time to time raking through the stair carpet. Usually when she did that, I shouted at her; but now I simply did not care. Kitty lumbered up behind.

My body seemed to burn as it touched the icy sheets; my head was throbbing. I looked at the crossword and then, turning over to put on the transistor set, realised that it was still downstairs in the kitchen. This nightly vigil was absurd, I told myself. I must forget about Antonio, I must cease to imagine all the things that he and Pam might be doing at this moment in the cockroach, I must get to sleep. I scrambled out of bed, went to the bathroom for a sleeping pill and swallowed it. Then I put out the bedside light. Hot a moment before, now I began to shiver, each rigor seeming to lift me up and then let me fall back, as though I were lying out naked on a stretch of wintry sand and the incoming sea kept lapping under me. I closed my eyes; and suddenly I found myself muttering a prayer to the God in whom I did not believe: 'O God, teach me to care and not to care, oh, teach me to care and not to care.' No, I could not wish not to care for him entirely; I did not wish to step down off that cross. But I wanted to have the intensity of love without this intensity of suffering.

Briefly I slept, then woke. I had left on the light in the hall, intentionally, since I knew that when it had been put out I would know that he had returned. It was still burning; it was past three o'clock. 'Oh hell!' I groaned against the sheet that I pressed with both hands against my mouth. I wondered whether to swallow another pill and then decided that, if I did, I should be unable to work in the morning.

Again I dropped off into a fitful sleep, to have the first of two dreams. I was in my bed and the hall light was on and I was waiting for Antonio to come back, as I had been waiting in reality. Then the gate creaked and banged, the door opened and also banged; he was climbing the stairs. 'Antonio!' I called, through my half-open door. But he went on into his own room without answering me. I lay there, in the dark, wondering whether to get up and go to him. Then I heard the creak of a floorboard, the faintest of raps on the door. 'Come in! Is it you, Antonio?' He opened the door wider, to reveal himself, wholly naked, in the dim light that filtered up the stairwell. Unspeaking he advanced, drew back the bedclothes and climbed into the bed beside me. He gave a kind of groan and then I was enveloped in the suffocating mass of him, struggling against the flesh against my mouth, the hair against my eyes, the weight of him upon my chest, the warmth of him cocooning around me. The struggle was brief against this Antonio suddenly grown to a superhuman stature; then I gave in, allowing myself to sink into oblivion with the thought, joyful not afraid, 'This is what dying must be. I must be dying.'

I woke with my whole body shaking in spasm after spasm: an orgasm like an endless bout of retching that produces no result. Half-crying and half-laughing, I remember saying to myself 'I suppose this could be called a *dry* dream.' I gripped the bedrail above my head and eventually the long, sterile spasms quietened and ceased. Only my eyes were moist, not with tears but with the fearful, involuntary effort of the seizure.

Again I fell off into sleep as though over some giddying precipice; and again I dreamed that Antonio had returned, this time his voice weaving in and out of another coarse female voice as they mounted the stairs, with sudden spurts of laughter from him and a high-pitched maniacal cackling from her. They had gone into his room now; but as I lay stretched out on my bed as on the rack I could hear an extraordinary din—shrill screams, shouts of laughter, thumps, a violent scraping noise and then a tremendous bang as though the cupboard had crashed over. Now the whole house was shuddering; even my bed was rocking from side to side and up and down. I put on the light, then got out of bed, thrusting my feet into my slippers and drawing my dressing gown around me.

I knocked on the door behind which I could still hear the same extraordinary tumult. I went in. The room was totally wrecked, the new wallpaper hanging in ribbons, the Sheraton chest of drawers piled in splintered pieces in a corner, the bed lopsided with a leg broken off, the electric-light shade a trampled oval at my feet. The window had been flung open, so that the night air blew in, icy gust on gust; and there, under it, their naked bodies sprawled across the red damask curtains now ripped off the rails, was Antonio grappling with a gipsy woman, all wild black hair, long, dirt-encrusted nails and writhing limbs. She was ancient, this hag; I had seen such gipsies in Greece, their faces lined with the deprivations of the centuries, their teeth rotting in their gums, their eyes bleary with a yellowing mucus. In a fury I rushed at them and began to kick and beat at their entangled bodies; but they were totally impervious to me, going on with their obscene fucking despite my presence. Suddenly with the intensity of my impotent attempts to kill them, I felt my heart swell within me and then halt with an agonising jolt. Falling into a furry kind of blackness I was conscious only of my forehead hitting a post of the ravaged bed before unconsciousness supervened.

I woke with my pyjamas drenched in an icy sweat. Now it was past four.

Looking for some pretext for my baffled fury—after all, if I were rational, I should have to allow Antonio, a grown man, the freedom of coming home at whatever hour he chose—I began to remind myself of how, when I had taken out a new insurance policy at the time of my move, the company had insisted on the provision of a number of security devices, including two bolts and a mortice lock on the front door. But what had been the point of having these installed if they could not be used? Again I reminded myself that within the last six months there had been two burglaries in the road. Of course if Antonio were seated with Pam in the cockroach outside the house then there was no cause for worry. I had better go to see. A tree made it difficult to scan the whole length of the road from the upstairs bedroom that faced out that way and I therefore descended to the drawing-room, still only half-decorated and still piled high with furniture and pictures. There were no curtains up.

I did not put on the light. Picking my way now over a stool and now round a table, I went into the magnificent bow and peered out, first up and then down the road, both hands pressed to the icy glass. There was no sign of the car.

Forgetting that I had fulfilled the purpose of my descent, I stayed on there, oblivious of the draught that swept along the floor of the uncarpeted, unheated room and through the cracks of the unpainted, uncurtained window. A drunk wove his slow way up the hill and while he was still in the distance I thought 'That must be Antonio!' But it was the Irish labourer who lived with a slatternly harridan and a brood of innumerable children not in my road but in the one above it, to the scandal of the neighbourhood.

Far off a clock struck five. In all my years in the town I had been unaware of its existence; yet now all my senses were so preternaturally acute that it reverberated with stunning power in my head. Five! What *could* he be doing?

At that I managed to take hold of myself. It was ludicrous to wait up like this; I might be some anxiously possessive mother looking out for her teenage daughter's long-overdue return from a date. What Antonio did with Pam was his business; I had no hold on him. He was my lodger—admittedly a lodger who now paid me so little that I was losing, not making, money—and as a lodger he was not accountable to me for his irregularities of behaviour. I must get back to bed; I must sleep, I must prepare myself for another day . . .

As I came into the hall, suddenly elated by a decision that I now felt I had the strength of will to put at last into effect, the door creaked open and the light, not where I had left it on but in the lobby, poured down on me, making me shrink away, a hand to my eyes.

'Antonio!'

'What is this?' He spoke with a fury I had never seen him display before. 'What are you doing here? Why are you waiting like this for me?'

In a rage as cold as his was heated, I replied, 'I want to talk to you. Come upstairs.'

'It is too late now. Anything you want to talk about you can talk about tomorrow. I am tired. I want to sleep.'

'No. Now.'

I had begun to climb the stairs and he followed me. At the entrance to his room he paused, hand on door handle.

'I want to talk to you,' I said.

'Well—what is it?' Reluctantly he began to follow me up the remaining stairs to my bedroom.

I climbed into bed, still in my dressing gown, and pointed to the chair. 'Sit.'

'I prefer to stand. I wish to sleep. It is very late.'

It was then that I looked at his face closely for the first time since he had come home. I was appalled. The skin was grey and puckered; the eyes seemed to have receded far back into their sockets. His jaws were clenched, making the cheeks bulge oddly and drawing the lips into a taut line. Anyone seeing him then for the first time would have thought of him as neither young nor handsome. His hands plunged deep into the pockets of his trousers—he had evidently gone out without his coat—he was trembling all over.

'What's the matter with you?'

'The matter with me?' His voice was clouded with huskiness; it seemed to emerge after breaking through some damp, constricting web. 'I have told you—I am tired.'

'What have you been doing?'

'Walking.'

'Walking?'

'Walking and thinking. I took Pam home. Then I walked.'

'You look ill, Antonio.'

'I am *not* ill. But it is late.' He approached the bed. 'Well, what did you want to say to me?'

All the dammed-up reproaches seemed to have seeped away; there was nothing there. 'It doesn't matter,' I said. 'Forget it.'

'Then I must tell you something.' Though still weary, his voice became implacable. 'I think it is better if I leave this house.'

'Leave this house?'

He nodded.

'Why?'

'Because I do not like to make you unhappy.' I said nothing, staring at him in desolation. 'You *are* unhappy?' he pursued.

'I don't know. Yes, in a way I *am* unhappy, I have never been so unhappy in my life. But there's a kind of unhappiness so intense that it becomes a kind of happiness.'

He gave an impatient shake of his body. 'I don't understand that,' he said.

'No. You wouldn't.'

'I must feel free,' he went on. 'I must not think "If I am late tonight, Dick cannot sleep, Dick will be unhappy." I am not good for you. I must go. Yes, I must go,' he repeated, as my lips moved for an answer. 'If I liked you less, I'd stay on. It is convenient for me here, you charge me very little. But'—he shrugged.

'Please sit down.' I patted the bed and slowly he came over and perched himself on it, gripping one hand in the other to stop their trembling. 'You know, Antonio, there are advantages and disadvantages to living here with me. The disadvantages are that I'm possessive and jealous and fussy and you don't feel truly free. Yes, I know that. But you can do many things here that you couldn't do if you were an ordinary lodger. You bring back friends, you help yourself to food, you treat this house as though it were your own. I want you to do that, I like you to do that, but few other landlords would give you the same facilities. And then, Antonio'—I was speaking gently to him—'you pay me awfully little. You paid Penny eleven guineas a week, which of course was too much. But five pounds a week is really too little—if one includes laundry and drinks before dinner and wine with dinner. But I don't want to make money out of you, you're a friend, that's how I think of you—as a friend. And I know that you're in financial difficulties with your wife and the children and the flat to keep up in Florence. So there *are* advantages.'

'Yes. I know there are advantages. And—I am very grateful to you.' Gratitude was something he hated to feel and he said that last sentence with chilling contempt.

'You think you should be allowed to come home whenever you like. But there are a lot of landladies who insist on their guests being back by midnight. Did you know that? And certainly no landlady would allow you to make spaghetti in her kitchen or dance there into the early hours.'

'Ah, you mention that again!' he cried savagely. 'You tell me to treat your home as my home but when I bring back some friends—'

'Even in our own homes we have to be considerate of others, Antonio. When I stay with my brother and sister-in-law I don't come in at all hours and I don't bring people back late at night, because I know both of them have to work very hard in the morning and I know I may wake up their children. You must not be such an egotist.'

'Yes, I am an egotist. I am selfish.' Suddenly he slumped; one hand went to his forehead, to cover his eyes. His mouth twitched as though he were about to burst into tears. 'That is why I must go. You are too kind to me—too devoted.'

'I know I am at fault.' Suddenly the thought of his going became insupportable. 'I know I'm difficult—pernickety, quarrelsome, possessive. If you can be more considerate, then all the better. But if you cannot be'—helplessly I was now carried away from my original decision, like a drowning man from the spar he has almost grasped—'well, do as you like. I'll put up with it. I'll *have* to put up with it. That's all. I don't want you to go.'

'I could take a room, I could come to see you often. We should still be friends.'

'It'll cost you far more that way. And can you look after yourself? You can cook, I know that. But what about the cleaning and your laundry and the shopping and the making of your bed?'

'Dick—don't always treat me as a child! I have told you—all my life I have had to look after myself, all my life I have managed.' Again his fingers covered his eyes; I wanted to put out my own hand to touch them. 'I must think,' he said. 'Now I am too tired to think. I have many things I must consider.'

'What have you been doing, Antonio?'

'Doing?'

'Tonight. Since you left the house.'

'I told you. Walking.'

I shook my head. 'You slept with her for the first time tonight, didn't you?'

He stared at me, mouth open in amazement.

'It's strange,' I said. 'But I *know*.'

'How do you know?'

'Where you're concerned I seem to have developed this curious kind of hyperaesthesia . . . I *am* right, aren't I?'

His silence confirmed that I was.

Wearily he got off my bed, his shoulders hunched and his chin on his chest. 'I have to play football tomorrow. How can I play?' he asked in a fretful voice.

'Put it off.'

'No, no. I gave my word.'

'Then let me bring you breakfast in bed.'

'But *I* should bring *you* breakfast in bed.'

'I never sleep after seven-thirty.'

He looked at his watch. 'Then you have just one and a half hours of sleep ahead of you.'

'That is enough.'

'Dick—what am I doing to you?' There was a choking anguish in his voice.

'Nothing that I do not want. What you do to me I freely let you do to me. So you have nothing with which to blame yourself.'

'You must stop caring for me so much.'

'If I could!'

'Goodnight, Dick . . . You are a good man,' he added, pausing at the door to look back at me.

'No, Antonio. I'm not that,' I said sadly.

'Sleep well.'

He seemed to intend no irony.

'Sleep well,' I echoed.

9

The next morning Antonio was ashen when he came down to breakfast and I wondered if he had slept as little as I. 'Good morning, Dick.' As he passed behind my chair his hand rested lightly on my shoulder.

'Good morning, Antonio. How do you feel?'

'Fine.'

Slowly he lowered himself into the chair opposite me, shook out his napkin and reached for the packet of corn flakes I was holding out. Then he seemed visibly to make an effort. Peering out of the window, he exclaimed in a voice of spurious heartiness that I found oddly moving: 'What a beautiful day! A perfect day for a match!'

'You're not really going to play, are you?'

'Of course I am! Why not?'

'I could telephone to say you were not well.'

'But I want to play! After a week of sitting, sitting, sitting, it's the best thing for me.'

He went on talking, the voice effortfully fluent, as though in a despairing attempt to persuade himself as much as me that all the events of the previous night had never taken place. He spoke of a book he had been reading on the nature of historical explanation; he asked me about the forthcoming Lymstead festival: he even jumped up and, raising Kitty on her hind legs, waltzed with her across the kitchen.

Suddenly he asked: 'Will you come and watch me play?'

I had, in fact, promised to go for a country walk with Masa but I sensed that the invitation was in the nature of a gesture of reconciliation, of an assurance that things between us were as they always had been, and that if I refused, I should hurt him deeply.

I nodded. 'Yes, of course. I've never seen you play.'

'Pam is going to drive me out in her car.' He mumbled the name with some embarrassment. 'I promised to take two of the other players out as well. But perhaps we can all manage to—'

'No, no. Masa will be with me. We can come out by train. But thank you.'

'It will not be a very interesting match. Just an occasional side. Perhaps you would prefer—'

'I want to see you play.'

Soon after, he asked me if I could put through a telephone call to his wife in Florence for him. She had written him a series of plaintive and even accusatory letters—perhaps with the same kind of hyperaesthesia that I myself had developed she had sensed what was happening to him—telling him that her headaches were now almost continuous, that she was at her wits' end with the older child, that a remittance of money had still not reached her, that she knew that he thought less and less about her. Antonio, with that complete frankness he always showed me about everything except his affair with Pam, had even read to me extracts from these letters. Obviously Chiaretta had wished to make him feel guilty and she had succeeded in doing so; and now that he could no longer make the claim that his life in England had been 'pure' (whatever precisely he meant by that word), the guilt must be acute.

I could hear his voice from the dining-room, even though I had closed the door, as he spoke to her, at first cajolingly and affectionately, and then with increasing vehemence. The call went on for a long time.

'*Accidenti!*' He flung himself down into his chair, his face expressive of exasperation and despair.

'What's the matter?'

'Everything is the matter! She accuses me of not writing to her. But you know, Dick, that I write every day. Every day! Is it my fault if the posts in Italy are so bad? . . . And she tells me that her headaches are worse. I have told her that she must tell the doctor that she wishes to see a specialist. But she has not done so. She says the expense is too great. But what does the expense matter if her health is in danger?'

'I imagine the headaches are psychosomatic. She must miss you, Antonio.'

'Yes. She misses me.' It was characteristic of his vanity that he should agree to that with obvious satisfaction. If she did not miss him, if she were happy and at peace, he would feel aggrieved, I was certain. 'Ah-h-h!' He gave what was half a groan and half a cry of baffled rage. 'How wise you are not to have got married!'

'That's the first time you've ever told me that.'

'It's the first time I have thought it. But now I am sure . . . You know, Dick, I really wonder if after I go back to Italy at Easter I can return here.'

I looked at him, appalled. 'But of course you must return! What are you talking about?'

'She does not want me to return.'

'Then she's being thoroughly selfish. You *must* return. Doesn't she realise how important this year in England must be to you?'

'She realises nothing. She would die for me—yes, really—if it was to give me something she could understand. If I was hungry, for example, she would starve for me. If I needed a new heart she would offer hers. But philosophy, my career—they mean nothing to her, nothing at all. She thinks she is being forced to make all these sacrifices just for *un capriccio*.'

'Poor Antonio.'

Now he felt that perhaps he had gone too far. 'But she is a good girl,' he conceded. 'A simple girl but a good girl. One day, when you come to stay with us, you will see.'

'But Antonio—you must be tough with her. You mustn't give up. Really you mustn't.'

Antonio shrugged. 'It is difficult. Perhaps I shall never really be a philosopher. Perhaps I shall never be anything but a family man.' He paused: 'And a *donnaiolo*,' he added with an intense self-loathing.

It was only from the dictionary that I later learned that '*donnaiolo*' means 'philanderer'.

Masa was willing enough to watch the football match instead of going for a walk in the country. 'I will take some photographs,' he announced, disappearing into his room to reappear with two cameras, one a Minolta and the other a Bronica, slung about him and a leather case containing equipment held in one hand.

'You must be out of your mind,' Penny said. 'Watching a football match in weather like this! I've never heard of anything more crazy.'

'Why don't you come with us, Miss Ashleigh?' Masa suggested.

'Come with you! I've better things to do with my time than to watch Antonio kick a ball about. But what I *will* do, if you like, is drive you out to the University.'

Suffering from the chronic loneliness of those incapable of being interested in anyone but themselves, Penny soon made it clear that this offer had been prompted not, primarily, by kindness but by the desire to confide in me. A mutual friend of ours, an elderly actress, had retired from the stage many years before, on inheriting a substantial fortune from the married man, much younger than herself, with whom she had been having an affair at the time of his death. She and Penny had been extremely close, making weekly jaunts to London together and telephoning each other two or three times each day. But now they had quarrelled: over a beach-hut, which fortunately I had declined to share with them when they had first proposed renting it for the summer. The actress, according to Penny, had filled the hut with undesirables every weekend; Penny, according to the actress, was fussy and bossy and made free use of provisions she had not bought. By now I had heard so much about this feud that I could have recited every detail of it, first in Penny's version and then in the actress's, without a single slip.

'I saw Diana in the supermarket yesterday and I stared her straight in the face,' Penny now began. 'But of course she wouldn't meet my gaze—oh no! All at once she became tremendously interested in the meat-counter—and her a vegetarian! I couldn't help feeling a little sorry for her in spite of everything. She looked so old all of a sudden. And shabby. Pathetic really.'

'She was in excellent form at Sybil's party last week.'

'Oh, of course, she can rise to an occasion. She can always do that. But it becomes more and more of an effort for her. You've never seen her the day after a night out, have you? . . .

Well, if she's found someone else to go in and give her her black coffee and aspirin, good luck to her.'

From her tone good luck was the last thing that Penny was really wishing her enemy at that moment.

'I've always been told, Masa, that in Japan friendship is something sacred?' Masa nodded nervously, adjusting the strap of his Bronica. 'Some of us in England have the same feeling. But not all, by no means all. There was this woman, Masa, for whom I would have given my right arm. I nursed her when she was ill. I stood by her when everyone was gossiping about her. I even found the flat in which she's living. And what did I get in return?' Penny looked at Masa over her shoulder, as though waiting for his answer; again he fiddled with the camera-strap. 'Usually I'm a shrewd judge of character, everyone says that about me. But in the case of that woman Penny made a right old fool of herself.'

'Oh Diana's not a bad sort,' I remonstrated, as I had often remonstrated in the past.

'You should hear what she has to say about *you*,' Penny retorted.

'I prefer not to hear what my friends say about me. I've told you that before.' Penny, though she makes few malicious remarks herself, is one of those 'kind' people who act as general post-offices for the malicious remarks of others.

'It's no use living in a fool's paradise.'

'Better a fool's paradise than no paradise at all . . . Penny, dear, aren't you overshooting the University?'

'Am I? Oh, so I am! Oh, dear.' She began to reverse into an oncoming stream of traffic. 'Have you any idea where the match is taking place?'

'None at all. Do you know, Masa?'

Masa drew in his breath, with the same sound that he made when slurping soup.

'Well, that's a fat lot of use!' exclaimed Penny who, now that she had delivered herself of her diatribe against Diana, was eager to be rid of us. 'You'd better ask someone!' Masa began to wind down a window but impatiently she cried out: 'No, not you, Masa!', adding to me, loud enough for him to hear, 'No one is going to understand a word he says. *You* ask, Dick!'

Fortunately at that moment I saw a tousled youth, a pair of football boots slung around his neck and a canvas bag in one hand, who was about to enter the campus.

'Which ground did you want?' he asked with a strong Belfast accent.

'I've no idea.'

'Well, which is the team?'

'You've got me there too.'

'I suppose you're from American Express?'

'From *what?*'

'You must be one of the American Express team.'

'I don't belong to any team. But an Italian friend of mine is playing and I came out—'

'Oh, you mean Antonio!'

'That's right.'

'Well, we're playing the American Express team.'

'Then why don't you hop into the back of the car and you can direct us,' Penny cut in impatiently.

The boy clambered into the back beside Masa, at once filling the car with a smell of stale sweat.

'You'll be from the seven counties like myself,' Penny said, adopting a Belfast accent even thicker than his. Presumably she had learned this trick when in the services.

The boy, delighted, leant forward to her, gripping the back of her seat with a pair of swollen red hands.

Penny began to talk about an address she had given to the University branch of the Student Christian Union, not taking in the young man's blunt confession that he was an atheist. 'They were an awfully nice crowd. They restored my faith in the University . . . I hope you're not one of these students who take drugs and sleep around and indulge in all this rowdyism.' To judge from the boy's round, simple face, close-cropped blond hair, sticking up in dry tufts, and his bucolic manner, it seemed unlikely.

'Well, next time I address the S.C.U. I hope to see you there,' were her parting words to him, as she deposited us outside a pavilion that looked like a gardening shed afflicted with elephantiasis.

'I don't think that's very likely,' the boy replied with devastating candour. 'Though I hope we meet again.'

Antonio and one of the youths he had brought to the house the previous night were seated, already changed, at a table in the pavilion, with Pam and a fat girl I had not seen before facing them. All four of them were plunged in a viscous silence, from which our arrival took some seconds to stir them.

'Ah, Dick!' Antonio raised a hand in salute. It was unlike him not to leap to his feet and rush over.

'Hello, Pam,' I said.

I was always unnaturally polite to Pam, in the way in which, in my Foreign Office days, I used to be unnaturally polite to the wives of senior colleagues whom I either disliked or feared.

'Hello, Dick . . . Hi, Masa!'

There was a difference of tone between her first greeting, so coolly correct, and her second, so friendly and informal.

Antonio brought two more chairs and then, as an afterthought, introduced me to the fat girl, who went by some man's name—Bobby or Frankie or Tommy. The boy was gazing at me with what I thought was suspicion, even hostility, so that I began to wonder if he were still smarting from the way I had got Roger summarily to dissolve the gathering of the night before.

We all sat in silence for a while: a silence in which I was keenly aware of the contrast on the one hand between my own tension and the tension of Masa, invariably shy with strangers, and on the other hand the gorged relaxation of the two couples. Pam was slouched far back in her chair, her legs, in dark blue ski-pants, outstretched in front of her and her hands, in huge fur gloves, clasped over her stomach. Her face, beneath the hood of her anorak, looked even more vulturine than ever; but it was the face of a vulture that has picked its carrion clean. Antonio was watching her in dreamy absorption, his bare legs, superbly muscled beneath the incredibly narrow hips and waist, also stretched far out ahead of him. I stared at those legs, seeing every detail of them with an illusion of magnification that I used often to experience at that time: each hair, each tiny scar, each trivial blemish seemed to stand out as in some Pre-Raphaelite picture. Then, looking upwards, I saw that again he had an erection; and at once, conscious of the changed direction of my gaze, he shifted in his seat, drew in his legs and put his hands on his lap.

I found something gross and even obscene in that post-sexual torpor; and the other two, the youth with the silvery scales of psoriasis on his forehead and chin and the obese girl whose legs bulged out from what Penny, with her schoolgirl ribaldry, liked to call a 'crotch-curtain' seemed merely to be miming the same mood. Had they, I wondered, had sex again just before they drove out? It seemed not impossible.

It was a cold but clear day of spring. The football ground itself had thawed out but where the sun had not touched the far corners of the field the frost still glittered. Antonio ran off with the other players—at one moment he linked arms with the youth to whom we had given the lift, evidently the captain—and I found myself walking towards the ground with Pam. Neither of us spoke until she turned:

'Antonio says you work awfully hard.'

'Yes, I suppose I do.'

'We shouldn't have come to your house so late.'

'Oh, I was glad to see you all,' I replied with perfunctory politeness.

'A writer must need peace. I know so little about it but I'm sure he must need peace.'

'Yes, he often needs peace. But he also often needs chaos.'

She gave a little laugh. 'Antonio must provide that for you.'

'Yes. But it's no bad thing to have an unrest cure from time to time. What baffles me is how he gets anything done himself. After all, philosophy is an arduous discipline. And to pursue it one's life must have its moments of tranquillity. There seem to be no such moments in Antonio's life. At least not since he came to Lymstead.' I might have said, 'At least not until he met you,' and she sensed, I am sure, that that was what I intended.

'Do you like football?'

'It bores me stiff. I used to hate to play it, I hate even more to watch it.'

'Then Antonio should be flattered that you've come.'

'I want to see if he's as good a player as he's always telling me . . . And you, do you like football?'

'Very much.'

It was one of those uneasy conversations, in which both participants keep wondering what, if anything, lies behind the conventional words and phrases. 'Is she getting at me?' I kept asking myself; and no doubt she, too, was putting the same question to herself.

We sat together on a bench, one at either end of it, while Masa scurried from one end of the field to another, clicking the shutter now of the Bronica and now of the Minolta. The youth and the fat girl had gone to another seat where they sat, two heavily overcoated figures, their arms round each other's shoulders. Neither Pam nor I spoke; but from time to time when the ball came to Antonio she would half-rise from the bench, with an animation unusual for her, and sometimes even shout his name or some word of encouragement. He was playing badly, with frequent miscalculations and a tendency to throw in his hand as soon as he came under pressure. Certainly, though once a well-known professional, he was now no more skilful than most of these amateurs.

Shortly before half-time Masa approached, zigzagging towards our bench as though unsure whether he would be welcome or not. Some fifteen yards away he halted, until I called out 'Hello, Masa!'

'I have been using my telescopic lens,' he announced as he now drew near. 'My cameras are both Japanese but this lens is German. It is extremely powerful,' he added and then went on to explain its technicalities.

'Have you managed to get some good snaps?' Pam asked. The word 'snap' seemed hardly applicable to photographs taken with all the deliberate care and scientific expertise that Masa lavished on them.

'Yes. I am taking photographs of Antonio. I wish to send them to his wife. She will be pleased, I think, Mr Thompson?'

'I'm sure she will.'

He raised one of the two cameras and began to fiddle with its stops. Detaching one lens, he fumbled in the leather case he had placed at his feet and took out another. 'Now I will photograph Miss Mason with Mr Thompson.'

Pam's reaction to this suggestion was immediate and astonishing. Leaping to her feet and covering her face with both hands, she shouted: 'No! I don't want to be photographed! Please not! No!'

'But just one shot,' Masa pleaded.

'No! I said no!'

At first this almost hysterical refusal bewildered me as much as it obviously bewildered Masa. Then I suddenly realised the reason for her panic. Among the photographs that Masa said he was taking for Antonio's wife she was convinced that there would also be one of herself. Perhaps she even thought that there would be one of herself because I had put Masa up to taking one.

Masa giggled in embarrassment. 'If a lady is ugly, then I can imagine that she does not wish to be photographed. But if she is beautiful, Miss Mason, why should she object?'

Unappeased and still suspicious, she said in a small, sharp voice, as she slowly reseated herself: 'I don't like to be photographed. I never like to be photographed. That's all.'

Soon after that it was half-time and Antonio, having snatched a slice of lemon, ran over to us. He looked totally exhausted, and I noticed that one of his knees was bleeding.

As he approached, I smiled at him and pointed, saying 'Antonio—your knee;' but he looked beyond me to Pam, without any acknowledgement of my presence. Perching himself on the arm of the bench that was closest to her, he put out a hand to tuck a straying lock of hair under her anorak. 'Cold?' he asked in the same tender voice that he would once say to me 'Tired?'

Pam shook her head. Then she looked up at him and her hand emerged from its grey fur glove and touched, with its fingertips, the blood on his knee. 'I didn't see you do that. How did you do it?'

He smiled down at her. 'It's nothing. I had not noticed it till now. Someone must have kicked me there.'

'Does it hurt?'

He shook his head.

She put her smeared fingertips to her mouth, in a gesture that seemed totally unconscious; then, realising what she was doing, she hurriedly replaced the hand in its glove. Leaning right over, Antonio whispered something in her ear, his arm around her shoulder.

At that period my despair was like a toothache: when I was involved in something that interested me deeply—the writing of a review; listening to the record-player; talking to a friend—I would be conscious of it only as a dull, continuous throb, ever-present but not over-insistent. Then suddenly in a lull there would come stab on stab of pain that left me breathless and incapable of thinking of anything else. Such a sudden intensification was what I now experienced as I watched, again every detail extraordinarily magnified by my morbid state, as the large hand, the wrist caked with mud, massaged her thin arm through the protective layers of the anorak. I wanted to go away and yet felt too weak even to rise. Then I saw that Masa was staring at me, with an expression of surprise and even fright on his face.

The whistle blew, Antonio dashed off and Masa came up to me:

'You are cold, I think, Mr Thompson.'

'Yes, a little, Masa.'

'Come and walk with me.'

The voice, usually almost choked by shyness, now carried in it a note of clear, bell-like authority. 'Come,' he said again.

We began to walk round the edge of the field in silence while, from far off, there came to us the occasional shouts of 'Pass!' 'Goal!' 'Here!' and a thud when the ball landed on either of the crossbars. Masa stopped, raised his camera, the telescopic lens now attached to it, and said: 'I can take a perfect picture of Pam from here. And she will never know.' He laughed: not his usual laugh of embarrassment but one that seemed, perhaps only in my imagination, jeering and vindictive.

The shutter clicked.

'I will give you a copy,' he said. 'And Antonio one.'

'But not one to his wife.'

Again he gave that same laugh, totally unlike his laugh as I had ever heard it on any previous occasion.

'Perhaps not,' he said.

Suddenly I was aware that the ball was bouncing towards me and that behind it there was Antonio, his mouth drawn back in an agonised rictus of effort. I made no attempt to stop the ball and, without once glancing at me, he hurtled after it, picked it up and raced to fling it back into play from touch.

'Why did he run so fast?' Masa asked. 'The ball was out. He must have known it was out.'

But Antonio was incapable of not putting all his being into everything he tackled.

We strolled on, Masa from time to time kicking at the indentations in the ground where the frost still glittered. He seemed to take a pleasure in splintering the ice into glass-like slivers and not to care when the water beneath splashed up over his shoes to turn them grey.

'This is not a very interesting game,' he said.

'No. It's a very dull one.'

'I feel Italians are very far from us.'

There seemed to be no connection between the first remark and the second.

'How do you mean?'

'I feel close to the English, Mr Thompson. I feel close to you. But Antonio—it is as though he belonged to another species.'

'Is he really so different?'

Masa nodded, fiddling with one of his cameras, his head bowed. 'Our feelings are narrow and deep. And lasting. Like one of our mountain streams, with rocks on either side. Deep, fast-flowing. Making a channel for itself, deeper, deeper, deeper. But *their* feelings—it is like the estuary of a river. The estuary spreads everywhere, but there are only a few feet of water and the water is sluggish and—and muddy.' He looked up at me at that last word and gave a slow, radiant smile. It was almost as though he had successfully delivered a speech long since prepared and memorised. 'In a way,' he went on, 'Pam must be happy. To have won the love of a man like Antonio is something remarkable for her. But what has she won? She has won something that many other women have won and many other women will win. Not very difficult, not difficult at all. She has won it, she will lose it.'

The quiet vehemence with which he said all this convinced me that at some time—perhaps when he had been circling the field alone to take his photographs—he had planned a way to comfort me; and my conviction was strengthened when he touched my arm, a thing he had never done before and has never done since, and said, 'Pam is not really worthy of Antonio. But people seldom fall in love with those who are worthy of them. Do they?' He was now guiding me away from the football field, as one guides someone badly shocked away from the scene of an accident, and propelling me towards the pavilion. 'We can get some tea at the cafeteria in the pavilion. That will warm us. Make us feel a little less sorry for ourselves. Is that a good idea, Mr Thompson?'

'A very good idea, Masa.'

But after I had drunk my scalding cup of bitter brown Indian tea I could not remain waiting there in patience. 'Let's go and see the end of the match.'

'Do you really wish to see it?' His dark eyes were liquid with a patient compassion.

'Yes, I do.'

But as we began the descent a whistle pierced the dimming air and then spectators and players began to crowd up towards us. Pam came first, this time alone, her shoulders hunched and her hands deep in the pocket of her anorak. Not long after, the boy and the fat girl, staggering with their arms round each other's shoulders as though in a three-legged race, emerged panting on the terrace, the girl to give me a little nod, the boy to grunt 'Hi!'

Antonio was walking with the captain; and I noticed how repeatedly they linked arms with each other, threw arms around each other's shoulders, patted each other's backs. I was always deluding myself with 'signs' that were probably not really signs at all; and as they drew near my fury that he and this other man should repeatedly attain this degree of physical intimacy was moderated by the thought: 'That must mean something! There *must* be something in all that. He *must* be a suppressed homosexual. There *must* be something of it in him. Normal men don't behave like that.'

While Antonio changed we all five waited. Masa had brought more cups of tea with a generosity unusual for him, and Pam was gulping at hers, her chin almost touching the table, in a way that I found nauseating.

'How are you going to get back?' she asked me.

'We'll take the train.'

'I don't honestly think we could squeeze you into the car.'

'No. It would be out of the question.'

Suddenly I felt the desire to get away from the pavilion with its smells of sausage rolls and Indian tea and sweat; to get away from this quietly triumphant, sexually sated woman; to cease to wait for Antonio who, when he emerged from the changing-room, would probably not care whether I was there or not; to return to a life of sanity in which I could eat crumpets by the fireside of a friend or listen to *Winterreise* on my record-player or read the books that had arrived the day before from the London Library. What was I, a middle-aged, moderately successful, intellectual of a writer doing out here, watching two scratch sides play a bungling game of football?

'Shall we go, Masa?'

'Now?'

'Yes.'

He rose slowly to his feet. 'Perhaps it is better.'

10

Until the night of my house-warming party, several days later, 'love' was never a word either of us used to describe my devotion to him. 'You care too much for me,' he would say; or 'You should not feel this way about me;' or 'I cannot return the kind of friendship you have for me.' In turn I would use similar euphemisms—'the affection I have for you,' 'I've never felt like this for any man before,' 'this absurd attachment.' I think that both of us sensed subconsciously that if that monosyllable 'love' passed between us then this curious relationship, still fluid between us because it was never defined, would come to a crisis; and that crisis, oddly, was what he as much as I wished to avoid.

I know that he was fond of me—indeed, is fond of me still; but once he acknowledged to himself and me that he knew that in my fondness for him there was an element of sexuality, then to return the fondness would be fraught with embarrassment and even shame. He needed my devotion, both because he had more than his share of Italian vanity and because, as he told me later, he saw in me the protective, all-loving, all-forgiving father he had lost so young. But if he were to acknowledge that the source of that devotion beyond the ordinary was an affection beyond the ordinary, then for a man so jealous of his maleness the situation might become insupportable. It was essential, therefore, to maintain the pretence that, though in my friendship there was something eccentric—the result of my loneliness, my singleness, my childlessness—there was in it nothing abnormal. I should have allowed him to maintain that pretence. But I could not do so.

I had no heart for the party at a time when I wished to concern myself with no one but him. But the invitations had long since been sent out, the food had long since been ordered; and Antonio himself was looking forward to it—I had given him a dozen invitations for his friends and he regarded it as much his party as mine. 'I wish I hadn't ever decided on anything so foolish,' I said to him, and in amazement he replied 'What do you mean? It will be *fun*, Dick! You will see.' For me parties are rarely fun; for Antonio they always are.

Exhausted and tense, I swallowed early in the afternoon one of the purple-hearts prescribed for me several years before when my doctor had told me to lose weight. It worked so efficiently that a number of my guests said to me afterwards 'You were in such wonderful form.' But even with a pill to give me a spurious gaiety, I was in far less wonderful form than Antonio without one. He seemed to be everywhere: rushing forward with a tray of drinks; handing round the canapés; introducing one person he did not know to another person he did not know; flattering the plainest women and the dullest men and even finding time to come up to me at intervals to demand 'O.K.?' or to assure me 'It is going very well. No reason for worry.'

Pam was there, of course, looking even paler and limper than usual, with her hair rinsed to the same silvery colour as her nails, her lips and eyelids, and her frail, slightly round-shouldered body swathed in a dress, unfashionably long in the skirt, of a washed-out green. Penny, who had met her before, had greeted her in front of everyone with a booming 'Hello, my dear! How pretty you look! Each time I see you, you seem more and more Italian.' The remark was an idiotic one, since no one could have looked less Italian than Pam; but Penny is rarely malicious and I am sure that no malice was intended. Pam, however, began to flush painfully, first her throat and then her face reddening as she frowned down into her glass of tomato juice. Soon after that she disappeared upstairs into Antonio's bedroom, whither I saw him leaping the stairs in twos or threes to see what she was doing. A few minutes later he came down, slowly now, with one hand trailing along the banister, as though he were deep in thought. Pam herself did not descend until the party was almost over, and then I noticed that her face looked curiously puffy and her eyes slightly inflamed as though from shedding tears. I wondered whether she had been upset by Penny's heedless greeting, whether she and Antonio had had a quarrel, whether she had missed a period or whether she was merely desperate about a love that, on any long-term prognostication, was likely to be no less fruitless than mine. It was cruel of me since she had never done anything consciously to injure me, but I was exhilarated by the spectacle of her manifest suffering. I hoped that he had been brutal to her; that he had told her that their relationship must end; that she had become conscious of the untenability of her whole position.

But when at last all the guests had gone except for my brother and sister-in-law, my sister, her teenage daughter and Pam, and Antonio had prepared a vast bowl of *tagliatelle bolognese* to which we then sat down, I saw at once, with a mingling of exasperation and despair, that, whatever had made her cry, it was certainly not any diminution in his love for her. He had reached that stage when it is impossible not to touch the loved object as though perpetually to assure oneself that it still exists. He had placed himself near her and even as he ate, sucking up the strands of tagliatelle and gulping them down like some famished Tuscan peasant, his free hand would stray now to her hair, now to the nape of her neck and now even to her thigh. Both of them, it was evident, were in a state of febrile excitation; my brother even remarked on it to me—'I do wish people would wait till they get to bed to start that kind of thing, but perhaps I'm being old-fashioned'—as I saw him and the rest of my family off in his car.

'The party was a success,' Pam said when I returned to the house.

'Thank you.'

'Yes, a great success,' Antonio confirmed.

'And so were you. I'm no good at parties.'

Desultorily the three of us talked for a while among the ruins of the party and our dinner—Antonio wanted to know the identities of a number of people to whom he had spoken and did not scruple to remark on the beauty of my niece in front of Pam. Then Pam got up, smoothing down first her dress with both hands and then her hair.

'I must be going,' she said.

'I will take Pam home,' Antonio told me, as though I did not know that already. 'But please wait for me to help you with the washing-up. I will be back soon.'

'I'll expect you when I see you,' I replied with the first onset of the pill-induced aggressiveness that was later to precipitate our crisis.

'Only half an hour,' he said, with the cajoling smile that I had once found so irresistible but that now only filled me with exasperation.

'I know your half-hours!'

Perhaps Pam sensed the tension between us; and perhaps because of it she let fall the little Sung celadon bowl she had been self-consciously examining while we were talking. She let out a scream; and I remember that what enraged me almost as much as the breaking of a treasured possession was the nature of the sound—a common, screeching 'Aowh!'

She and Antonio knelt facing each other, while I looked down on them.

'Is it very valuable?' she asked.

'It *was* a Sung bowl. Not that it matters. Don't worry about it.'

Antonio was picking up the pieces, taking the few she had collected out of her cupped palm. 'I will mend it for you,' he said.

'No, I don't think that would really be much good. But thank you all the same.'

'Keep the pieces,' he insisted, placing them on the hall-table beside me. 'I know how to mend china.'

'As you know how to fill in holes in paint!' I smiled; but it was not a joke but a gibe. 'Oh, forget it, Antonio! I said forget it! Accidents will happen, as people say on such occasions.'

'I'm awfully sorry,' Pam said. 'It was a pretty bowl.'

'Yes. I liked it. One might call it pretty.'

She said goodnight and the two of them left. From the window of the sitting-room I watched them as, talking to each other, they stood first at the gate and then outside the cockroach. What were they saying? I speculated. 'I'm afraid that upset him.' 'Serve him right!' 'With all those possessions fancy making such a fuss! Just a little bowl!' 'Did you drop it on purpose?' 'What an idea!' She would giggle at that. 'Well, not on purpose, but I can't say I was sorry when I let it fall and I looked up and saw that expression on his face.' 'Come on! Let's go!' 'You don't want it again tonight, do you, you greedy boy?' 'Tonight and every night.'

... Now they were driving off but the inane conversation, with its shared intimacies and its mockery of me, continued to speak itself in my head. I know now that Antonio and probably Pam would never and could never have talked in those terms. But in my then madness I was convinced that they might. Oh fuck them, fuck them, fuck them, I cried out not to myself but aloud, as I came into the hall. Heedless, in my rage, of the fact that the thousand-year-old shards of broken china still had considerable value, I swept them off the table and flung them into the dustbin. Then I set about washing-up.

I had of course finished long before Antonio returned; but in spite of the party, the endless glasses to dip in water and to dry and the lateness of the hour, I felt no tiredness but instead an implacable energy, engendered by the pill. I would wait for Antonio, but I would wait for him as I had never been capable of waiting for him before: without impatience, serenely, in total self-confidence. Going into the sitting-room I put on a record of the fifteen-year-old Menuhin playing Elgar's Violin Concerto and lay back on the sofa, my eyes closed.

It was during the slow movement that Antonio returned, apologising for not having come home earlier.

I took the arm from the record and switched off the current. 'I didn't really expect you any sooner,' I said in a voice that amazed me by its calmness.

He began to peel off his coat. 'Come! Let me help you with the washing-up.'

'I've done it.'

'Oh, Dick!'

'I had nothing else to do until your return.'

'But you should have waited for me.' He came across to me, laying one hand on either of my forearms. 'I am your friend. You must let me help you.' He looked into my eyes with a troubled affection.

'Oh, you have better things to do,' I answered drily.

'May I take a cigarette?'

Antonio never smoked.

'Yes, of course. But why?'

'I feel like one.' He lit the cigarette and as he did so, I saw that his hands were trembling. Inexpertly he puffed. 'Pam was sorry about your bowl.'

'She didn't sound very sorry.'

'Of course she was.'

'She probably didn't realise its value. It cost me seventy pounds in Japan. That means much more here, I should imagine.'

'Impossible!'

'Do you think I'm lying?'

'But seventy pounds, Dick! That's a terrible lot of money.' Again he puffed inexpertly, perched now on an arm of the sofa, while I stood above him.

'Yes. It's a terrible lot of money. As you say.' My voice still remained calm: so calm that I had an illusion that it belonged to someone other than myself.

'It's lucky she did not offer to replace it!' he exclaimed with a smile.

'Yes, very lucky. Though it might have been better manners if she had done so.'

He looked sharply at me; I could see that again I had angered him and I felt surge within me a sense of power at having succeeded in doing so. 'She apologised. What more did you expect?'

'I expected nothing more. From her.'

It is painful for me now to remember my coolly insulting answers; but I must do so if this story is to serve the purpose I have designed for it. It is easy to blame my conduct on certain chemical changes in the blood; but they merely precipitated what was already there, as a hot compress draws out the pus that lurks deep in an abscessed wound.

'What do you mean by that?'

'No more than I said.'

'It is not really the breaking of the bowl that has made you angry. That is only your excuse.'

'And what has made me angry?'

'You are jealous!'

'Jealous?'

'Jealous.'

I thought for a moment. I had a curious sensation in my head, as though suddenly a hole had been made in it without any pain and the light and the air were flooding in, brighter and brighter, colder and colder. 'Yes,' I said. 'I *am* jealous of her. You're right. I *am* jealous. But I also think her a careless and ill-mannered slut. So don't think that when I say she's a careless and ill-mannered slut I say that only because I'm jealous.'

He stared at me. 'I cannot understand you.'

'What you mean is not that you cannot understand me but that you don't want to understand me.'

'But what is this—this crazy jealousy?'

'Haven't you ever been jealous?'

'Of course! But how can one man be jealous because another man who is a friend of his is having an affair with a woman?'

'Oh, very easily, Antonio.' I bent forward to take the cigarette from between his fingers; it was almost burnt out. But he started away as though I were about to touch him. 'Very easily. But to understand what I mean you have to face the truth.'

'What truth?'

'The truth that you already know but refuse to acknowledge . . . That I love you.' Now at last it seemed simple to say it.

He got up and then sat down again. He drew a handkerchief out of one pocket and wiped first the palm of one hand and then of the other. This last action he performed in a perfunctory manner, as though the confession I had just made was of no importance at all. But when finally he looked at me there was both shock and a lurking panic in his eyes.

'Don't be foolish, Dick.'

Trying to make a joke of it, he gave a short laugh.

'No, I must be foolish. I can't help it, Antonio. I love you. In a way that I haven't loved anyone, man or woman, for—oh—the last fourteen years.'

'But it's—it's absurd.'

'Why? You've heard of such things happening before, haven't you?'

'Of course. But—'

'Then why is this absurd? If you were ugly and stupid and disagreeable then perhaps it might be. But you know you're none of those things. If one man has to fall in love with another what better choice could there be?'

'A better choice would be someone who was capable of returning that love,' he said in a quiet but deadly voice.

Suddenly, with one of those sighs of his that were almost groans, he stretched himself full length on the sofa, pulling a cushion under his head. At any other time I might have said to him, with my usual fussiness, 'Oh, Antonio, your shoes!'

'You've never felt that kind of love?'

'Never.' He raised one hand, forefinger extended, and shook it from side to side.

'But I can't be the first man to fall for you. I don't believe that.'

'Oh, from time to time, men—if you can call them men—have made—suggestions to me. But never anyone like you.'

'What do you mean by that?'

'Well, all those were only half-men.'

'You must accept the fact that I'm a half-man too.'

'No one would guess, seeing you in the street—talking to you—'

'Any homosexual would guess.'

'I am not a homosexual!' He put both hands up to his face and then drew them down his cheeks. 'I worked in a garage when I was sixteen—seventeen—and there was this Czech—a refugee—married—who was always kind to me. Then he started trying to play with me and I had to go—had to leave my job. He was a good man, the job was a good job. But I had to go. . . As a footballer, I often had suggestions made to me. All the *finocchi* are crazy about footballers in my country. Do you know?' He mentioned a prince of a famous Florentine house.

'I knew his brother.'

'Well, this one was the protector of another footballer, a friend of mine called Bruno. He would buy Bruno these beautiful suits made in Rome and these diamond cuff-links and finally this car—an Alfa Romeo. And then he took Bruno to America with him and Bruno met all these people—the aristocracy, you understand, and the intellectuals. Then this man got interested in me, he was bored with Bruno. He used to follow the team around Italy, he became a joke to us all. But the other boys could not understand why I said always 'No, no, no.' I remember one of them said to me "If Paris is worth a Mass then surely an Alfa Romeo is worth a *pompino*"!' He gave a mirthless chuckle. 'But I could not do it!'

He said all this with a curious bitterness that suggested that he was both bewildered and exasperated by his inability to do what others could do and so earn, with a minimum of effort, the car, the expensive Roman suits, the trip to the States.

'And the missionary?' I asked.

'What missionary?'

'Joe.'

There was an infinitesimal pause. Then turning his head aside on the cushion, so that I could see only the left temple and cheek-bone, he answered with the monosyllable 'No.'

Often since I have read into that answer an unwilling admission of guilt; and often in consequence I have felt a consuming hatred and jealousy of this stranger for having enjoyed what I can never enjoy.

'No?'

'Of course not. He was a good man. A man of God.'

'How naïve you are! When I lived in Florence the male-whores used to refer to the Pope as "La Mamma".'

Suddenly he turned his face back to me, to ask in a taunting, almost brutal voice: 'Why are so many Englishmen like this?'

'Like what?'

'Homosexual.'

'There are a great many homosexuals in Italy.'

He shook his head.

'Of course there are! Not in your class perhaps. But among the aristocracy there are many people who do it for pleasure and among the working class there are many people who do it for profit.'

'I can take no pleasure in it. And though I am often short of money, yes, I could not do it for profit. I regret.' He gave a short laugh.

Still with the same composure I now sat down in the chair opposite to him. 'It's sad,' I said, as though talking not about my own situation but about the situation of some mutual acquaintance or even a stranger.

'I do not have any moral feelings about it—you know that, Dick. I am not a religious man, I am not even a particularly moral man. But—the idea of making love to someone of the same sex as myself—it disgusts me.'

'Really?'

'Perhaps you see'—the two hands went again up to his face, to cover the eyes—'perhaps I am frightened of it because there is something of it in myself. Perhaps.'

He was never to make that admission again to me; and when later I was to make the suggestion to him that his desire to be admired, his ceaseless pursuit of women and his affectation of boyishness might all perhaps be construed as symptoms of a latent homosexuality, he would indignantly repudiate it.

'What am I to do?' I said; and such was the effect of that single pill on me, it was again as though I were talking about the problem of someone remote from us.

'You must stop feeling like this, Dick. Before it is too late.'

'It is too late.'

'I want to be your friend. All my friends are men, I am not like you, I have no women friends. But we must be ordinary friends, friends as we were before—before all this happened.'

'We were never ordinary friends, Antonio. I was attracted by you from the first moment you entered Penny's house.'

He was obviously pleased by the implied flattery of this confession; it always pleased him to have confirmation of the effects of his charm and beauty. But he went on:

'You must find someone else. Someone who can care for you as I cannot care for you, Dick.'

'You talk as though falling in love were like buying a suit. If one does not fit, then try on another. Perhaps for you it *is* like that. But not for me. I'm afraid not for me.'

'You must have will power.'

'Do you think that I've not tried to will myself *not* to love you? But it's like willing oneself not to have cancer or heart disease. Don't be silly, Antonio.'

'You are very different from me,' he said in a voice of wonder.

'You've said that before, Yes, I'm afraid I am. I don't love many people—perhaps only three or four in my whole life—and I love them for years and years. There it is. You're lucky. You love innumerable people, many of them simultaneously, and the love lasts for a week-end or a week or at most a month.'

He laughed at that, swinging his legs off the sofa and exclaiming: 'I must go to bed! And so must you. It is late.' He went to the door, then turned: 'Perhaps after all it is best if I find a room out.'

'No, Antonio.'

'I will come to see you often as I came to see you when I lived with Penny. But it is better for you if I am not always so near you.'

'No.'

'No?'

'I want you near me.'

He shook his head.

'Yes, Antonio. I've told you this before. Either way I'll suffer. But this way it's better. I know what I'm doing. If you go away it will be merely—death.'

I think that it was the calmness of my tone that convinced him.

'Well, if you want it like that . . .' he mumbled.

'I want it like that.' Then I added: 'Of course it would be easier if you *tried* to make it easier.'

'How do you mean?'

'Well, Antonio, you don't think very much about me these days, do you? Only about yourself and Pam. That's all . . . But I can take that too. I think I can take anything—anything at all. Your rushing off to be with her. The lies you tell in order not to hurt my feelings. Pawing her in front of me. All that.

I don't like it, actually it's hell, but'—I smiled at him—'I can take it.'

'You have a low opinion of me.'

'I have a high opinion of you. But like all people who are deeply infatuated you are now shut up in this little world of only yourself and Pam.'

'But Dick, you are wrong! Pam is not all that important to me. She is only a *passatempo*, I have told you.'

'She *was* only a *passatempo*. Now things have changed.'

'There has been no change!' He said it with a vehemence that seemed intended to convince himself as much as me.

'Of course there has. Do you think that ten days ago you would have sat at the dining-room table caressing her as you did this evening—in front of me and my sister and my brother and sister-in-law and my niece? Of course not, Antonio!'

'What is wrong with touching her?'

'Nothing is wrong as far as I'm concerned—though I found the sight of it painful. But these are things one just does not do. You would not do them in Italy. You would not do them here if you were not, in a sense, mad.'

'I do not care what your relatives think of me!' he shouted in sudden anger. 'Let them think what they like.'

'But it's not a question of what they think of *you*,' I pursued, remorselessly calm still. 'It is what they think of Pam. She is a nineteen-year-old girl, not much older than my niece. She is an apparently respectable girl. But if you, a married man, caress her like that and she allows you to caress her like that, then it is obvious to everyone that she must be your mistress. That's all.'

Silent, he stared down at the carpet, one foot kicking at a leg of the chair from which I had risen. His mouth was bunched, his chin drawn down on to his chest; he looked—with a sudden exultant sense of power I realised it—as though he were about to burst into tears.

Then he turned on me: 'And what about you?'

'About me? What do you mean?'

'You criticise me for caressing Pam in public, but what about your behaviour to me? Isn't that equally embarrassing? Equally *compromettente?*'

Amazed, I said, 'I have never touched you in public. I have hardly ever touched you in private for the matter of that.'

'You have not touched me, no! But all your behaviour to me—your fussing over me, your watching me as I walk about a room—your watching me at the party this evening. The way you say my name even. It's obvious to everyone. Everyone must think that I am your lover.'

'No one thinks that,' I retorted drily; but my heart was thumping painfully and my head had a feeling of ever-increasing constriction. 'They think merely that I'm a foolish queen who has lost his head over a handsome and normal Italian. And that's only the truth. Yes, I *have* made myself look ridiculous. But not you, Antonio. Not you.'

He shrugged. I think that I had convinced him.

'It is all too difficult,' he said, with the pettishness of a child given some study-task beyond him.

At those words I felt a terrible remorse and pity. Life for him in England, as an exile without a wife and infatuated with another woman, would have been hard enough; I had made it even harder, perhaps untenable, by introducing into it a problem strange, alarming and—who knew?—potentially disruptive to all he had so carefully achieved by ceaseless self-discipline and labour. But though I felt a sudden weight of guilt crushing down on me, and though, as he stood there before me with his shoulders hunched and his stance, all his weight on one leg, limply drooping, the pity I felt for him was almost as consuming as the love, yet I also wanted to disrupt that life yet further, to blast it into fragments that I could then remake in a pattern in which I should at last achieve pride of place.

'Go to bed, Antonio,' I whispered, as to an overwrought child.

He went without saying a word, dragging his feet as though already half-asleep.

I sat for a long time in the empty room, thinking not with alarm but with a cold curiosity 'What have I done? What is to become of me?' I had no thought of abdicating from the struggle. All my life I had become used to achieving the things I wanted to achieve, until I had developed an irrational, almost mystical belief that if one cared enough about something and was prepared to sacrifice enough to its pursuit, then it could not evade one. I had wanted a beautiful house and I had wanted beautiful possessions; and now, by dint of hard work and sacrifice and scheming, here were both around me. In Greece I had wanted a young, married policeman who had feigned a complete indifference to me; but by courting him and spending money on him, he had eventually been mine. In Japan I had won the Japanese wife of a colleague in the same way.

Part of me said that in the battle on which I was now gambling all that I possessed, I was certain to be defeated; but part of me still persisted in believing that, whatever the cost, I might still come through the victor.

If I could not be the victor, then I was satisfied to go down mortally wounded into the darkness.

11

In the days that followed, our separate madnesses seemed to whirl in an ever-increasing tempo along their parallel grooves; but whereas I was only too willing to admit that I was, in a sense, insane, it was only shortly before he left for his Easter vacation in Florence that Antonio would do so. I saw him as a man lost in a tropical forest, where lianas, tangling voluptuously about him, threatened to make him a prisoner forever. Myself I saw as a traveller through a desert, circling aimlessly under a broiling sun with the constant illusion that the next few steps would bring him stumbling to the oasis that everyone assured him did not exist.

Being a person who had all his life exercised a rigid, almost self-mutilating discipline over himself, I was far better able than Antonio to carry out a hundred-and-one tasks exasperating in their now seeming triviality but necessary to the business of earning a living and keeping my insanity a secret. I read the books I had to read, I watched the television programmes I had to watch; and then, waiting at two or three in the morning for Antonio to return from one of his sessions with Pam, I would thump out a review on my typewriter, shivering from the early morning cold and fatigue and a curious sense of bloodlessness that had started to afflict me. I even went to literary parties and queer parties and parties, given by neighbours, that were dismally neither. I felt a certain pride in my 'professionalism' when I contrasted it with Antonio's total inability to get to grips with his work. His professor in Italy wanted a report on his progress; there was a paper he had agreed to read to a philosophical society at Oxford; there was an article he had promised to write for *Mind*. I would often ask him about these commitments, taking a cruel pleasure in hearing him groan and in seeing him clutch his head with both hands. 'Yes, yes, they will be done, I am working on them.' But he was working on nothing. Sometimes when Pam could not or would not see him—she was cunning, I used to think, in the way she would practise a sudden withdrawal, though perhaps in truth each withdrawal was unavoidable—he would settle down in his room or, more often, in the sitting-room since he hated to be alone, and would start to read a book. But whereas, thinking of him with part of my mind, I could force another part of my mind to take in the matter before it and even form a literary assessment of some kind, poor Antonio, thinking of Pam, could do nothing but think about her. His eyes would stray out of the open window or would gaze aimlessly at the fireplace; until, suddenly, he would jump to his feet and exclaim: 'Come, Dick, it's such a beautiful afternoon—let's go for a stroll.'

'Why not?' I would answer.

Usually we walked in silence.

I found that I now developed a craving for food, that sent me down to the kitchen late at night from my bed, to wolf biscuits or bananas or slices of fruit cake. I started to put on weight. Antonio, on the other hand, ate hardly at all; and when he did eat it was with a fastidiousness at odds with the way in which he would once snatch and gulp at food. He sang endlessly, in his slight, nasal tenor, and that, almost more than anything else, filled me with exasperation. 'Antonio—how do you expect me to concentrate?' I would yell from my study and he would call back 'Sorry, Dick. I did not know that you could hear me.' But I could always hear him; though slightly deaf, I could hear even the faintest of his movements.

I have never been a fetishist but now, when he was out, whether at the University during the day or with Pam in the evening, I would go into his room and examine his clothes. His soiled things he would throw into the bottom of the wardrobe for my daily to recover and wash. He was never scrupulously clean in his person as I have always been: the socks, too long unchanged, were often smelly; the vests, of a cheap cotton even at that time of winter cold, were stained orange under the armpits with sweat; the exiguous Y-fronted pants, wrinkled like autumn leaves, were often almost the same colour. But I would pick them up, hold them to my face, breathe in all the different odours of that beautiful but all-too-human body that had left on them all its all-too-human traces. There was his navy blue track-suit, pungent, almost peppery in its smell; the football boots into which I would slide a hand to feel their slippery dampness; the jock-strap and the towel smeared with mud and the shin-pads. There were, above all, his pyjamas, with the traces of a dry encrustation at the flies. All filled me with an excitement that was like a choking nausea.

In his drawers—the only neat things in them—were piles of letters, the envelopes deckle-edged and a pale green in colour, arranged by the week, each with an elastic band around it and the dates pencilled in. I knew that handwriting, slantingly immature, was his wife's, and I was often tempted to slip off a rubber band to see how she wrote to him. What endearments would she use? How frankly would she speak of their love-making in the past or their love-making in the future? Would she refer to me? But whereas at home and at public school I had never been told that a gentleman does not examine another person's soiled underclothes, I had often been told that a gentleman does not read another person's letters. It was absurd but the taboo was too strong; the letters remained untouched.

Lying awake as the night-hours passed—Kitty would be snoring under the bed, Selima would be stretched across me—I would indulge in curious fantasies—partly, no doubt, produced by the pills that I swallowed to so little other effect. I would imagine myself somehow concealed in that bedroom of his—in the cupboard, behind the curtain—while he and Pam writhed together on the bed. I imagined a threesome, Pam between us, a hampering object through which we both thrust to reach what each of us really craved—each other. I imagined blackmailing him—'Do what I want or your wife will learn all.' I imagined drugging him or knocking him unconscious or even killing him, in order to have my way.

Never consciously a sadist, I would now imagine a whole sequence of brutalities—tied to his bed while still asleep, he would wake at the sting of my hand across his cheek or the sting of a whip across his flanks. Impotently he would struggle to free himself; impotently he would attempt to jerk his head away as I bit deep into those lips. He would cry out; he would groan; he would beseech me to spare him. Then suddenly, by a miraculous reversal, the sheets thrown back from the body off which I had ripped the pyjamas, he would show his growing excitation. He would welcome, as though famished, what he had previously rejected: the bondage, the subservience to my will, the ever-watchful, unremitting devotion. I would pluck apart the knots, I would unwind the ropes, I would staunch the blood and lick the wounds. 'Forgive me,' I would murmur as we lay close to each other; and 'Forgive me,' he would murmur back.

Sometimes in these fantasies he would be hideously maimed in a motor-accident or hideously emaciated by some illness. He would be on a hospital bed or in a wheel-chair and I would walk down a long corridor to see him. 'Dick! You are the only person who ever comes to see me now.' He would grip my hand in a hand no longer powerful but clammy and bony. 'Dear Dick.' Pam had forgotten him, all his friends had forgotten him. But each day I would visit him, with flowers and books and chocolates. We would make plans for when he could walk again—'I'll take you to Greece. There's no more beautiful place in the world. You'll get well there, Antonio.' Often the face would be dreadfully scarred or a leg or arm would be amputated. His sexual attraction had been totally extinguished—no longer would anyone, man or woman, look at him in the street except with a brief glance of horrified compassion. But for me he was still as beautiful as he had ever been.

Often during these fantasies, I would in desperation resort to masturbation, a practice I had abandoned in my twenties. But the desired self-placation was seldom achieved. I no longer dropped off into a satiated, if shamefaced, sleep as long ago; but instead I felt only a deeper despair, a more arid fatigue, a more violent craving for that body that I had summoned up, for a few seconds, under my own.

Once, when I had just indulged in this useless quest for release from bondage, he had suddenly knocked on my door, back far sooner than I had expected from a visit to Pam. I was even muttering his name into the pillow 'Antonio, Antonio, Antonio.'

'You are not asleep.' It was a statement, not a question, even though the light was off.

'No, I'm not asleep.'

'Pam is not feeling very well.'

'Oh. I'm sorry.' I presumed that she was menstruating and felt a surprise that he should have allowed that fact to terminate their evening. I had no doubt that, whatever her innocence when they met, he had taught her a variety of sexual skills since.

'Besides, I wanted you to hear me read my paper.'

'Have you really finished it?'

'Yes.'

He was proud of that because for days I had been nagging at him to get it finished and only the day before I had told him that he had better write to the secretary of the Oxford society to say that he would not, after all, be able to come.

'Oh, good, Antonio.'

I was glad as I was always glad when he achieved something in his work. That I could be glad shows that my love was never wholly selfish.

'Let me get it and I'll read it to you. Or is it too late?' he added as an afterthought, knowing full well that I should never say that it was.

I looked at my watch. 'It's nearly two. But it's not too late.'

He came and sat on my bed and began to read; and just as I was able to indulge in long reveries about him and yet form a critical assessment of some book I had to review, so now I was able to stare at him with a growing excitement, sitting there at the foot of my bed, and at the same time correct now a fault of grammar and now a fault of pronunciation. I even seemed to understand, as I had never understood philosophy before or have never understood it since, the whole tenor of his intricate argument. It was then that I realised for the first time 'This is a most remarkable mind'; but while realising it I was also thinking: He has never looked more beautiful, no one has ever looked more beautiful, with that massive chest twisted on that incredibly narrow waist and those curious, sherry-coloured eyes and that marvellous line of the jaw. There was a terrible pressure between my loins, my heart was racing; until all at once, just as he was nearing his final paragraph, the orgasm which I had achieved with so much difficulty before his arrival, repeated itself unbidden, the warm stream spurting out over the hand I lowered to protect the sheet.

He looked at me when he had ended; and I am sure that though I had made not a sound or a visible movement he knew what had happened.

'So that's it,' he said; and with a sigh of seeming exhaustion his whole body then stretched across my legs, one arm going out to dangle to the ground.

I have often thought since that at that moment I should have taken him in my arms; that some part of my extreme excitement had communicated itself to him and had prepared him for the action. But instead I remained rigid, one hand over my eyes, the other under the sheet and my head far back on the pillows.

'You are a good friend,' he said, as though realising it only now for the first time, such was the note of surprise, even wonder in his voice. 'I have no other friend who would allow me to read to him something so boring until nearly three in the morning.'

'It wasn't boring. It was really remarkable. So lucid—and in English too. Don't waste yourself, Antonio.'

'Oh, I have nothing to waste.' He shrugged it off.

'You have. Of course you have.'

He got slowly off the bed and then stood over me, smiling down.

'It is good to have one person who believes in one.'

'Goodnight, Antonio.'

That secret, sudden orgasm had been like a long-delayed, minutely desired consummation of my love for him; and now those words, seemingly spoken out of a genuine gratitude and affection and not with the spurious 'sincerity' he so often affected in his desire to please and charm, came like the kiss which the beloved brushes on one's lips before, exhausted by a night of love-making, he or she slips off the ledge of consciousness into an abyss of sleep. Suddenly I knew that I could close my eyes and find the oblivion that, night after night, had eluded me. My eyes were closing even now.

He put out a hand and extinguished the bedside lamp for me. Then he tiptoed from the room.

12

I often asked myself whether Pam was aware of the nature of my affection for Antonio. Because I myself was in love with him I had developed an astonishing intuition about all those, men and women, whom he attracted. Might not she have developed the same kind of intuition about myself? More than once I asked Antonio if he had ever told her the truth and always he was angry: no, of course he had not; what kind of friend would he be if he had done such a thing? He would then invariably end with the same phrase 'I have told you, Dick—this is only something between the two of us;' and since, as I have said, he rarely lied except to flatter, I believed him. 'But she knows?' I would sometimes pursue and he would then answer, 'Why should she know? How should she know? She is a very simple girl. She would not understand such a thing.' Evidently he was unaware of the extent to which even the simplest of English girls understand such things today.

Fearful that she would discover a secret that could only make me appear pitiable or ridiculous or both in her eyes, I used to adopt to Antonio a manner that was subtly derisive or even hectoring when we were all together. Oddly, Pam seemed to take my part on such occasions: smiling at the more bitter of my remarks or giving me a look of covert agreement; saying 'Dick's right, you know, Antonio,' when I had made fun of some dogmatic assertion of his; once even laughing so loudly and so long at a gibe of mine that his face flushed deeply with anger, not so much against me as against an apparent betrayal by this woman who increasingly obsessed him.

Having myself always had more women than men friends, I had been amused in the past by the manner, at once impeccably polite and nervously distant, adopted to women by so many of my homosexual friends. But now, in my relations with Pam, I found myself behaving in precisely the same way. Antonio's considerateness to women was always intermittent: if he felt the need to exert his charm, he was adept at opening doors for them, leaping to his feet when they entered a room or hastening to remove their coats. But there were many occasions when his behaviour to Pam was rough and even discourteous. 'I will drive,' he would say, taking from her the key to the cockroach and leaving her to open the door on one side while he got in on the other. Or I would bring in a tray of coffee and at once he would grab a cup and drop in three or four lumps of sugar before I had an opportunity to serve her first.

I, on the other hand, was at pains to look after all her needs. When she sat down in a restaurant I was there to pull out her chair; when she had a shopping-bag full of groceries, I at once took it from her. 'Dick has such beautiful manners,' she said on more than one occasion, not so much to compliment me, I feel sure, as to make an oblique criticism of Antonio.

She had read little and regarded as serious writers, worthy of discussion, novelists popular but irremediably second-rate. It embarrassed me when she would ask me what I had thought of this or that best-seller, because if I replied that I had thought very little of it, she would be vaguely affronted and refer to what she always called 'the crits'. 'It had awfully good crits,' she would say; and I would reply gently 'Yes, I believe it did.' She had taken to reading all the ephemeral journalism I produced and more than once chided Antonio for not telling her that I had an article in this paper or a review in that. I remember her excitement, all the more touching because the news left me cold, at hearing on the wireless some passing reference to one of my novels.

At first she had been frightened of me, as Antonio had told me, and her attitude had been akin to that of a typist to the managing director of the firm in which she works—I had almost expected her to call me 'sir'. But that had passed. Then, for a period just after she had become Antonio's mistress, I had persuaded myself that there was a deliberately ill-concealed mockery and even contempt in her attitude to me (I was then like a man who has been flayed alive, sensitive to everything) and that made me hate her. I could not bear to have an adversary so confident of victory. But perhaps what I had thought were mockery and contempt were merely embarrassment and shame. Slowly her behaviour had warmed; until there had come a time when anyone seeing the three of us together would have been tempted to assume that she was not Antonio's girl-friend but mine. If we sat at a restaurant table she would at once take the chair next to mine, leaving Antonio to face us; if we were with a group of their friends, secretaries and students, the latter usually foreign, it was with me that she opted to walk. She would defer to me and refer to me in any discussion and to any newcomer she would talk with apparent pride of my literary achievements.

I was mystified by all this. Did she really admire and like me? Was she, like so many women, stimulated by my indifference and, on occasions, my hostility? Or was she deliberately attempting to give the impression to her circle that it was with me, an unmarried man, that she was having an affair, rather than with Antonio, a married one?

As my obsession with Antonio intensified, so did my preoccupation with her. I used to sit, watching her surreptitiously as she talked to Antonio, as once I used to watch Antonio himself, excited and yet stabbed through with anguish when I detected the physical excitation that he produced with so much ease and concealed with so much difficulty or indifference. I would find myself speculating, in a kind of daydream, what form their love-making could have taken during those long hours in the cockroach or—who knew?—in one of those sleazy hotels around the railway station. I would stare at those lips, smeared with a lipstick that gave them the pallor of tarnished silver, or at those hands, oddly clawlike, with nails also silver, or at the tiny breasts under the Shetland jumpers she so often wore. In a strange way, almost against my own volition, I would find my personality coalescing at such times with hers, so that it was briefly my own mouth or my own hands or my own body, not hers, that had felt the thrust of his passion.

Occasionally such examinations, however furtive, would be noticed by her and she would give me a twitching little smile or sometimes merely a look, as though the two of us had been conspirators in some nameless crime, unknown to the rest of the world.

I had often told Antonio that I did not want to see her—'She exists, and for you she has to exist, but I do not want to be reminded of her existence' was how I expressed it once—but he was always trying to arrange entertainments in which the three of us could participate, together. If I cried out in exasperation 'No! No, Antonio! I don't want to come along! It's too painful for me—don't you understand?' he would reply that it was Pam who had particularly wanted me to join the party. Often in front of me, as on the night of the house-warming party in front of my relatives, he would caress her with a total indifference as to what I or anyone else might think; and then, like some cat purring under the hand that sends electric sensations of pleasure crackling along its spine, she would unsmilingly fix on me those pale green eyes that seemed to be watering slightly as a preparation to the shedding of long-withheld tears and I would gaze back, feeling the same excitement that I should have experienced had the hand been stroking my own neck or calf or thigh.

One week-end Antonio went off to Oxford to deliver his paper. 'Shall I come with you?' I asked. 'I'd like to see my old college again after so many years.' But he brushed aside the suggestion, with obvious embarrassment: I had a lot of work to do; it was a needless expense for me; and besides he had a number of philosophers he had to meet and he would be able to spare, little time to spend in my company. I guessed that he was afraid that if he arrived in my company, the people, many of them influential, whom he had to visit, would assume that he and I were lovers. This dread had recently come to obsess him.

On that Sunday afternoon the bell rang while I was lying on my bed listening to a broadcast concert, and there, to my surprise, was Pam.

'Is Antonio in?'

'Oh, no.' Since they had been together on Friday evening, Antonio not returning home till the early hours, the question surprised me. 'He's in Oxford. Didn't he tell you?'

'Oh, perhaps he did,' she replied vaguely, turning round and round between forefinger and thumb a huge button that was loose at the neck of her coat. 'I'd forgotten. It's this lecture thing of his, is it?'

'Yes, that's right.'

Surely, I thought, a woman does not so easily forget that the man with whom she is having an affair is going to be away?

'He's back tomorrow?'

Again I was astonished, since she must have known the answer to her question. 'Yes, tomorrow afternoon. At least, that's what he *said*. You know he's not always all that reliable.'

She gave me a nervous little smile, lids lowered and one hand still fiddling with the button, at that last remark. She did not seem disposed to go away.

'Can I offer you a cup of tea?' I asked in a voice that made it clear that this was merely a politeness.

'Well, it *would* be fun to be shown round your house. I've never really *looked* at things properly. And you have so many treasures.'

'Yes,' I felt like saying, 'and among them I once had a Sung bowl.' But I merely gave a little bow: 'Then do come in.'

Aimlessly we wandered from room to room, with her asking me about this or that object and my then delivering a little lecture about it. 'This must be awfully valuable,' she would say from time to time, looking up at me with a glance the nervousness of which contrasted bafflingly with the composure, even lethargy of her manner.

It is malicious to write this, but invariably in each room she picked out for particularly enthusiastic comment the one object that, if I had had something to put in its place, I should certainly have removed. Worst of all was the huge Satsuma vase, covered with an intricate red-and-gold pattern of peonies and writhing dragons, in which I kept umbrellas and walking-sticks in the hall. She knelt down beside this, one hand caressing it with wonder. 'It must be terribly old,' she eventually looked up to say.

'Not all that old. Perhaps a hundred years. It was given to me by a business man I helped in Japan. I managed to get his son into a university.'

'What a marvellous present! Oh, I do think it's beautiful!' I had never heard her talk with the same enthusiasm about anything before.

'When you have a home of your own I'll give it to you.'

She looked at me first with amazement and then with delight. 'Are you being serious?'

Something in her manner touched me deeply; and it was then, for the first time, that I felt for her some emotion other than contempt, exasperation or hostility.

'Of course I'm being serious. I have far too much junk in this house. It's time I got rid of some of it.'

'But this isn't junk.'

Again her hand moved over the hideous vase, touching it with the same tenderness and the same wonder with which, I thought with a pang of desolation, it must so often have touched Antonio's most intimate parts. There was a long silence. Then she rose slowly to her feet. We went on with our tour.

In the doorway of my bedroom, with its peacock-blue walls, its reddish Victorian mahogany furniture and its twin gold Japanese screens, one on either side of the four-poster bed, she let out a little squeal, that unattractive 'Aowh!' of hers. 'But what a bed! You don't sleep in *all* of that, do you?'

'No one else does.'

She giggled. 'But it's a double bed and a half,' She went over to it and bounced on the edge. 'Marvellous! The springing is super!' Then she touched the bedspread, made of three Japanese brocade *obis* stitched together. 'And I love this bedspread.'

I explained how the bedspread had been made, adding: 'Japanese women wear those things wrapped round and round their middles.'

She looked at me; then she said reflectively: 'You do know a lot.'

'Not more than Antonio.'

'Oh, he knows such uninteresting things. Things I wouldn't understand in a hundred years.' She pulled a face.

'Well, that's the end of the tour.'

I had not taken her into Antonio's room, assuming that on my visits to London she must have seen it often enough.

'I'd love to live here,' she said in the same reflective voice. 'Antonio is lucky.'

'If he is, I don't think he knows it.'

'Oh, he does!' she said quickly. 'He takes such a pride in this house. As though it were his own almost.'

I felt she was being generous; I hoped that she was also being truthful.

We wandered into the kitchen and I offered to make her some tea.

'Let me do it! It's a woman's job after all.'

Reluctantly I agreed and then watched to see if she knew where to find the cups and saucers, the teaspoons, the milk-jug, the sugar. Unerringly she went to the right place for each; she was used to my kitchen. But strangely I felt none of the expected resentment or jealousy.

'China or Indian?' she asked.

'Well, I prefer China in the afternoon. But have which you like. I don't really mind.'

'I suppose I ought really to like China. But the awful thing is that I don't.'

'Then don't drink it. Make the Indian.'

'But is that awful of me?'

'Why should it be awful to like one kind of tea and not another?'

Now she was examining the caddy: one in which, some years before, a Japanese friend had brought me a gift of green tea. 'This is one of the most beautiful caddies I've ever seen. Even these unimportant things in your house are so—so *fine*.'

If she and I had ever had occasion to be present at the same auction, each of us furnished with unlimited funds, it is unlikely that we should ever have come into competition; but in that other auction in which Antonio was the prize and my resources were so meagre in comparison with hers, she had unerringly picked out the one object which I wanted more than anything else in the world.

Sipping her tea, her long, thin neck bent forward as though the ash-blonde hair were too heavy for it, she suddenly said: 'Do you think I'm behaving badly?'

Absurdly, I thought for one moment that she was worried about some possible breach of manners. 'Badly?'

'With Antonio, I mean.'

'We all behave badly when we fall in love. Or most of us do.'

'A married man. With two children. It's not very nice of me really. Is it?' Still without looking up, she pensively swirled her teaspoon round and round the cup. 'My mother says it's not right.'

'"All's fair in love and war." When we're not concerned ourselves we're quick to criticise those who don't play fair. But when we are concerned ourselves, then we're as bad as the next man.'

'I never chased him you know. It was he who went for me.'

I could believe that: Antonio 'went for' most women he met. I nodded.

'I tried to make a break,' she went on.

'But it didn't work?'

'I lasted out two days and then I thought "Hell, I don't give a damn for what anyone thinks or for that wife of his or for those two children."' She spoke with a vehemence so at odds with her usual tentativeness of manner that I felt an icy shock. I had always suspected this single-minded ruthlessness where Antonio was concerned; now it had been revealed to me. She giggled and at once she reverted to her usual self: 'You must think me a bitch for saying that.'

'Not at all.'

'Antonio's weak,' she said. 'He appears to be strong, everyone thinks he's strong. But really he's weak.'

That was unusually perceptive of her, I thought. 'Yes. You're right about that.' Then I added slowly 'But you're not weak, Pam.'

Suddenly she looked frightened, as she used to look frightened when I addressed her at the beginning of our acquaintanceship. 'Aren't I? My family all say that I'm far too—'

'You're tough,' I said. 'You fight for what you want.'

She looked at me and the lingering fear was now diluted with wonder. 'You understand people,' she said, in a voice so soft that it was almost inaudible. 'I suppose that comes from being a writer.'

I felt an urge to say 'No, in this case it comes merely from the fact that I'm in love with Antonio like yourself.' But I just shrugged my shoulders.

'I ought to go,' she said hurriedly, as though that shrug had been a gesture of dismissal.

I rose to my feet. It was in silence that we walked to the door.

'Shall I give Antonio any message?' I asked, as she turned to say goodbye.

'Antonio? Oh, no, I don't think so. I'll probably see him in the refectory tomorrow at lunchtime... Thanks, Dick. Thanks a lot.'

'Thank you for coming.'

'Bye!'

She raised a hand in a limp salute, and then with the same hand brushed the hair away from her face as she hurried, head lowered, for the cockroach.

Suddenly I felt a fury against that car. I wanted to kick at it with my feet, to pound at it with my hands. I wanted to smash the glass of the windscreen and to rip the leather of the seats on which he and she had, night after night, made love.

She had climbed into it and now she called again: 'Bye!'

'Goodbye, Pam!'

As I watched the ramshackle little car chug down the hill and then swivel to the left, I found with horror that I was wishing: Let the brakes fail, let some huge lorry swerve round and hit her, O God, let the steering wheel come away in her hands!

But on chugged the tough little car and vanished out of sight.

13

Five days before his departure for Italy Antonio and Pam had a quarrel. It was obvious when he came home for dinner that he was deeply upset, but when I asked him 'What's the matter, Antonio? What has happened?' he answered in a choked, peevish voice 'Nothing, nothing at all. What do you think has happened?'

He ate little, pushing most of the expensive fillet steak I had bought for him—he liked steaks and by then I always spoiled him—to one corner of his plate.

'You're not your usual cheerful self,' I needled him.

'One cannot always be cheerful.'

'How right you are!'

We finished the meal in silence. Then, as I washed up, he walked up and down the kitchen, puffing at one of my cigarettes—on the rare occasions he smoked, it was always one of mine—and from time to time peering out of the window at the darkening garden. Suddenly I felt exasperated that he never offered to help me with the washing-up—after all he was paying me only five pounds a week, a sum that barely covered the cost of the enormous meals he ate. 'Do you think you could dry these plates for me?'

He sighed, pulled a face and then reluctantly took up the tea-cloth.

'What is it, Antonio?'

'Nothing, I told you, nothing. Can't one sometimes be silent?'

'You are not often silent.'

He finished wiping the plate and then, tea-cloth in hand and cigarette in mouth, again wandered over to the window.

'It's Pam, isn't it?'

'Pam?'

'You've had some trouble with her.'

He said nothing. Then suddenly he threw himself down into one of the kitchen chairs, legs thrust out so that the trousers were pulled tight against his crotch. His face sagged, like a little boy's when he is about to burst into tears.

'Isn't it?' I pursued implacably.

He nodded; the urge to unburden himself was too great. He began to mumble out details of their quarrel, in a voice so muffled that often, stooping over the sink as automatically I washed and dried the plates and knives and forks, I could not catch the words.

She had told him that he was using her; that they were 'getting nowhere'; that he was selfish and ruthless and heartless—all reproaches that I myself might also have made. She thought it better for them to part. It would be easier now that he was due to leave so soon for home. She had to think of the future, she had to think of herself.

When he had finished this recitation, he raised his head which until then had been kept perpetually lowered, and looked at me, waiting for a comment. But I could find nothing to say. I should have been triumphant at what might yet prove to be a victory; but I felt curiously detached from him in a way that I had never felt before and also curiously brutal. Let him suffer now; let him know what rejection could mean.

'You say nothing.'

'What is there to say?'

'I am unhappy, Dick.'

'Perhaps it's for the best.' Even the obvious sincerity of that 'I am unhappy, Dick' left me unmoved.

'How can it be for the best?' Suddenly he was angry, the voice high and querulous, like that of a child set some problem too hard for it to understand.

'The affair has to end some time. Doesn't it?' He was silent. 'Doesn't it?'

With that sigh of his that was almost a groan he put his arms across the kitchen table and then rested his head on them. 'I do not know,' I heard faintly.

'But of course it has, Antonio. Or do you want to break up your marriage?'

'I love my wife,' he said stubbornly, as he had said to me so often before, in the tone of someone who says 'Lord I believe, help thou mine unbelief.'

Suddenly I relented. I sat down opposite to him and stared at the bowed head, with the copper-coloured hair curling over the far from clean collar and the ears that had a strange orange sheen. 'Poor Antonio,' I said. 'It's a problem, isn't it? She's got you.'

In the past he had always rejected angrily any suggestion of mine that he might be in love with Pam; but now he merely said in that same voice that was so much muffled that it was almost inaudible: 'What am I to do, Dick? What am I to do? I must see her again.'

'Well, I know what you feel,' I said. 'You feel about her as I feel about you. We're in the same boat. But your chances are better. She's not going to give you up until she has to—you can be quite sure of that. This is only another move in the game, that's all.'

'It was no game, Dick.' He raised his head now and looked at me with a bewildered despair. 'She was serious. I know when she is serious.'

'You thought she was serious the last time and within two days you had seen her again.'

'This was different. And she is right, Dick, she is right. I could never give up my family for her, she knows that. Never. But I want her. These last five days I must see her. I must see her,' he repeated in stubborn anguish.

'Don't worry, you will. But if you do—as I am sure you will—there will have to be another separation later. You will have to go through all this again.'

'Never mind later!' he shouted.

'But you can't live always in the present, you must think sometimes of later. You say you can't give up your wife and family. But the longer you carry on this affair with Pam, the easier it will seem to give them up and the harder to give her up.'

'You do not understand my character—it is too much unlike yours. I want to—to burn all this—Pam, all I feel for her—out of my mind.'

I looked at him and I still felt dispassionate in my pity, like a doctor examining a stranger brought in hideously wounded from an accident.

'I thought you strong,' I said. 'I thought you ruthless and strong. But you're not, Antonio. You're really a weak man who must play at being strong.' Now I saw how right Pam had been.

He seemed not to hear. 'Usually you are the pessimist,' he said, 'and I am the optimist. But now you say that I will have her again and I know that I will not have her. Ever.'

Again he raised his face, the skin of which had a greenish sheen, as though he had just vomited. We stared at each other, until with an involuntary gesture he put one hand over mine.

'You are a good friend,' he said. 'Come—let us go drinking. Come!'

I could not help admiring the way in which, from dreary pub to pub, he put on a performance of light-hearted bonhommie. In the dim-lit bar in which the pianist with the dyed hair would alternately sing out-of-date Italian love songs for him and go off into peals of idiot laughter, Antonio joined in, in that nasal, not unpleasing tenor of his. In a bar frequented by students he got into conversation with three lumpish girls, never met before, whom he flattered outrageously while from time to time winking at me.

But then his spirits began to flag. He had been drinking enormous quantities, allowing me, as he usually did, to buy double after double for him, and for once so much alcohol was beginning to produce a visible effect in a slurring of speech and a tendency to ramble.

In the last pub at which we called, my local, we sat in a corner of the smoke-filled room.

'What is wrong with me, Dick?' he suddenly asked.

'Wrong with you?'

'There is something wrong with me. You have often told me that and I know that you are right.'

'Have I told you that?' I was surprised. It was something I had often thought but I did not remember putting it into words for him.

'I love my wife,' he said in the same stubborn, peevish voice he had used earlier that evening. 'Truly I love her. And I love my children. But there are times when to be with them is like a—like a prison. I feel I must go away, that I never wish to see them again. All that love, I cannot be possessed! . . . And with you it is the same. Part of me says "Here is a wonderfully kind man, who will do anything for me", and that part feels for you affection and respect and gratitude. But the other part is—is—' He sought for a word, his eyes blinking as they travelled around the smoke-filled bar.

'Exasperated?'

'Exasperated.' He gulped down his double whisky neat. 'And then there are all these women, Dick. Now I am thirty-four, a respectably married man, a university teacher. But I must have these women, not one woman, not just two women, but women, women, women. Here, in Lymstead, you know, it has not only been Pam. There have been others—light women, women of the streets. But in a way I cannot explain I never find with any of them, not even with Pam, the thing that I want. What do I want? I don't know.'

The lights dimmed for a second; it was time for last orders. Antonio jumped up with his glass and tried to take mine; but I shook my head. 'I've had more than enough. And you too, Antonio.'

However, he ordered himself yet another double, asking me to lend him some money since he had emptied his wallet.

This drink too he gulped at one go. Then thickly, swaying slightly before me, he said 'Let's go.'

In the street he took my arm, dragging so heavily on it that it was an effort to walk. As we trudged slowly up the hill, he began again: 'I have to escape, Dick. I always wish to escape. Wherever I am—however happy I am—I want to escape. But to what? Where?'

'You don't seem to want to escape from Pam.'

'Sometimes. Not now. But sometimes. And I will, Dick, one day I will.' He tripped on a flagstone of the pavement and only by clutching at my arm prevented himself from falling over. 'It is strange,' he said. 'I have no *women friends*. Do you realise that? You have many women friends and you are a homosexual. I am a normal man and I have none. Pam is not a friend'—the words came more and more thickly—'not a friend like you. She is—what do you say?—a good fuck.' I wondered, briefly, where he had heard that phrase. Could it have been from her? 'That is all. A good fuck. The best fuck in the world.'

We had reached the house and I had to let go of him as I fumbled for the key.

'Perhaps I do not really *like* women,' he said in a high-pitched, querulous voice, leaning against the wall. 'They tell me—all of them tell me—that I am a good lover, but perhaps I do not really like them. What do you think, Dick?'

I was both excited and appalled. He seemed to be disintegrating before my eyes in the light that now rained down on us.

'For someone who does not like them you spend a great deal of time courting and sleeping with them!'

He raised an arm in a clumsy gesture of brushing away. 'Yes, it is true, I like to sleep with them. Pam—I must sleep with her again. But that is all—the fuck, that is all.'

Suddenly he was so drunk that, propped against the wall, he could barely keep on his feet. His eyes flickered upwards. He gave a prolonged belch.

'Come, Antonio. You had better go to bed.'

I put out a hand; and as I did so he lunged at me so abruptly that I thought for a moment he was about to strike me. He gave a groan. 'Toilet.' He was about to vomit.

Somehow I got him there in time. I held his head as he stooped above the bowl and watched, pitying, even deeply moved but not for a moment disgusted as he retched and retched again, bringing up the sour-smelling drink. At last he was finished and he lent back against the lavatory wall, chin streaked with mucus, face clammy and green and eyes closed.

'Thank you, Dick. I am sorry.'

Slowly he raised one arm and then the other as though in sleep, his eyes still closed, and placed them, dangling, over my shoulders. 'Poor Dick,' he breathed. His face approaching mine, the stench of the vomit entering my nostrils but causing me none of the expected nausea, he put his forehead down on my right shoulder, holding me to him with the two limp arms, so that I seemed to be supporting all his weight. Then, his head twisted sideways, the extraordinarily pallid lips drew back from the teeth and pushed themselves outwards in what at first seemed to be a grimace of disgust, and next—all at once it struck me, with a feeling of wild exhilaration and terror—seemed to be an invitation for a kiss. Eyes always closed (there were the tears from his effortful vomiting glistening below them) he gave a murmur that was almost a groan: 'Oh, Dick!'

In our relationship so many of my actions were bad and even unforgivable; but when I think of those actions I console myself with the thought that then, and perhaps then only, I behaved well. I remember that I stared down at him, with the realisation that this was his cracking-point. I had only now to prod deftly into the cracks and a total disintegration would follow. But (of course the thoughts did not at that moment pass in this logical sequence through my brain) he had worked so hard to achieve a perilous integration and the disintegration might finish him. I could not do it: not while he was wild with distress at his abandonment by Pam; not while he was away, an exile, from his wife and family; above all, not while he was drunk.

'You must go to bed. Antonio, you must go to bed. Come, I will help you.'

I think that he knew the extent of his escape, and that mingled with his disappointment there was also relief and gratitude.

Somehow I lugged him up the stairs, our legs twining with each other so that repeatedly we almost fell; somehow I got him on to the bed and then began to strip the clothes off that beautiful body that I had never before touched. But now, my decision made, I felt no excitement; only a terrible chill that made my body shake, my hands jerk spasmodically as they fumbled at his buttons, my teeth chatter.

I drew the blankets over him, almost lifting him in order to get him between the sheets. By then he was near unconsciousness.

'Dick,' he murmured. He took my hand, gripped it for a moment with an extraordinary force; then let it go. He began to breathe stertorously.

Often, as I now lie awake at night, thinking of him, I see again that strange movement of the lips, first drawing back from the teeth in a rictus of agony and then thrusting themselves outwards, and I touch again that sweat-soaked body from which I eased off the clothes as though they were bandages. What a fool I was! The pearl of great price had rested on my palm and I had let it drop. But then I tell myself: in rejecting him, you did more than Pam was able to do; more perhaps than even his wife has ever done for him.

14

I had, of course, been right about Pam: though the next day, when Antonio had telephoned to her, she had hung up on him, on the day after that, when he awaited outside her lodging, she at first agreed, reluctantly, to talk to him and then asked him in. The result of this reconciliation was that he seemed to ascend to a peak of exaltation far beyond any I had ever seen him inhabit before, while I sank into a trough of profound depression. He could hardly be bothered to speak to me, unless about Pam. I gave him some letters to post on his way to the University and he left them on the breakfast table. If he ate a meal in the house, he bolted it in a matter of minutes and then jumped up, long before I had finished, saying that he had to hurry. He would return home at four, five or six, so that the next morning, under the febrile gaiety of his manner, there would always be the same deadly weariness: I remembered one of my Oxford friends, a manic depressive, and thought how similar were Antonio's present moods of restless euphoria to those from which that friend would suffer before collapsing into a numb apathy from which nothing could stir him.

It was during this period that an old friend of mine, Maisie Bridges, visited me after seeing an aunt of hers into an old people's home in the town. Maisie had once lived with me for four months in Athens—a liaison that had created all the scandal that in my previous surreptitious affair with a Piraeus electrician I had so discreetly avoided. She was one of those women whose attitude, predatory and frankly sexual, to the men who attracted her was far closer to that of the typical 'queen' than to that of the majority of her sex. Sporadically we had made love to each other during that period in Greece; but she also liked to go out 'hunting' with me, trailing Evzones in the Zappeion or watching the male passers-by from a table at Zonar's, with frequent comments on their endowments—'Just take a look at *that*, my dear! . . . Well, there's a packet and a half . . . I shouldn't think much of a tune could be played on that penny-whistle . . .'

At that period, ten years before, she had been a handsome woman, with a skin tanned a deep brown by the sun, pale blue eyes and tawny hair that she wore sometimes loose and sometimes coiled into a bun on the nape of her neck. She had had a little money from her divorced husband and a little more of her own, and she was always generous, too generous, with it. But now she was conscious of being in her fifties; of the possible humiliations of pursuing men half her age; of the lack of money that had made it necessary for her to work for one of those organisations claiming to be able to solve all one's problems for an appropriate fee; and, above all, of the fact that she was not married and would probably now never be married again. People tended to say of her that she was 'so brave'—a tribute both to her stoicism, whether when she had lost a considerable part of her capital in a restaurant started by one of her lovers or when she had had to submit to the amputation of a breast, and to her never-failing gaiety in a life which, though crowded with friends, was essentially lonely.

Antonio had happened to be, not at the University, but at the house that day, and inevitably he had flattered and fussed over Maisie as he flattered and fussed over every woman with whom he first came into contact. But Maisie, usually so responsive on such occasions, remained cold. Antonio must have sensed this and his efforts to charm became even more exaggerated. Eventually, telling her that when he was next in London he was certain to ring her up, he dashed off to play in a game of football.

As the front-door banged, Maisie looked at me, shook her head and smiled. 'Well!'

'You weren't awfully impressed?'

'No. Not really. Once I would have been. But if the charm is quite that professional—well, no. He was like one of those screen performances of a glamorous Italian lover—a combination of Mastroianni and Gassman. I couldn't really take it.' She glanced at me. 'But you can?'

I sighed. 'Oh, yes, *I* can,'

'You're mad about him—I could see that at a glance. But you don't get anywhere, do you?'

'Nowhere.'

'And you never will. Sorry to be brutal, but you never will.'

'I know that. But there it is.'

'God, you *are* persistent! Remember that highly respectable married Swiss you insisted on repeatedly asking to join us on our expeditions in Istanbul? God what a bore! And what did you get out of it? Precisely nothing—except the suggestion that you were "sick" and ought to see a psychiatrist. Oh, Dick, when will you learn? When will you learn?'

Her kindness and consideration after days of Antonio's lack of either moved me deeply. I crossed over to the sofa where she was placed and sat down beside her.

'Perhaps subconsciously I want to frustrate myself. Perhaps I want these pointless affairs. It makes me feel less guilty if I suffer.'

'Poor Dick. Poor, poor Dick.' She put a hand to the back of my neck and began gently to massage it. 'You should go away. It's the best thing. Escape physically and nine times out of ten you escape emotionally as well.'

'That's not necessary. He leaves in three days for the Easter vacation. I don't know how I shall live without him. I don't know how I can live *with* him.' I felt a humiliating desire to burst into tears.

Slowly she drew my head down towards her shoulders and I smelled the heavy, musky odour of her scent.

'Let's go upstairs,' I whispered.

'Really want to?'

'H'm. Yes.'

'Well, I'd be only too delighted.' She released me and began to get to her feet. 'It's been—how long? Three years?'

It had been since her near-fatal illness and her operation, but I did not tell her that.

'It didn't really work, did it?'

I did not answer.

'Did it, Dick?'

I threw myself away from her, a hand going up to cover my eyes. 'I can't get him out of my mind. Not for a moment.'

'But you did it beautifully, you know. You've never done it better. That's the odd thing.'

'Oh, Maisie, I'm sorry! It was not a very nice thing to ask of you. Was it?'

'Oh, I'm always glad to give an old friend a helping hand.'

'Nothing is any good,' I said. 'Nothing at all. I could do it again and I should still think of him and when it was over I should go on thinking of him.'

'You've got it bad, poor thing.' She swung her legs off the bed, her arms crossed over her chest to conceal the bluish puckered scar. 'I know what you're going through. I had those six miserable years over Tom. In a way the situations are parallel. Why couldn't you have fallen in love with a queer like Tom and I with a normal man like Antonio? Well, that's how it is.' She shivered and reached for her brassiere.

'That's how it is. But thank you, Maisie.'

'Il n'y a pas de quoi.'

15

On the night before Antonio left for Florence I arranged to take Maisie to a theatre in London. Partly I wanted to make some amends to her for that afternoon in Lymstead; but chiefly I wanted to spare myself the anguish of sitting at home, wondering what Antonio and Pam might be doing and what time he might come home.

Maisie did her best to cheer me up but the evening was a glum one. At the restaurant at which we dined after the show was over, I found myself eating almost nothing set down before me and drinking far too much; and in the train back I went on with the drinking.

It was past midnight when I reached home and, though the central heating was on, the house felt strangely chill to me. Lights were burning in the sitting-room and the ashtray on the table in front of the sofa was thick with lipstick-stained cigarette ends, most of them abandoned after only a few puffs. There were two glasses, at which I sniffed: whisky, my whisky. Antonio had forgotten to put coasters under the glasses and since he always liked his whisky iced, there were milky rings on the table at which I rubbed ineffectually with a handkerchief. Lights were also on in the dining room and in the kitchen; plates were piled higgledy-piggledy on the draining-board and on the kitchen table, and there was a splash of red wine forming a crust on the linoleum. I surveyed it all with a growing rage and a growing desolation, Kitty and Selima one on either side of me.

Perhaps he is back and upstairs and sleeping, I thought. He has his packing to do. He must have a good sleep before the long journey by boat and train. But I did not really believe he would be there.

The dog pattering behind me, I made my way to his room and knocked once and then a second time more loudly. I went in. There was that smell of his sweat, which I still catch faintly when I open the drawers into which he used to stuff his dirty underclothes or his football things and which still gives me a fearful jolting sensation as though a blow had been struck upwards inside me, hammering through my guts to land against my diaphragm. But with that smell there was mingled another smell.

The bedspread, of Brussels lace, was ruffled; and there (I peered down in fascinated horror) in the centre of it was a large pale-yellow stain. I touched it and felt its stickiness; I stooped and sniffed it, drawing in its bitter odour as a condemned man draws in the bitter odour of the dissolving cyanide capsule.

There was something so insolent, even brutal about that patch of semen. God knows, I had often enough had such accidents in hotels or even in the houses of friends; and appalled I had then done everything possible to erase the traces. The two of them had done nothing. It was as though they had struck me in the face and said 'Take that, you queen!'

Again my fingers lingered on that stickiness, imagining his shuddering body over hers and then the semen spurting out to ooze beneath her.

Slowly I turned out the light and went into the bathroom, feeling an overmastering nausea.

Talcum powder spotted the floor; in the bath a long strand of blonde hair curled around the plug-hole. I picked up the hair and twisted it round my forefinger; then by clenching my fist I managed to break it.

Suddenly I saw my towel. It lay on the floor, half under the bathroom chair, and when I picked it up, again I touched that same dreadful stickiness. There, too, there was a patch of semen and, stuck to it, some hairs, not long and blonde but short and black.

I was still clutching the towel to me when I leant over the basin and began to vomit.

16

Antonio started in astonishment when, returning home at three, he came face to face with me at the top of the staircase.

'Dick! . . . What are you doing up so late? Why aren't you in bed?'

'I wanted to see you on your last night.'

He peered at me. 'You look ill. Are you ill?'

'You look ill too.'

His skin seemed to be wrapped over the flesh, fold on fold, like greying cerements; the eyes, red-rimmed, gave the appearance of remaining open only by an effort of the will, the lips were bloodless.

'I am tired.'

'And I am tired. Tired of it all.'

'You must go to bed. Come.' He put a hand on my shoulder and began to propel me roughly up the stairs ahead of him.

'Have you done your packing?'

'I have little to do. I will leave most of my things here.' It was typical of him not to ask if this would be convenient or not. Later I was to find all the drawers stuffed with his clothes.

'You shouldn't be so late when you have this long journey ahead of you.'

'One must enjoy oneself while one can enjoy oneself,' he replied with a dreadful attempt at a smile. 'Now the time of enjoyment is over.'

We had been talking on the threshold of his room; he entered and I followed. Involuntarily my eyes went to the stain on the bed—drier now and therefore yellower—and I wondered how he would react to the knowledge that I had seen what, whether subconsciously or consciously, he and Pam had wanted me to see. But he was so deeply absorbed in some inner problem of his own—or perhaps merely in the memory of his last, desperate, impassioned love-making with her—that he obviously did not notice.

He sat on the edge of the bed, body crouched forward and hands dangling between his knees.

'Did you say goodbye to Penny?' I asked, knowing the answer.

'No.'

'And did you remember to buy Mrs Black some cigarettes?' (Mrs Black is my daily.)

'No,' he said in the same toneless voice, almost a sigh.

'Well, I have some you can leave for her. You've thought of nothing. Except one thing.'

He did not flash back at me as so often in the past. His head hung lower.

'Antonio—before you go there are two things I want to say to you.' Often in the past I had rehearsed all day some such speech as this, but now the words spilled out with unbidden fluency. 'Firstly'—I crossed to a straightbacked chair and sat on it, hands folded in my lap—'I know that you think that what I feel for you is something ridiculous, but don't

A DOMESTIC ANIMAL   193

despise it, don't despise it, Antonio. It's not often in life that you find someone to care for you with complete devotion—unquestioningly—permanently—with no thought of any return. It's rare, Antonio. What I'm offering you may seem to you something wrong and something silly and something disgusting, but it's rare, it's very rare.'

Suddenly he jerked up his head; and when his answer came it came with the same kind of insolent, even brutal slap as the sight of that sticky yellowness on the bed.

'What is rare? It is not rare. Hundreds, thousands of women feel as you do. They want to humiliate themselves and subjugate themselves and indulge in a hopeless passion. What is rare about that?'

I controlled my anger at his tone; my voice was still quiet when I answered. 'But Antonio, they *do* have some hope of some return. They may not have any hope of a return of love but at least they have the hope of sexual gratification. I haven't even got that hope. I have—nothing.'

Suddenly he seemed to relent. 'You have my friendship,' he said. 'Why are you so foolish? You have my friendship. Forever. Next year or even this year Pam will be nothing to me. Forgotten. I will hardly remember her name. But when we are old men, we shall still be friends, Dick.'

'Yes, Antonio. That *is* something.'

'It is everything.'

There was a long silence, broken only by his gentle whistling under his breath '*Ciao, ciao, bambino.*'

'Then the second thing,' I said; and again I was surprised by the way in which the unpremeditated words spilled themselves out. 'I don't know what you are planning to do about Pam. But Antonio, if—when you get back—you want to continue with this—this madness of yours—then please, please, Antonio, go somewhere else, find somewhere else to live. I can't go on like this. These last days have been like nothing I have ever had to live through. I can't live through them again. Ever. If I have to, I don't think I'll survive.'

'I understand, Dick.' He spoke with that almost feminine tenderness of which, from time to time, he was so astonishingly capable. He got off the bed and stripped away his jacket and then his vest. I watched him reveal his body with a sensation that was at once the most piercing anguish and the most intense rapture I have ever known. There was no sexuality in it now but only a wonder that, even when he was so exhausted by the excesses of the night and so beaten down by the problems of his divided nature, any human being could still be so beautiful. The strange pallor, so far from detracting from that beauty, only gave it a marmoreal permanence, as of some antique statue of a gladiator or discobolus. 'And now I want to ask you something, I want you to do me a favour.'

'Anything, Antonio.'

'I have thought.' He slowly unbuttoned his trousers and slipped, them off, revealing those footballer's legs, immensely sturdy, with the orange hair thick upon them. 'I am in a very difficult situation. You were right. Now I care for Pam too much. She has become an obsession for me. He tugged off one sock and then the other. 'If I am to save my marriage I must bring my wife and children over here.'

'Over here?'

He nodded. He was now standing before me in nothing but his Y-fronted pants, his hands held stiffly to his sides as though on parade. 'But you know about my means, Dick. I cannot afford to rent for them a furnished apartment. I have been enquiring, I should have to pay eight guineas, nine guineas, ten guineas. It is impossible. Dick, let me have your apartment. I will pay you what I can afford and Chiaretta will cook for you—she is a good cook—and look after you and you need not have Mrs Black to work for you any more.'

'But Antonio . . .' I stared at him, seeing that magnificent body as though lit by some destroying flash of lightning. I had always thought in the past that it was a masculine body and indeed in its extraordinary musculature it was. But I noticed the size of the nipples, standing out from the fuzz of orange hair, the narrowness of the waist, as of a young girl, and the curious stance in which he was now held, one foot in front of the other to bear the whole weight of a torso that had a pliant, androgynous grace I had never noticed before. 'But you know, Antonio . . . I had promised that flat to Masa.'

'You could tell him he could not have it.'

The heedless egotism of the reply shocked me deeply.

'But Masa is a friend.'

'Aren't I a closer friend?'

'Of course you are.'

'Then, Dick, is it so difficult?'

'But he is *your* friend, too.'

'I need that flat, Dick. If I do not have my wife and children here, I am afraid of what will happen. I am terribly afraid.'

'But Antonio . . . You must see . . .'

I broke off. I could not say 'Don't you see that what you are asking of me is dishonourable?'

'You say you care for me—that you will do anything, anything in the world for me—and when I ask you for something—something that is terribly important to me . . .'

'But I *must* think of Masa.'

'Yes, you must think of Masa.' He spoke with extreme bitterness; and as he did so he reached for his pyjamas, jerking them from under his pillow and thrusting first one leg and then the other into the trousers. He was now in a cold fury with me. 'I do not matter. My happiness—my marriage does not matter. Masa only matters.'

'Masa is your friend,' I repeated.

He was buttoning up his pyjama jacket, his hands twisting with nervous anger at the buttons. 'Now I must sleep,' he said.

'Yes, we must both sleep.' I made for the door; then I turned, my hand on the knob. 'Is—is Pam going with you to Farhaven?'

'No. She is not going with me. She must be at her office.'

'Then may I come?'

'If you wish.'

'I do wish.'

'Very well—then come.'

17

Our journey to Farhaven passed almost in silence. Antonio had refused all breakfast except a cup of coffee; I had forced myself to swallow a slice of toast that tasted as though it were made of brown paper. 'Did you sleep well?' I had queried and had got the reply 'How could I have slept well?' As we were leaving the house, he asked me if I had any remedy for diarrhoea and I gave him some Enterovioform tablets.

Gloomily he stared out of the train window at a countryside as grey as his face. Suddenly he was looking what he was: a man on the threshold of middle age.

'It has been a strange experience,' he said suddenly.

'What has?'

'England.'

'And soon it will all seem a dream. Or a nightmare.'

'A little of both.' He put both hands up to his face and then slowly drew them downwards as though to rub off an invisible film left there by this country he was leaving. 'You know, Dick, I have never in all my life met so—so many people like you as I have met in England.'

'Like me?' For a comic moment I thought that he meant writers or intellectuals or even collectors of oriental art.

'Homosexuals. So many. England is full of them.'

'You haven't met more than two or three at my house.'

He considered. 'Derek,' he said, naming one friend. 'And that friend of yours who is a music critic. And Ronald. And of course Ralph and Mervyn. But I have also met homosexuals at the University.'

'I met many in Florence.'

'Not as many as in Lymstead.'

'I'm afraid I don't know the comparative statistics,' I retorted with sarcasm.

'Ralph and Mervyn—I cannot understand two men living together like that.'

'Can't you? Why not?'

Suddenly his tone of contemptuous superiority began to make me angry.

'Two men living together like a married couple—it is ridiculous.'

'I think your marriage is far more ridiculous.'

His head swivelled round, so that he was no longer gazing with a moody intensity out of the window of the train but gazing at me. I had astonished him: that, and not indignation or anger, was his dominant emotion.

'What do you mean?'

'Ralph and Mervyn have lived together ever since they were students. Ten years, eleven years. As far as I know they've never been unfaithful to each other, I've never once seen them quarrel. I see nothing "ridiculous" in a relationship like that. Whereas your marriage—writing letters every morning to your wife and fucking Pam every evening—*does* seem to me ridiculous. A farce.'

It was one of those occasions when I felt the sadistic desire to hurt him for all the hurts he had inflicted on me, and I could see that I had succeeded. His face went taut, the eyes glazed over like those of a person who tries to will himself not to feel an intolerable pain. He turned back to the window, he said nothing more.

In silence we left the carriage at Farhaven Harbour and in silence we walked the echoing platform and turned into the hall—empty but for a group of weary Spanish truck-drivers—in which he would have to wait for passport control.

'Ah, it is cold here,' he said, wrapping his arms around himself.

'You never bought an overcoat.'

'Now it is not necessary. Soon I shall be in the sun. And when I return you will have the summer here.'

'Don't be too optimistic.'

Suddenly he turned to me. 'We have both done badly, Dick. Badly.'

'We have not done well.'

'But when I come back it will be different.'

'Yes, it'll be different.'

But I could not see how that difference could possibly be achieved.

'I am grateful to you, Dick. You must know that. I am grateful to you. You think that I am an ungrateful man because it is not in my character to be able to say thank you easily, but truly, Dick, I am grateful. Truly. You have been kind, kind, kind to me.'

'It's not difficult to be kind to the people of whom one is fond. There's no merit in it. I've told you that before. But perhaps if I had been less kind—if I had tried less hard—if I had left you alone more . . . Well, don't let's think about it.'

At that moment a tiny passport official with a wrinkled purplish face stepped into the hall from his cubby-hole of an office and barked 'Right you are!'

'You can show your passport now.'

'Don't wait, Dick. Go. I prefer that. You will miss your train.'

'Well, goodbye, Antonio.' I took his hand in both of mine; I had a terrible desire to lean forward to place my lips on his and wondered, for a brief instant, what would have been the reaction of the fiery-eyed little passport officer if I had done so. 'Forgive me, Antonio.'

'Don't be foolish.'

'Good luck.'

I did not look back. I walked back along the echoing platform on to which the London boat-train would come and then crossed, knifed by icy gusts of wind, along by the quay to the other, little station from which the Lymstead train would leave. In a corner of my vision the ship loomed up; but I forced myself not to look at it and not to look for him. Probably now with his suitcase and his battered briefcase he was making his way along the gangway; probably even now, I thought with a sudden access of bitterness, he was examining his fellow-passengers, to decide which of the women would deserve his attention.

There was no train for almost thirty minutes and I wondered whether to try for a bus or to walk into the town and warm myself with a cup of coffee. But eventually I sank down on to a bench, hands deep in pockets, with the sense of relief that one has on coming out of a dentist's surgery after a difficult extraction: one knows that soon the local anaesthetic will wear off and that then one will suffer far more than one has suffered up to now; but though in a sense the worst is still ahead of one, the worst is also, in another sense, behind one.

I remember that there was a piece of yellowing paper—lavatory paper, it seemed—fluttering between the railway lines. It had got hooked on to something and with each gust of razor-sharp wind I wondered if this time it would succeed in wrenching free. At last it did so, fluttering off out of sight, and, I don't know why, this little event gave me a lift of elation.

He had been good to speak those final words, especially after that brutal remark I had made about his marriage. He was a good man. '*Sei un ottima persona*,' he had often said to me, when I had performed some little service that gave me far more pleasure than it could ever have given him. But of me it was not true; of him it was. All at once I was seeing the past weeks, not subjectively, through a distorting mist of frustrated love and jealousy and resentment, but objectively, as they had really been. He had been at times selfish and inconsiderate and even savage in his behaviour to me; but could I call him to account for that? How many normal men would have behaved as well? I had fussed him and bullied him and pried into the most intimate of his secrets, and had tried to possess him as a parasite enters and then sets about making its host a part of itself. He had rejected the parasite. How else could he survive?

Suddenly, unbidden, there came back to me the memory of a little hunchback, a Scotswoman in late middle age, who had worked as an accountant in Chancery in Tokyo. It was a joke among the secretaries, many of them girls who were young and beautiful, that this brilliantly efficient but physically repellent little woman, had, as they put it, 'a crush' on me. She was always finding some excuse to enter my office; she would coo at me, in a voice of mincing refinement quite unlike the staccato Scots voice with which she bossed around the Japanese beneath her, that she had so much enjoyed that story of mine in the *London Magazine* or *Encounter* or wherever it might be;

she would even stage-manage casual encounters outside the block of flats in which I lived—'Fancy running into you, Mr Thompson! My little hairdresser is just around the corner!'—or in the restaurant, far too expensive for her means, in which she had learned that I took official guests for luncheon. I was conscious of her watching me; of a kind of invisible, viscous ooze, emanating like ectoplasm from her stocky pigmy-like body and reaching out to submerge me. I was brutal to her, increasingly maddened by a devotion of which I wanted no part at all. When she told me that if I ever wanted a manuscript typed she would be delighted to do it, I replied 'Thank you, Miss McGregor, but I have a professional I always use.' When she invited me repeatedly to dinner—'I have some Aussie friends, this brilliant surgeon and his wife' was one of the baits she dangled before me—I hardly bothered to make any excuse at all for my refusal, let alone a convincing one.

How much better had been Antonio's treatment of me! The phial of precious ointment that I had wanted to break over his feet must have stunk as much in his nostrils as poor Miss McGregor's devotion in mine. But he had been patient with me; he had been affectionate; he had even been grateful.

'*Sei un ottima persona.*' Yes, within his limits, which were the limits of most human beings, fearful of the shadows around them and even more of the unacknowledged shadows within their own selves, he was a good man; and as my now dead philosopher friend had sensed, that extraordinary physical beauty was no more than the external manifestation of an extraordinary beauty of nature.

The train came into the station, thrusting the icy air ahead of it. I got into an empty carriage and, chin propped on elbow, now at last allowed myself to look back at the ship.

There he was—yes, it must be he—standing alone in the stern, looking down into the water. I had an irrational desire to pull down the window, to shout, to wave. But at such a distance he would probably not see me and certainly not hear me. I remained where I was.

I have no memory of what happened before the train stopped at the University station. Did I sleep? Did my brain, exhausted by all the exertions and emotions of those last few days, temporarily cease to function? Did I suffer some brief fugue?

All I know is that suddenly I was roused by someone leaping into my carriage as the train began to move off again, with a 'Hello, there! I saw you from the other end of the platform as the train came in. I thought I'd never make it.'

I stared bewildered at the plump, youthful face, much as, coming round from an anaesthetic, a patient looks into the face of his nurse.

'Don't you remember me?'

'Yes. Yes, of course I do. You're the friend Antonio once brought to my house for spaghetti.'

'So late at night. That's it. Roger.' He threw his briefcase on to the rack and now sat down opposite me. 'I wanted to see you long before this but, you see, I was ill.'

'Were you? What was the matter?'

'Appendix. The day after we met. Acute. Perhaps it was that spaghetti! I had to be rushed into Lymstead General and I was carved up that night. While I was in hospital I reread two of your books.'

He talked on with that same febrile excitement, sexual in origin, that had so often made friends say to me after an evening spent by all of us with Antonio 'You were in terrific form last night.' But now I felt nothing but an accelerating agony, an intensifying despair.

Suddenly the boy broke off:

'Are you feeling well?'

'Not terribly. I think I'm getting flu,' I lied.

'You shouldn't be out.' He was solicitous, with exactly the same nannying tone in which I would be solicitous about Antonio.

'I suppose not. But I was seeing Antonio off.'

'Has he gone?'

'Yes, he's gone.' As I spoke the words, I felt my lips tremble and the lids of my eyes burn. 'Only for the vacation.'

'I don't really know him. Not well. I met him through that girl, Pam. She was also there that evening. Remember her? He seemed rather taken.'

'Yes. I remember. Yes, he was—rather taken.'

He got me a taxi and put me into it and even insisted on accompanying me to my door. I knew that he wanted me to invite him in—'Can I cook something for you? Or do your shopping? Help in any way?'—but I kept saying that he was very kind, that I mustn't waste any more of his time, that once I had got to bed I should feel much better.

'Do ring me if you need anything. Or shall I ring you to see how you're getting on?' He was tugging a sheet out of his pocket diary in order to write his number, as he had written it once before.

'I'll ring you.'

He was what my friends would call 'a dish': young; fresh-looking; eager; kind; intelligent. But my one desire at that moment was to get rid of him. He was as exasperatingly obtrusive as the head at the theatre that continually prevents one from keeping the leading actor in view.

He telephoned two or three times but I never saw him again.

18

It had been a long and terrible day; the anaesthetic wore off, my whole body began to ache, the invisible cavity seeped an invisible blood and pus until I grew weak and dizzy with their constant flux. I sat, hugging myself, on a straightbacked chair in the kitchen, as though afraid that the jolt of any movement would only make the life drain out of me more quickly; or I lay on my bed, Selima pressed purring to my side, to stare up at the ceiling with eyes that kept going out of focus.

But at last night came; and I thought of the sleepingpills I would take and of the unaccustomed silence and the freedom from having to lie awake and worry—'What time is it now? What is he doing? Is he with her? Are they making love now?' Then I felt a voluptuous relief, as though after hours of prolonged and debilitating love-making. Teeth chattering I began to strip off my clothes, got into my pyjamas and, unwashed, climbed into bed. It was only ten o'clock.

'Now I shall sleep because there is nothing else to do. The frontdoor will not bang because no one will enter and voices will not reverberate up from the kitchen as he and she drink those endless late-night cups of coffee. I do not have to call out "Is that you, Antonio?" when the light shines under my bedroom door and the feet mount the stairs. I do not have to say "Did you have a nice time?" when what I mean is "Did you fuck her?" and I do not have to urge on him, exhausted from the hours spent in her company, "Talk to me a little" when what I mean is "Make love to me too." I do not have to say "Goodnight, Antonio" knowing that he will drop off into a profound slumber but that I shall continue to be unsleeping, the arm that supports my head going rigid with cramp and the eyes that stare into the darkness itching with a weight of unshed tears. I shall sleep because I have taken three sleeping pills though the doctor has told me never to take more than two and because I do not wish to wake again and because though that other agony was preferable to oblivion this one is not.'

I slept.

Then, hours later it seemed, the telephone began to ring, endlessly, on and on, its shrill sound like a hook that fastened in my entrails and dragged my struggling body up, through fathoms of water until, aching from the terrible decompression, I was floating on the surface of consciousness.

I reached out a hand. Flicked on the light. Picked up the receiver. 'Yes.' My voice sounded as though I had a heavy cold.

There was a jumble of French and English sounds. Then, razoring through them: 'Dick, is that you?'

'Yes . . . Antonio!' (So he has telephoned all this way to ask how I am! He cares, he cares, however little.) 'Where are you, Antonio?'

'In Parish.' (I had often told him that the word was Paris, not Parish, but he could never get it right.) 'Dick—you must help me.' Now the voice was urgent and, curiously, far clearer than when he would call me from the University. 'I need your help.'

'Yes. What is it?'

'I have lost my work. It is terrible.'

My first thought was that he had lost his job and I wondered how that news could have reached him in France. But he hurried on: 'All my notes. Everything I have done at the University. I thought they were in my briefcase but I cannot find them. Perhaps they have been stolen. Perhaps I have left them somewhere. Maybe in my room. Maybe at the University. Maybe at the room of Pam. Please look for me, Dick.'

'Yes, yes, of course I will.'

If he could mislay his notes, so essential for his future, then that was the worst of all the symptoms of the derangement of those last days.

'I rely on you. I trust you. I know that you will find them.'

Yes, he knew that I would find them: not in his bedroom, not in his room at the University (I was to travel out there the following morning), not in Pam's room (she was frostily suspicious when I called to see her) but in the Wine Lodge where she and he must have gone to drink together either before or after that flurry of untidy love-making in my house.

'If I can find them, I will find them.'

'Dick—something else.'

'Yes?'

There was a silence.

Again I said 'Yes?'

'About the flat. You remember—last night—I spoke about the flat. All this journey I have been thinking, thinking, thinking. Dick, I must have the flat. You must let me have the flat. If I cannot bring my wife—'

'But Antonio, I've told you—how can I break my promise to poor Masa?'

'Dick—if I do not have the flat—don't you understand?—I cannot return. *I cannot!*'

The voice seemed to be in the room with me; he himself, now wheedling and now threatening, seemed to be there.

'What do you mean? Of course you must come back. Don't be idiotic. Your career . . .'

'My marriage is more important, Dick. My family is more important. I must save them. If I come back—then—you know how weak I am. You are always telling me how weak I am. If I start again with Pam . . . Please, Dick!'

'I'll have to think about it. I just don't know.'

'Please!'

'I'll think about it, I'll write to let you know. And if I find the notes I'll give you a telephone call.'

'Thank you, Dick . . . Then—ciao.'

'*Ciao, ciao, bambino*,' I answered idiotically.

I lay back on the bed and thought about it; but the sleeping pills had confused my mind, my eyelids kept closing irresistibly. Did he really mean what he said? Or was this just a subtle form of blackmail? Of course if his wife were below, I should cease to be the person from whose authority, order and discipline he perpetually craved to escape and I should become instead the person to whom he escaped from the authority, order and discipline of family life. Probably he would have to stop seeing Pam. If he did continue to see her, it would be surreptitiously. I felt consoled by that thought, vindictive though it was of me.

But Pam did not matter, either way. All that mattered was that I should see him again, however acute the agony. Masa did not matter. Masa's wife and his child did not matter. I must see Antonio again. I must see him.

Sleep descended with the sweep of a leaden curtain, crushing life out of me and obliterating for a moment the shameful decision on which, at the moment of its fall, I had already embarked.

19

One evening, some ten days later, the bell rang and there, standing without either umbrella or coat in the rain, was Pam. She seemed to cringe at the obvious hostility of my gaze before she said placatingly: 'I'm afraid I've come at the wrong moment, Dick. I know you like to be telephoned first, Antonio often told me you did. But I was passing and I thought—'

'Well, why not come in?'

'Thanks.'

She sidled through the door with a bobbing movement of her slender body, almost like a curtsey.

'Are you very wet?'

'Oh, no, thank you. I came in the car, you know.'

'How's it going?'

Obscurely I wanted to hear that the horrible little vehicle was disintegrating.

'Oh, it's terrific. I never have any trouble with it . . . Are you sure I'm not disturbing you?' Usually so composed, she was now nervous as she fumbled in the bag slung over her arm and fished out a packet of cigarettes.

'Of course not. I was just sitting here feeling depressed and wishing that some friend would either telephone or call.' That she should call had, however, certainly not been my wish. 'Do sit down.' She sat, folding her legs neatly under her and placing her hands in her lap, rather like an applicant at an interview for a job. I picked up a box of matches and lit her cigarette.

'Did you find those papers?' she asked.

'What papers?'

'Those papers of Antonio's.'

'Oh, yes.' I had forgotten that I had never told her of their eventual recovery. 'They weren't at the University and they weren't here. I found them at the Wine Lodge.'

She looked down at the tip of her cigarette, a slow flush seeping up over the pale skin of first her neck and then her face.

'I sent them off Express to him at once—it cost me quite a packet. I also sent him a telegram. Needless to say he hasn't acknowledged either.'

'Haven't you heard from him?'

'Oh, yes. Twice. But one was a short letter that merely asked me to order for him some Stationery Office publication that he needed for a colleague. And the other was just a postcard of the Duomo in Florence.'

'Well, you've done better than I.'

'Haven't you heard from him?' I asked, hoping that my voice did not betray my pleasure.

She shook her head miserably. 'Not a line. He told me not to write until I did hear—he was going to arrange with some friend for me to write there instead of to his home address—but . . .' Her voice trailed off; she shrugged her shoulders.

'I suppose he has so much to do on his return.'

'Not *that* much surely.' Her lower lip quivered as she raised the cigarette with a trembling hand to her mouth. 'I suppose it's the brush-off.'

I thought with a sudden pang of guilt of the telegram I had sent—'As always you have your way the flat is yours'—and wondered what part I had played in that brush-off.

'Well, he warned me,' she went on. 'I can't say that he didn't warn me. He was always truthful, was Antonio. "You must understand, Pam, I'll never break up my marriage", that's what he would tell me. And "I'm selfish" he would say. "I'm an egotist. Don't expect any gentleness from me when the time comes to part." Oh, he warned me all right. I knew what to expect. But it hurts nonetheless.'

She took a handkerchief out of her bag, stooping to do so, so that the long, ash-blonde hair fell across her face. A strand of it, I noticed, was curled on the dark blue cushion against which she had been leaning; and I remembered that other hair, curled around the waste-pipe of the bath. She put the handkerchief to her mouth and at first I thought that, her shoulders shaking wildly, she had succumbed to a fit of coughing. Then I realised that she was crying, the effortful sobs jerking out of her while her hair screened her face.

Dispassionately I watched her for several seconds.

'I—don't—know—why—I'm doing this,' the words jerked out of her.

The question passed through my mind: did you come here with the intention of doing it?

'Oh, I'm so unhappy!'

Suddenly the truth of this pierced through to me: like myself she was 'so unhappy'. Unlike myself, she could find relief in this wild, jagged fit of tears. I went over to where she was sitting on the sofa and stood above her, looking down. I had never thought that I should pity her, but now I did; and the pity, perhaps no more than an extension of the pity I felt for myself, similarly entrapped by Antonio, all at once took on a physical dimension, like a blinding headache or an acute attack of cramp.

'Pam.' I touched her shoulder. 'Pam. Don't do that.'

She caught at my hand; the tears fell hot across the thumb. She was now whimpering, eyes tightly shut, like a terrified child.

I sat on the sofa beside her, trying to ease away my hand; but still she clung to it. Incoherent words spilled out of her as she put her face, the hair rough against my cheek for all its silken appearance, on to my shoulder '. . . Unhappy . . . might have known . . . cares not a damn . . . So lonely . . .'

Suddenly the limp arm that hung over my neck stiffened; I felt fingertips first lightly brush along my nape and then move, more insistently, up through my hair. 'The loneliness of these days . . . The wretchedness . . . You've no idea . . .'

I had no idea! I felt a hysterical desire to laugh.

'One waits and each day one waits one knows that it's increasingly useless. But one goes on waiting. I wake in the morning, oh, terribly early, and I know that the postman can't possibly have been but I go downstairs and I look for the letters. And then ten minutes later I go down again. Isn't that crazy?'

Yes, it was crazy; but I did just the same.

'I miss him so much!' she moaned. 'Oh, I miss him so much.'

Suddenly, with a feeling of horror, I felt her lips first on my cheek and then, curiously salt, brushing my mouth. But the horror turned to a sensation, at once acutely disagreeable and acutely exhilarating. My hands went out to feel this brittle, bony body: the narrow knees; the boyish thighs; the shoulders that were so pitifully emaciated, the breasts that were so pitifully small. At that last touch she gave a little moan and I felt one of the nipples hardening between my fingers. I lowered my mouth again to hers, thinking with a desperate violence that was neither wholly hate nor wholly love but a mixture of both: 'His saliva has mixed with this saliva; those peasant's hands have gently brushed the aureoles of these nipples; his hair has tangled with this hair; and through this passage, opening out to my touch, opening, opening, his manhood has thrust and pulsated.'

Her hands were now at my flies; she was tugging at a button, gasping now with as much excitement as she had recently gulped with grief. She lowered her head. Yes, he had taught her well. I knew that few Italian women would do that same thing.

'Let me get something,' I whispered.

'No, it doesn't matter.'

'But we've got to be careful, Pam.'

'It doesn't matter. It's all—arranged.'

I wondered then, as I have often wondered since, if it was 'all arranged' because she had known all along or had hoped all along that this would be how her visit would be consummated or because, naturally promiscuous, she was a girl who as a matter of course took contraceptive precautions.

Now she was tugging at my clothes. 'Not so fast, Pam. Gently. Slowly.'

But the frenzy of her haste soon communicated itself to me. Pulling down her stockings I caught my nail on the mesh and left a jagged snag.

'Put out the light,' she muttered, her eyes now closed.

I did as she said; but not before I had stared down at the thin, defenceless body, a crinkling of the skin around her waist where her suspender-belt had been, a large mole on one thigh, the knees drawn up as though for protection.

In a savage despair I sank myself abruptly into her; she gave a little scream, those silvery nails digging deep into the skin of my neck. His body has sweated on your body, as I am sweating on it now. His odours have lingered here as mine will linger. Deep inside of you some essence of him lurks and will, however vestigially, lurk forever, just as some essence of me will also lurk there, a part of your physiology as much as of your memory. With each stab that brought from her a shuddering moan, whether of pain or of pleasure, I seemed to be obliterating her, to reach through to him. I remembered my recurrent fantasy of the two of us possessing her simultaneously and that recollection drove me to an even wilder frenzy.

At last motionless but still panting we lay side by side on the narrow sofa; and the absurd thought came to me 'I wonder if I've made the same kind of mess on this velvet as he made on that Brussels lace.'

A forefinger, the silver nail pointed like a lance so that it rasped as it moved over the stubble of my chin, caressed me slowly.

'You know—he's—never done that to me.'

I did not know what she meant; I do not know now. Was it that I had given her the orgasm that she had never achieved in her love making with him? It was possible: he would, I felt certain, be a precipitate and selfish lover. Or did she mean that he had never penetrated her, either from some scruple of his own or some scruple of hers? That would explain the stickiness on the bedspread and the stickiness on my towel.

She giggled sleepily: 'You know, Englishwomen are supposed to ask men if they feel better when it's over. Aren't they? Well, I do feel better.' She turned her head, her lips seeking out my ear. 'Do you?'

I did not answer. I did not know.

'Are you disgusted with me?'

'Good God, no.'

'It's strange.' She spoke musingly. 'Kinky really. It was as though when—when we were—doing it—you were only partly yourself and partly—partly Antonio. Oh, don't be offended that I say that. I suppose I'd been thinking about him so much and wanting him so much, that it was natural . . .'

Perhaps I should have been equally frank with her; it would have been both more courageous and more generous to have been so. But I merely murmured 'Perfectly natural.'

'I'm glad we're friends now, Dick. That other time I came to see you—you know, when *he* was at Oxford—you were kind to me, very kind, and very, very polite, but I felt that, well, really, underneath it all, you just hated my guts. You know—' again she gave that little giggle, again the sharp silvery nail moved from my chin up my cheek—'I used to be frightened of you. And I used to be jealous of you.'

'*Jealous* of me?' I was amazed.

'H'm.' She nodded. 'It was silly, I know, but you and Antonio had this life of yours, this intellectual life, of books and philosophy and politics and art and music, in which, well, I just couldn't share. He and I really had so little to talk about. And of all the men I've known he was the least interested in hearing anything I had to say—which admittedly isn't up to much.'

Her lips sought out mine; but now the taste of the saliva had begun to repel me.

'I got sick of hearing about you. About what you thought of this or that. About what you were writing. About what you had said. He said you were the most *spiritoso* Englishman he had met.' She sighed. 'Yes, I was very jealous of you. More jealous, really and truly, than of that wife of his or those children. Odd, isn't it?'

'It's cold. We'd better get dressed.' I got off the sofa and put out a hand for my vest. She was staring at my body.

'Physically he's not really my type, you know. That's also odd. I've never gone for a muscle-man before. All those muscles usually revolt me.' Dreamily she got off the sofa and began to dress too.

'I suppose this sort of thing is only a temporary kind of relief,' she said, slipping into her brassiere. I noticed that she had started to shiver.

'Cold?'

'A little. But I'll be all right when I've got all my clothes on again.'

'These things are palliatives,' I said. 'And a palliative is better than nothing.'

Her words about being jealous of me ought to have filled me with joy, but strangely they hadn't. I was feeling increasingly depressed and ashamed.

'What's that?' she said.

'What?'

'A pally—whatever-you-said?'

I tried to explain.

Dressed, she refused my offer of a drink: 'No, I'd better buzz . . . If you hear from him, please let me know. Will you?'

'Of course.'

'Thanks, Dick.' She turned on the doorstep. 'You don't think badly of me, do you?'

'Badly of you? Why?'

'Some men do, you know. I think Antonio did.'

'Well, I suppose an Italian might.'

'He never said anything, but I think he thought badly of me. I was too easy.'

Antonio's references to 'light' women passed through my mind. But what man could have been 'lighter' than he?

'We'll meet again,' she said, more as a question than as a statement.

'Yes, we'll meet again.'

She put her face up to mine and I forced myself to touch her mouth with my lips.

In the event we did not meet again until Antonio's return.

20

Antonio had come upstairs from the flat below to ask a favour of me. By then both he and Chiaretta had grown used to asking favours and to knowing that I would grant them; but on this occasion he was obviously uneasy.

He began by saying that Chiaretta was eager to make for me the *polpette* that were one of her specialities; they had eaten so many dinners in my house since their arrival, I had eaten so few in theirs. Would I be free on Thursday of next week? I consulted my diary and said that yes, I should. It was, in fact, unnecessary to consult the diary since I should have said yes whatever the engagement.

'I wish also to invite Pam,' he went on.

'Pam!'

Whether he had been seeing her, I did not know: I had not met her to find out and since his return to England, though he always spoke of me to others as his 'closest and best English friend', the former intimacy had begun to bleed out of our relationship. I had referred to her once or twice and he had looked vague and had answered vaguely. It had been obvious either that he wished to forget her altogether or at least not to discuss her with me.

'She has always wished to see the children.'

'But Antonio, is it really wise to ask her? And is it kind?'

'I invite her only as a friend, Dick. As a friend. As I invite you. All the rest—is finished.'

'Do you sometimes see her?'

He shifted uneasily, his hand going up to a chin that had plumpened as the result of a life of orderly hours and Chiaretta's delicious if heavy meals. 'Sometimes. Just for a cup of coffee in the refectory. This is all.' I remembered that more than once Chiaretta had complained to me, in that voice that at such times took on an unattractive nasal whine, that Antonio was working far too hard, often not leaving the University till eight.

'But, Antonio, wouldn't it be better not to risk a confrontation? I can't see the point. It'll be upsetting for the poor girl. Possibly dangerous for you. And certainly embarrassing for me.'

'Dick, you try to make everything more difficult than it is. Pam is a sensible girl. We had our amusement, she knows that it is over. She does not have a broken heart—our relationship was not of that kind. She has always wanted to see the children. She is fond of children.'

I saw that to argue with him was useless. Out of some motive obscure to me—an unconscious sadism possibly but more likely out of no more than the insensitive desire to show off to Pam the children to which he was so devoted—he was determined she should come.

I laughed; and he was aware of the note of contempt in my laugh, and flushed as he heard it. 'Really, Antonio! You are quite incredible!'

'Why do you say that? What I am arranging is not so strange . . . But, Dick, you must do one little thing to help me.'

His voice became gently confidential; he gripped my arm in one hand. 'I will tell Chiaretta that Pam is your friend—your girl-friend. You will not mind? Pam can come here and you can then bring her down to us and I will tell Chiaretta that I met Pam through you and that I am inviting her for you.'

I stared at him. 'Yes, you're incredible,' I said.

'You will do this for me?'

Still staring, I sighed. 'When have I refused to do anything for you?'

'I don't know why I let myself in for this.'

Pam was making up her lips in the mirror in the hall; I noticed that the shade was no longer that silver that gave her the look of having just been host to a vampire, but a brilliant coral. 'I just don't know.'

'Did you really want to see the children? They're very sweet if totally spoiled.'

'I once said I wanted to see them. Yes. But I'm more curious about her. That's why I eventually decided to come. I wrote him a note at the University to refuse the invitation and then—as I was taking it along to the post—suddenly—well, my curiosity was too strong for me.'

Now my curiosity was too strong for me too. 'Do you see him often?' I asked.

'We meet in the refectory.' She spoke with a simple, dignified frankness that I found moving. 'Two or three times we've been for drives in the car. To Roland's Park, to the downs.' She blushed slightly; but even without that blush I knew what she meant. 'But really it's over. It has to be over.' Her upper lip trembled, as she began to slip the lipstick back into the bag at her feet. Then she straightened, to gaze again into the mirror.

'Do I look a fright?'

'Of course not.'

But whereas Antonio these last weeks had looked healthier than I had ever seen him, before, I was shocked by her chlorotic pallor, a thinness that now verged on emaciation and a nervous tic that from time to time made one of her eyelids flutter as though a smut had embedded itself beneath it.

'I feel a hundred.'

'You certainly don't look it.'

To me Chiaretta was always charming in a vaguely flirtatious way; and because she had obviously accepted the story that Pam was my girlfriend, she was charming to her too. Her English was minimal and so between us Antonio and I acted as interpreters for the two women, while we sipped at our glasses of sweet vermouth. The baby was asleep—later Chiaretta was to insist on us all tiptoeing in to view her—but Carlo, the delicately beautiful five-year-old boy, was playing in a corner with a doll. Bored with translating back and forth when Chiaretta admired Pam's shoes or Pam asked Chiaretta where she had gone to have her hair set, I wandered over to the child. But though there were days when he was prepared to be friendly with me, even to the extent of accompanying me on a walk with Kitty, this was not one of them. '*Va via!*' he cried in the voice of a Roman housewife dismissing an importunate beggar or salesman. Such rudenesses were common; neither parent ever rebuked him for them.

Eventually Chiaretta took him off to bed and Antonio, Pam and I were left alone, with the pink frosted glasses empty on the table before us, each resting on a doily. Antonio knew that I liked gin, he liked it himself. Had he himself decided that to buy a bottle was an unjustifiable extravagance or had Chiaretta decided it?

There was a long silence.

Pam, who had made such an effort to be cordial with Chiaretta, now looked sad and strained. My own predominating emotion was one of ennui: and ennui was something I had never felt on any previous occasion when Antonio was present. Antonio cleared his throat two or three times, a sure sign that he was nervous or embarrassed. Then suddenly he shouted out to Chiaretta in Italian:

'Hurry up! We must eat! Masa and Hiroko will be here before we have finished.' It was the first that I knew about Masa and his wife having also been invited.

Chiaretta screamed back: 'I can't do anything until I've got the child off to sleep.' She and Antonio seemed to spend much of their time shouting at each other, not necessarily in anger, and their voices would reverberate up into my house above them. 'Why don't you come and see what you can do with Carlo and I can go to the kitchen?'

'Excuse me,' he said, leaving the room.

Chiaretta next hurried through the sitting-room into the kitchen. Pam and I were alone together.

'Carlo is a beautiful child,' Pam said.

'He is exactly like his father, isn't he?'

'He'll never be as strong or tough.'

We talked on with an increasing constraint; I asked her about her work at the architect's, she asked what I was writing now. From next door we could hear Antonio singing '*Volare*' to send the child to sleep. For some reason the light, nasal tenor gave me a terrible pang of sadness. In the days when he had lived in my house and he was at his happiest over his affair with Pam, he had sung both that song and '*Ciao, ciao, bambino*' ceaselessly—in his room, in the bath, even while we were eating. But now the jaunty tune, muted and slowed to a lullaby, had acquired a quality of pathos.

'He still sings that,' Pam broke off at one point to say.

'How it used to get on my nerves!'

'Mine too.'

Eventually the child had settled down, the meal was on the table. Antonio once again put on his stage-Italian performance, as he piled our plates with far more spaghetti than either Pam or I could eat, splashed wine into our glasses and then announced 'Now you are going to eat the most delicious spaghetti in the world, prepared by the best cook and the most beautiful wife in the world.' He watched first me and then Pam take a mouthful. 'You like, Dick? You like, Pam? All right!'

Chiaretta ate stolidly, seeming neither pleased nor displeased by his extravagant compliments and equally extravagant mugging. She was, even now, when her face was beginning to get jowly and her figure to spread, a far more handsome woman than Pam; but contrasting her ample, almost crude voluptuousness with Pam's etiolated lack of it I could see why Antonio had been attracted to the Englishwoman—she was so unlike any other woman he could ever have had. Chiaretta alone of all of us seemed totally at her ease and totally composed; but I knew, from the sounds of scenes between her and Antonio no less than his accounts to me of all her trivial ailments, that beneath that apparent complacency there lurked a vein of neurosis.

The food was, like all her food, excellent; but I had to force myself to get it down and I knew that Pam had to do likewise, with frequent gulps at her wine-glass.

'Aren't these *polpette* the best you have ever tasted?'

'Quite the best,' I replied—as indeed they were.

'Now you see the advantage of having a wife, Dick. You like your freedom, I know, and freedom is fine. But think if you had a wife to cook for you and look after you. You waste so much of your time on running your house and cooking for yourself.' He turned to Chiaretta and began to translate what he had said, and she kept smiling at me and nodding, one plump hand all the time stroking her coarse black hair. 'Don't you agree, Pam? Dick must marry. He loves children, he needs someone to look after him. Am I not right?'

Pam said nothing.

Chiaretta said in Italian: 'Perhaps he will marry Pam?' She was joking, but she also believed that it might be a possibility. 'Then I will teach her how to make *polpette* and Dick will be happy always . . . Tell her, Antonio.'

Antonio merely said: 'Chiaretta says that she will one day show you how to make *polpette*.'

'Thank you.'

Eventually the dreadful meal was over. It had taken a long time, with the result that Masa and his wife arrived just as Chiaretta, unaided by Antonio but with the assistance of Pam, was carrying out the dishes. At once Hiroko also offered to help. The Japanese woman had put on kimono and *zori* for the occasion and now, as, smiling endlessly, she took small, tripping steps between sitting-room and kitchen, always with only a single plate or dish in her hands, held high up against her flat chest, she seemed, in contrast with the coarse-grained voluptuousness of Chiaretta and the rangy clumsiness of the English girl, a marvel of elegance, self-assurance and dignity. I thought, as I have often thought, that if I were to marry anyone—an increasingly remote possibility—it would be for an oriental that I should opt.

Masa had greeted me with the chill courtesy that had characterised all our encounters since I had told him that I must give the flat to the Italians. 'You see, Masa,' I had said, 'I really do feel that his marriage is at stake—it's essential for him to get his wife and family over here before it is too late,' and Masa had nodded his head at each explanation, with a taut smile cracking his face in two. 'Yes, Thompson-san, of course I understand. I will find something else,' he had assured me at the end. 'It is difficult for you, and naturally we must do all in our power to assist Antonio.' I had repeatedly offered to help Masa in finding alternative accommodation, but each time he had quietly and politely repelled me. No, I was too busy, he did not wish to waste my time. There was the wife of one of his colleagues who had promised to take him around in her car. Penny was going to speak to a house-agent who was churchwarden of the church she attended. Eventually he and Hiroko had gone to live in a flat above a garage in some remote suburb, the property of a friend of Penny's.

The women returned and sat in one corner of the sitting-room while Masa, Antonio and I stood in another.

'So you are well!' Antonio exclaimed with the dreadful false bonhommie he had shown all that evening, thumping the Japanese on the back. 'You are glad to have your beautiful wife with you, I am sure—as I am glad to have my beautiful wife. Now we can really enjoy our life in England.'

At that he began to ask Masa about his baby son.

The Japanese's eyes were curiously cold and wary as he answered.

Suddenly Carlo was at the door, in an extravagant pair of pale blue silk pyjamas with scarlet facings.

'Carlo—what are you doing here?' Chiaretta demanded; but her tone, as always with the child, lacked any true authority.

'Carlo—go back to bed!' Antonio ordered.

The child sidled into the room, smiling at Pam, who stared back gravely. He then ran to his father, flinging himself into his arms.

'What is the matter with my little *pupo*?' Antonio asked, sitting on the sofa and lifting him on to his knee.

Carlo answered tearfully: 'I don't wish to sleep. I want to be with my *babbo*.'

Hiroko said something to Masa in Japanese: it was impossible to tell from either her tone or her expression whether it was approving or not.

'He is a handsome boy, isn't he, Dick?' Antonio appealed to me, not for the first time.

'What am I expected to say? Everyone remarks that he's so like his father.'

Antonio laughed, jigging him up and down on his knee. '*Un bel bambino*,' he chanted more than said.

Masa said 'Excuse me. I had almost forgotten.' He went out into the hall and returned with a small package, beautifully wrapped and beribboned. He bowed before the child who stretched out his hand. 'A little present for Carlo.'

The child wriggled loose from his father's arms and then began first to tug off the ribbon and then to tear away the paper, scattering it over the floor. There was a wooden box and coffined inside it there was an exquisite doll, looking surprisingly like some tiny effigy of Carlo himself. The child tried to pull up the doll's kimono but was unable to do so since the silk had been stuck to the wood. He dug a forefinger into the *obi*, trying to prise that away, and then picked at the lacquered hair. We all watched.

Chiaretta got up from her seat and came behind the sofa, so that she could lean over both Antonio and the child, a plump hand on Antonio's shoulder.

'*Ma è bello, Carlo! Non è bello?*' she said in a wheedling, artificial voice.

Intent on his examination of his present Carlo did not answer.

Suddenly he tried to move an arm of the doll; but this was no jointed western doll, such as he possessed in an abundance odd for a boy, and the arm would not budge. He began to tug and push at it in fury.

'Don't do that, *pupo*!' Antonio said.

'*No*, Carlo!' Chiaretta cried.

Hiroko raised a hand to her little diamond-shaped mouth and began to giggle behind it. Pam and I looked on, impassive.

There was a crack and the arm broke off. Carlo let out a scream. Then he flung both doll and severed arm against the fireplace.

'*Ma, no*, Carlo, *no!*' Chiaretta shouted; but again there was no authority in her voice.

'Carlo, *basta!*' Antonio commanded.

But the child continued to scream.

Chiaretta dragged him off Antonio's knee. 'I will take him to bed,' she said in Italian. The child kicked, squirmed and let out a series of piercing squeals.

'Let me take him,' Antonio said.

'All right, take him.'

Attempting to soothe the boy in a crooning, high-pitched voice, Antonio carried him shoulder-high out of the room.

'Please tell Masa and Hiroko that I am sorry about the doll,' Chiaretta told me in Italian as she picked both it and its amputated arm off the floor. I translated. 'It is too beautiful a present for such a young child.' Again I translated and Masa and Hiroko nodded their heads gravely in unison. It was impossible to tell what they felt about the incident. 'Antonio will mend the doll,' Chiaretta went on. 'He is very clever at mending things. He will make it as new.'

We began to talk of other things, Chiaretta asking the questions in Italian, I translating, Masa translating again for his wife and then answering for the both of them; and meanwhile the screams from the next room became first intermittent and then ceased altogether. Antonio was again chanting '*Volare*.'

Eventually he tiptoed back, to close the door gently behind him. I thought of all those nights when he had returned home at three, at four, at five, and the front-door had been banged and his bedroom door had been banged and he had raced up the stairs, making the whole house vibrate. 'I am sorry, everyone. Carlo is very *capriccioso*.'

'He takes after his father in that too,' I said.

Masa again said 'Excuse me' as he had when he had fetched the present and went once more into the hall, to return with a large envelope in his hands. 'I have been meaning to give these to you for a long time. Do you remember? The photographs I took at the football match.'

'You must see these, Chiaretta,' Antonio exclaimed. 'Chiaretta has not seen me play football in England because the season had ended when she arrived here.'

Masa drew the glossy enlargements out of their envelope and handed them to Antonio. Then he stood and watched, his hands clasped before him and his lips parted in a small, prim smile. Chiaretta was again behind Antonio, that plump hand on his shoulder.

Antonio gave his explanations: 'Ah, this is where the halfback made a foul... *Sì*, here I am—I almost kicked a goal but the wind was too strong... This is our captain, Chiaretta, you must meet him, and this is me.' English and Italian alternated; obviously he took an intense pleasure in looking through these records of his prowess. He laughed, 'Ah, Masa, you are a *brilliant* photographer—brilliant! You have caught me when I slipped, exactly when I slipped. See, Dick!' He held out the print for me to look; but my eyes were on the one beneath it.

Antonio stared down in momentary shock. Then he cried out gaily 'This is one you brought for Dick! Dick, Masa has brought you this souvenir. Look, Pam!'

I have often wondered subsequently whether Masa inserted the 'souvenir' among the other photographs in innocence or malice. I shall never know.

I took the photograph of Pam and stared down at it. She had not, of course, known that she was being photographed through the telescopic lens at that moment; but hands deep in the pocket of her anorak and face turned outwards to the invisible game she was, strangely, smiling, as though at the photographer's behest. I suppose that at that moment some incident had occurred on the field to make her smile; but that smile gave to her that same appearance of replete contentment that had made it clear, on that now seemingly so distant day of the match, that she and Antonio had become lovers.

Pam said: 'But when did you . . . ? I never knew . . .' She broke off. She had been looking over my shoulder.

I handed her the photograph and she took it with her back to her chair.

'Is that like me?' she asked in a curiously disbelieving voice. She stared down; then she raised her head, her chin thrust outwards, and with the lance-like nail of her forefinger scratched between her eyebrows as though to rub out some sudden pain.

Antonio was looking at her, like myself. Chiaretta was standing behind him still, and still that plump hand, ugly in its well-fed formlessness, rested on his shoulder, with an impression of weight, even deadness that suddenly filled me with an irrational horror.

I glanced back at Pam, the nail still rubbing away at her forehead, the chin trembling as though at the onset of tears and the photograph gleaming up from her lap at us. I felt that pity for her that was always also a pity for myself, so that I never really knew if what stirred me was the hopelessness of her predicament or of my own. Then, yet again, my gaze went back to Antonio: and astonishingly my pity for him, never felt before, was even greater.

That hand was like the ball of lead attached to the ankle of a prisoner; and the smile he had forced as our eyes met was like a grimace of agony. But what was most terrible of all were the eyes, dazed, almost stupefied, with their unfathomable silent cry of 'Free me, free me!'

'Italians are not really domestic animals'; but all three of us had been determined to make of him a household pet. Pam and I had failed, as we had always been doomed to fail; Chiaretta had succeeded, having caught him young enough and trained him soon enough. He would always want to escape and he would never escape. Perhaps on other occasions in his life he would see a possible refuge in the devotion of a man like myself or of a woman like Pam. But that plump hand, the ball of lead, would always be there; the two children, and how many more to follow, would always be there; and that terrible, stultifying morality of a class to which he did not really belong but to which he felt he must belong would always be there.

Pam and I were unhappy; but ours was the unhappiness of those who have acknowledged the deepest needs of their natures and have achieved the perfect freedom that comes from service to those needs, however fruitless that service. Antonio was unhappy because he only knew obscurely what those deepest needs were, and because he was ashamed of them and frightened of them.

Now Chiaretta had put both her arms around his neck and I had a mad desire to cry out 'No! Don't! Don't! Don't strangle him!'

EPILOGUE

All these events happened almost a year ago.

Masa and Hiroko have returned to Japan. From there Masa sent me a short letter, little more than the single sentence: 'I wish to express my humble gratitude to you for all that you did for us.' Although I have written twice since, I have never heard again from him. I do not think I shall.

Last month Pam married: a man, eleven years older than herself, who has a garage in Norwich. She invited me to her wedding but I contented myself with sending her the Satsuma vase, which in her letter of thanks she described as 'a super present'. The sight of it, whenever I entered the house, always irritated me; I am glad it is gone.

Antonio, Chiaretta and the children are now back in Florence. Most of the basement flat had to be redecorated when they left it; much of the furniture to be either repaired or replaced. They did not offer to pay and I did not ask them to do so. Next month I am to stay with them for ten days during a tour of Italy. I am both excited and fearful about the reunion; perhaps I shall not go.

I started this book in the hope that the writing of it would be both cathartic and therapeutic, but it has proved neither. The demon has not been exorcised; I remain at once possessed and dispossessed.

I see myself now as the sufferer from an illness which all remedies—surgery, drugs, a change of scene, rest—may palliate but can never cure. Of course, like all such sufferers I hope for the 'miracle'—the spontaneous regression that, in an infinitesimally small minority of cases, even the scientists agree to be possible. The deeply-rooted growth may all at once begin to dissolve and be absorbed into a system that asserts its long-withheld authority. But somehow I doubt it.

It will be with me always—something to live with and something to die with and something that is now so indissolubly a part of myself that I cannot conceive of a future without it.

I can only pray again to the God in whom I have never believed: O God, teach me to care and not to care.

McNally Editions publishes singular, engaging works from off the beaten path. Headquartered at McNally Jackson Books in New York City, our editions are available in the US wherever fine books are sold and by subscription from mcnallyeditions.com.

1. Han Suyin, *Winter Love*
2. Penelope Mortimer, *Daddy's Gone A-Hunting*
3. David Foster Wallace, *Something to Do with Paying Attention*
4. Kay Dick, *They*
5. Margaret Kennedy, *Troy Chimneys*
6. Roy Heath, *The Murderer*
7. Manuel Puig, *Betrayed by Rita Hayworth*
8. Maxine Clair, *Rattlebone*
9. Akhil Sharma, *An Obedient Father*
10. Gavin Lambert, *The Goodby People*
11. Edmund White, *Nocturnes for the King of Naples*
12. Lion Feuchtwanger, *The Oppermanns*
13. Gary Indiana, *Rent Boy*
14. Alston Anderson, *Lover Man*
15. Michael Clune, *White Out*
16. Martha Dickinson Bianchi, *Emily Dickinson Face to Face*
17. Ursula Parrott, *Ex-Wife*
18. Margaret Kennedy, *The Feast*
19. Henry Bean, *The Nenoquich*
20. Mary Gaitskill, *The Devil's Treasure*
21. Elizabeth Mavor, *A Green Equinox*
22. Dinah Brooke, *Lord Jim at Home*
23. Phyllis Paul, *Twice Lost*
24. John Bowen, *The Girls*
25. Henry Van Dyke, *Ladies of the Rachmaninoff Eyes*
26. Duff Cooper, *Operation Heartbreak*
27. Jane Ellen Harrison, *Reminiscences of a Student's Life*
28. Robert Shaplen, *Free Love*
29. Grégoire Bouillier, *The Mystery Guest*

30. Ann Schlee, *Rhine Journey*
31. Caroline Blackwood, *The Stepdaughter*
32. Wilfrid Sheed, *Office Politics*
33. Djuna Barnes, *I Am Alien to Life*
34. Dorothy Parker, *Constant Reader*
35. E. B. White, *New York Sketches*
36. Rebecca West, *Radio Treason*
37. John Broderick, *The Pilgrimage*
38. Brigid Brophy, *The King of a Rainy Country*
39. Ariane Bankes, *The Dazzling Paget Sisters*
40. Vivek Shanbhag, *Sakina's Kiss*
41. John Gregory Dunne, *Vegas*
42. Charles Neider, *The Authentic Death of Hendry Jones*
43. Pamela Hansford Johnson, *The Unspeakable Skipton*
44. Carolivia Herron, *Thereafter Johnnie*
45. Todd Grimson, *Stainless*
46. Dinah Brooke, *Love Life of a Cheltenham Lady*
47. Kay Cicellis, *The Way to Colonos*
48. Francis King, *A Domestic Animal*
49. Felix Platter, *Beloved Son Felix*